WRITE ON MAIN STREET

STEVIE LYNNE

STANHY PUBLICATIONS

To small towns everywhere ~ who keep life interesting.

ACKNOWLEDGMENTS

I could not have done this without the help of many key people in my life. My husband, for allowing me the freedom to spend hours holed up inside my head writing. My friend and former coworker Adam Orth, for his insight into small town newspaper shenanigans and help with editing along the way. My friends who have cheered me on and given me the courage to do this even on days when I really wondered what the hell I was doing.

And most of all, to my mom who instilled an early love of reading in me and the desire to one day write my own stories. This one is for you, Mom.

CHAPTER 1

The night they found Sebastian O'Nary ass deep in a pile of Schweddy Balls marked the four hundred and twenty-second day since the last time I'd gotten laid, the three hundred and tenth day since my divorce was finalized, the one hundred and fifth day since I had rolled into Brownville, VT, and the fifth night since I had gotten a full night's sleep.

Not that I was counting or anything.

Shadows cast by the streetlight through the maple tree out front painted strange shapes in the little bedroom of this new-to-me duplex apartment. Absent were the noises that had lulled me to sleep in Chicago for the past eight years: the soothing sounds of traffic, voices, gunshots and sirens. Also absent were the not so soothing noises of my now ex-husband's snores and booming farts.

Instead, the darkness here was a riot of insect and reptile noises, piercing and disconcerting, the sounds of chirring frogs in the garden below filling my room with their sexually frustrated vibrations.

I wondered if it was possible to shoot a frog.

I punched my pillow up into another position and flopped back into it. A traffic accident earlier in the evening had dragged me out of bed yet again; the fifth night in a row of broken sleep. I guess this was the price I was paying for trying to haul my tattered reporting career out of the urinal in which it had resided for the past 309 days. I closed my eyes and forced myself to breathe deeply and slowly, feeling the tingly drowsiness spreading from my limbs to my core, falling slowly through layers towards unconsciousness...

"Beep, beep, beep."

"That fucking pager!" I rolled over in a tangle of sheets, the shrill beep, beep, beep on my nightstand, just out of reach of my searching finger. A glass of water toppled off onto the bed, liquid splashing up over my face. "SHIT!"

Fully awake now, I sat up, savagely yanking the light cord. The object of my wrath sat there, glowing with a blue light, beeping merrily away, the newspaper's number scrolling across its screen. I grabbed it and flung it across the room. The beep trailed away with a squeal.

Not even a week into it and the beeper had gone off every night, multiple times some nights. A one car crash into a tree. A drunken brawl outside of the town's saloon. A shed fire at a home out in the Meadows. Since clipping that cursed electronic device to my belt, it hadn't let me have a single night of uninterrupted sleep. Woozy, I sat with the sheets puddled around my waist, contemplating an entirely different career, something with less stress, like, say, an air traffic controller.

My phone started ringing. "What the hell?" I squinted at the clock, my contact lenses tucked away in their case in the bathroom, sleeping like I should be now at 2:27 a.m. My phone hadn't rung before, not at this hour, just that cursed pager. Leaning over, I snagged it off the sopping wet nightstand.

"What!?" I tend to forgo pleasantries after 1 a.m.

"Sandy? Did you hear the page?"

Kyle Giardono, our nighttime newsroom staffer, was stumbling over his words as they gushed out.

"Yes, I heard the goddamned page, I just got it. What is it this time? Cows in the road again? A farmer came home drunk and buggered the neighbor's goat?"

At the other end of the line, Kyle's voice quivered. "No! It's not Larry Johnson and the goats again. This time it's big, huge!"

Sighing, I rolled my legs over the edge of the bed, my foot searching for my bunny slippers. "What is it then, Kyle?"

"It just came across the scanner, over on Main Street. Every cop in town is over there. Holy shit, I can't believe this one!"

"Kyle. Slow down. What. Is. It?" I closed my eyes and shoved a chunk of tangled brown hair out of my eyes and started counting backwards from twenty.

He drew a sharp breath. "There's been a murder in town, Sandy! The first honest to God murder since Hezzie MacLaine got shitfaced and gunned down his wife. This one is the real deal, though. Guess who they're saying the victim is?"

I rubbed my already aching head. "Kyle, I don't have time for guessing games. Who is it?"

"John Peckham."

The name rang a bell. Straightening up, I searched my cloudy memory. "Who is John Peckham, Kyle? And where is this crime scene?"

"He's running for Mayor, Sandy. And the scene is his store, A Pint of Peck's on Main Street."

I was already up and running for the bathroom.

I'm Sandy Case, formerly of Virginia, then California, and lastly of Chicago (which sounds a hell of a lot better than saying Illinois). Now I suppose I'm from Vermont. For how long, who knows? This wasn't exactly on my bucket list of places to live.

I had landed here in Brownville, Vermont, just a few short months ago after spamming every paper in the country with my resume. I wasn't that particular about where I ended up; it simply needed to be as many miles from my ex, Benjamin Morven, as I could be and still be within the continental United States of America. When the offer came, I hadn't thought twice: I'd packed my car and left.

Ben Morven has that effect on people.

On a chilly March day, I rolled into town, my car packed to the roof with my belongings, still in a state of suspended disbelief over the chain of events that led me here. Over the next couple of weeks, I experienced an odd culture shock. Oh, I had expected the transition from a major metropolitan area to a rural one to be a bit of an adjustment, and I wasn't disappointed. But my beliefs had always been that New Englander's were stodgy and talked with funny accents. What I hadn't realized was that they could be just plain weird.

The town was attempting a Renaissance of sorts, with the current mayoral race bringing a slew of ideas about potential businesses for Brownville. During my interview with Russell White, the Brownville Reporter's editor, he had spoken of broadening opportunities for this sleepy town, chances to reawaken and become a national or even global center. I had silently empathized with that idea; after all, I needed my own Renaissance right about now.

Russ had told me how I would be given a chance to become an integral part of the team, my big city experience giving me an edgy view they lacked. With a glimmer of hope that this was finally the way out of the pit I had fallen into, I had signed on the dotted line.

Then they promptly put me on the obituary desk. A task I

had spent countless hours on before moving to Chicago, a real fast track to nowhere. Something I had convinced myself I wouldn't have to do here.

Well, where ever you go, there you are. It was starting to feel like I would never get away from writing about dead people.

I had just resigned myself to a future of endless obituaries, and a meal plan that was going to have a lot of Ramen noodles in it when, six days ago, I was called into Russ' office.

Russ had a distracted look when I walked in, his hands worrying at a rubber band that lay like a latex snake on his blotter. He started twisting and stretching it.

"So, uh, Sandy, how are things going so far?"

"Well, I'm getting the feel of the town, getting to know the players and characters. Russ, I can do more than obituaries, you know." He nodded absently. "Good, good. Listen, I got a call from Dan earlier,"

Dan Rand, our nighttime police reporter, worked the second shift. He was usually in at 3:00. My eyes flicked to the clock over Russ' head. It was 3:12.

"His mother is sick again, and he has to stay with her, possibly for the rest of the month. He asked if he could use some of his vacation to do that. I can't have him leaving his mom, so I said yes. But I don't have anyone for his shift while he's out, and I wondered if you, uh, might be interested in trying it? If you do okay, maybe, um we can send more work like this your way."

Would I? I thought of the pieces waiting for me on my desk; three more dead people and the results of the grade school coloring contest. Trying to keep my reaction neutral, I casually told him, "Hell yeah!" I refrained from pumping my fist in the air.

He looked a bit startled. "You don't mind working until 11? And being on call until tomorrow morning?"

"Bring it on. Where's the pager?"

Overnight reporters slept with a pager. After 11 p.m., the paper had one staff member awake in the newsroom, manning the phone and listening to the scanners. If anything of note happened, the on-call reporter would be called to cover the story.

He shifted in his chair; the latex stretching between his fingers. "I, uh, still need your help on days too, you know." My enthusiasm started to evaporate. "Like... what kind of help Russ?"

"Well... what you are doing now. But you can come in a little later, too, like 10 a.m."

"You want me to work 13-hour days and be on call all night?"

I was incredulous. Even for a small paper, this was unheard of. "That gives me all of three hours a day off!"

He shifted uncomfortably again. "This is Brownville, Sandy. There's a lot of nights where nothing happens. And it's just for a week or two. But if you don't want it, I'll see if Lizzy will do it."

Lizzy? I stared at him incredulously. "You'd put an intern on night shift? And leave me with dead people and fluff pieces? Come on, Russ! If you're going to use her, why not have her do the fluff pieces for a week?"

"Because you could give her a piece on the Fourth of July and she'd write it in such a way you'd feel like you just read about the death of our democracy. She's a great kid, but she hasn't developed the well-rounded perspective on the world that our readers want. I tell you what, how about you come in at noon then? And we make it for two weeks. If it works out, I'd like to talk to you about making you one of our mainstream writers. I need someone with the background you have to cover the town's major events."

There it was. That damned carrot again. I took a deep breath and held it for a moment, slowly expelling it. Dammit. "OK, Russ. I'll do it. But I come in at noon, and it only lasts two weeks. We clear on that?"

He nodded, glasses twinkling in the fluorescents. I barged on before he could open his mouth again, "AND if I bag any stories during this, I get to keep them, you understand?" I wanted to make damn sure I didn't catch anything of value overnight just to lose it to the regular day reporter.

He blinked slowly but nodded again. "I doubt we will have anything huge happen, but you get to keep whatever you find."

"Okay." I had barely suppressed a goofy grin. "Hand over that pager, then."

Hard to believe that had only been six days ago. The days and nights had morphed into a gray blur, everything colored by my severe sleep deprivation. Tonight, dancing around on the cool hardwood floor as I jammed my feet into recalcitrant socks and shoes was the first jolt of feeling alive I had experienced since taking the pager. Of course, if mega doses of adrenaline can cause people with two broken legs to get up and run, it can probably wake me up from my stupor.

I hastily ran a brush through my hair. A murder! This could be a game changer for me. Maybe I would finally get a chance to prove my skills, repair my reputation and do some real journalism. By God, maybe this job would work out after all!

CHAPTER 2

*B*lue and red lights danced off blackened windows on Main Street, turning the sleepy street into a discotheque. I heard electronic chatter from the radios, multiple voices laden with confusion, urgency.

Between its darkened neighbors, A Pint of Pecks was lit up like a neon sign. Shapes were moving around inside the plate-glass window… or where the plate-glass window had been. Jagged shards hung from the corners, glinting like colored icicles. Behind yellow tape sagging across the sidewalk, small groups of citizens huddled in their pajamas and sweat pants, craning to see into the storefront. Abandoning my car across Main Street, I hustled toward the doorway.

"Ma'am, MA'AM! You cain't go in there!"

I had a fleeting glimpse of a prominent Adam's apple, and a too large police shirt that looked fresh out of the wrapper sagging on his slight frame. My press ID was already out and in my hand. I jammed it in his face. "Sandy Case, Brownville Reporter correspondent!" My credentials were approximately three inches from his nose. All I could see was the blue police hat above it and a substantial

Adam's apple below it. "I want your press liaison officer right now!"

He stammered, "Ma'am. We don't have no press officer. And I cain't let you in there. Now please step away and go back behind police lines." His Adam's apple bobbed as he swallowed nervously. Christ, this kid didn't even look old enough to shave, let alone be wearing a uniform.

I straightened up to my full, towering 5' 5" and pinned him with my cold-eyed stare. "I am a member of the press and I have a RIGHT to be present at this scene right now! And if you don't allow me access right this minute, then I will lawfully insist that you get your boss out here immediately, or I will write you up under section 1871, obstruction of the press by intimidation!" There was no such law. I was banking that this prepubescent police officer wouldn't know that.

He stammered. "Ma'am! I cain't let you in there right now! We have a murder to investigate! And you cain't see my boss, neither, because he's in there with the State Police!"

Shit. The state police would see through me in a nanosecond. Time for a change of tactic. Whipping my pad out, I snuck a peek at his name tag, "FELLOWS".

"Well then Officer Fellows, consider yourself deputized through the General Emergency act of 1972 to act as Official Press Officer for the Brownville Police. Please bow your head and say, 'Amen'." Startled, he did so.

"Alright then. Tell me what they have here, Press Officer Fellows."

"Shit... Ma'am, I don't think I can do this without my bosses' permission!"

"Press Officer Fellows, you've been formally deputized, as per the President of the United States of America. Now please report on the current situation."

He glanced at the busy scene inside, sweat trickling

down his cheeks now. "Well, ah, damn… we got a call at 2:10 about shots being fired. We scrambled everyone down here. When we arrived, we found a real firefight had happened. There's bullet holes all over the place, and one deceased male."

I craned to see over the crowd inside the store. "Where is he? Was he found on the floor? Is he truly dead?"

"Oh, he's dead alright, got himself a hole the size of a half dollar right smack in his forehead. He's not on the floor, he's settin' in the ice cream cooler."

Startled, I looked around at him. "Say what?"

"Yes, ma'am." Warming up to his new role, Press Officer Fellow's eyes were shining. "Looks like he staggered backward when he got shot and just sat down, ass first, right onto the cooler. Busted the glass, so he's just settin' there, his feet sticking straight out and his ass jammed down on top of a bunch of pints of Schweddy Balls ice cream."

I stared at him in fascination, seeing the words spooling out beneath my fingers onto my front-page story. "And how long would you say Mr. Peckham's been dead?"

Fellows looked confused. "Peckham? It ain't John Peckham. It's Sebastian O'Nary. Peckham's alive and over yonder in the chief's car."

"What… wait… then why is Peckham being held?"

Fellows shrugged. "They think he set O'Nary up." Leaning closer, he stage whispered, "And Schweddy Balls ain't the only thing they found under his ass." I leaned in closer, "What else did they find?"

Glancing over his shoulders, he whispered, "About a kilo of hashish."

My mouth drooped open momentarily. Hash? I leaned closer back to him, stage whispering, "Are you sure it's hashish?"

"Oh yes, ma'am." He swiped a bead of sweat off of his face.

"Ah know my Schweddy Balls and I know my drugs, and that was definitely Schweddy Balls and Hashish."

A shadow loomed beside me. "Tim! What are you doing?... you can't be talking to her!"

"Um, I uh, but she just deputized me as the press officer being as we don't have one, so I was just fulfilling my duties, Sir!"

Beside me, a blonde beefy steer of an officer swung around to give me an incredulous look. "She... she what?"

I jammed my credentials in his face. "Sandy Case, Brownville Reporter, and you are..." I spied his name tag, "PIM," and jotted it down, "Officer Pim. Can you elaborate on the situation? Is it true that John Peckham is being detained? And that he had Schweddy Balls in his freezer?" Schweddy Balls was like gold; you just couldn't find it any old place.

He stared at me, an incredulous look in his eyes. "Wha.... what? What the hell did you just tell her, son?"

Behind him the door to the shop opened, and a large blue uniformed man filled it. Pim's face flushed a dangerous red.

"Pim! What's going on here?"

"I, uh.." He shifted his body, blocking Tim from the view of the Chief. "We're just clearing her out from the scene, Sir."

"What the hell is she doing IN the scene in the first place? I told you to maintain a perimeter out here!"

"Chief, do you have a statement about the death of Sebastian O'Nary yet?" What the hell, I had his full attention right now. Brownville Police Chief Bill Hanniford fixed me with an icy stare. He didn't respond to me, but to Officer Pim. "WHAT the HELL did you tell her?"

Pim stammered. "Nothing much really... we were talking about Schweddy Balls." Behind him, Tim seemed to shrink down into his uniform shirt.

"Really. I bet she could tell you a thing or two about

Schweddy Balls." I glared at him. Being married to Benjamin Morven for eight years left me with balls bigger than his. "Chief, is it true that John Peckham is being detained at the moment? On what charges?"

He cast a withering look at Officer Pim, who seemed to shrink beneath his gray-eyed laser beam. Instead of replying to me, he directed his next comment to Officer Pim.

"Get her the hell out of here, Pim! This is a sealed crime scene. Don't let ANYONE else inside the tape!" Then to me: "No comment!" He turned and stomped back inside the shop.

His face beet red, Officer Pim grabbed my elbow, turning me toward the street. "Hey, hey, hey!" I twisted against his grip. "Slow down, Officer Pim! I need to talk to you for a second!" He grabbed the crime scene tape and thrust me under it. I was aware of the hungry stares of the citizens gathered outside the tape. This would be around town by daybreak. "C'mon! You guys were only doing your job!"

He shook his head in mute frustration. "Ma'am... you... I... damn it! No comment!" He marched back to the doorway.

Oh well, I at least got some damn good quotes out of that interview, as brief as it was. Pulling my notebook out of my bag, I stepped around the cars parked along the curb to find a place to lean and write. A rectangle of darkness just past the end of the crime scene tape caught my eye. It was an alley, running between A Pint of Pecks and the building next door. I glanced back over my shoulder at the front of the store. Officer Pim stood at attention right in the doorway, studiously ignoring me. I casually started down the sidewalk and eased around the corner of the building.

Inside the alley, the darkness was complete. I stopped for a moment, allowing my eyes to catch up to me. Vague outlines took shape. Cardboard boxes leaned against the wall in a miniature mountain. An empty beer can rattled under my feet, tall weeds scratched my ankle. Cautiously, I edged my way down the alleyway farther, my fingers trailing along the rough brick of the building to my left. The wall disappeared under my fingertips. Groping blindly, my fingers felt deeper, found old wood, a metal doorway. This had to be the side entrance to the ice cream shop. I fumbled around for the handle, found it, tugged on it without much hope.

To my utter shock, it turned smoothly; the door swinging open freely. I could hear the voices of the police officers inside the store.

"Hoo-yah!" I whispered under my breath. I entered the store.

CHAPTER 3

*T*he door snicked shut behind me. The voices were louder now, coming from the front of the storefront. Light glowed from the front room, spilling into the back storage area where I apparently now was. As my eyes adjusted, I realized why the back alley wasn't secured; the door was concealed behind rows of shelving packed full of boxes of ice cream cones, cups, boxes of spoons, napkins, all the things needed for an ice cream shop. A narrow walkway ran the length of the shelving. They must have taken deliveries straight onto the shelves from the alleyway with that setup. I peered down one end, then the other, searching for access to the front.

Seeing nothing, I carefully began edging my way along the wall, working closer to the retail area, where the cluster of blue and green shirted officers gathered, a long, low cooler the object of their attention. I froze when I saw Chief Hanniford again, facing my direction. He was talking to a gloved State Police technician who was carefully photographing the cooler and its contents. I spied a brown tasseled loafer sticking up in the air, visible between two Vermont trooper's derrieres.

Holding my breath, I carefully began edging boxes to one side to widen my view. The technician shifted position, opening up a full view of the late Mr. O'Nary. He was most certainly dead, and in exactly the fashion Officer Fellows had described. A round, blackened hole filled the center of his forehead like a third eye, and his mouth drooped open revealing years of golden dental work. The cheery ice cream shop looked like it was located in Beirut; bullet holes stippled the walls, the little iron tables and chairs lay on their sides, paper, glass and candy covered the floor from one end to the other. Overhead, the pretend Tiffany lamps were shattered and left dangling like bizarre used pinatas.

Beyond the cooler and its gruesome contents, I could look straight out onto Main Street, and Officer Pim's broad back planted squarely in front of the doorway.

Hanniford's voice reached me over the babble of voices, "Get a couple more shots of the writing on that package." The flash popped as the technician leaned into the cooler. "Sergeant, what's the count on the number of shots fired?" The ruddy-faced sergeant flipped open his notebook and consulted a page. "We have 23 counted so far, sir."

Holy shit! They had an outright firefight in here! I flipped open my pad, writing feverishly in my version of shorthand. Glass and candy crunched under the cops' feet as they milled around. So much for CSI type shows, I thought, watching them working without gloves, and with seven people inside. Better for me, though. Those CSI types never would leave a wide open hole for a civilian to crawl through like I just did. My pen flew over the paper.

A thought struck me. Peeking between two cartons of waffle cones, I noted the distance to the late Mr. O'Nary and the lighting. I eased my cellphone out of my bag, carefully aimed it toward the folded up corpse and waited. The broad backside of the cop between me and O'Nary refused to move. I swore inside my head, recalled something I had read about the powers of concentration. I stared at his backside, picturing it moving away, concentrated on it moving... pictured the muscles bunching and shifting, the derriere moving to the side by 6... 7 inches. A butt cheek twitched, shifted... and a hand came around and scratched surreptitiously at it. He refused to move. Some people can move mountains with their minds. My mind can make your ass itch.

The front door thumped open again, Tyvek clad technicians crowding inside, plastic cases in hand. Hanniford turned and glanced over at them. "Alright everyone, the cavalry is here. Let's clear out and let them get to work. Pim!" he bellowed out the door.

"Yes, SIR!" Pim stood at full attention.

"Get the civilians back another hundred feet or so. We need a bigger perimeter out front. And make sure no one can get down the sides of the building either."

Shit! Sneaking in while the locals were here was one thing; getting trapped with the big boys was another. Sure as shit they would look further into the scene and find the back doorway.

The butt that obscured my vision shifted and moved out of the way, revealing the very dead Mr. O'Nary again. I steadied my quivering hand and popped off two cell photos in quick succession. Hanniford was ushering his troops out the door onto Main Street. Time to get the hell out of Dodge. I carefully drew back and turned to leave the way I came, stepping carefully down the dim pathway behind the shelving. I felt a brief tug on my shoulder from my bag... and John Peckham loomed into my face and crashed into me.

$\mathcal{L}$izzy had a bright copper streak in her hair. That was new. Last week it was navy blue. She handed me a mug of fresh coffee without a word. I smiled my thanks. Inside Russell White's office, I could hear the men yelling at each other.

He had been closeted in there with Chief Hanniford and Lieutenant Daven from the Vermont State Police for almost 40 minutes now. I sat in a plastic chair outside his office, where I had been unceremoniously dumped by Officer Pim, who now stood glaring at me from 10 feet away, arms crossed over his chest. Lizzy tossed her hair over her shoulder and studiously ignored Pim, settling instead onto a chair next to me. I gave her an appreciative look. Right now, I really needed anyone I could get on my side.

In Russ' office, the yells grew louder. I heard phraseology like, "degenerate press bastards" and, "fascist police pricks." I was a bit surprised at Russ' backbone; when he had come racing in here an hour ago, still clad in pajama bottoms, I had looked at him and seen an aging, beaten down, small-town editor, who probably still slept with a Teddy Bear. I had figured the conference would take ten minutes, tops, then another five to gather my personal effects and be on my way out the door. Permanently.

I spent the first fifteen minutes consoling myself that it would be better this way, anyway. Maybe I could put some more miles between me and my ex and his hellacious new blog. Maybe I could go some place where no one had ever heard of him, like Uzbekistan. I could learn to wear a burka. Maybe I should learn to wear one now, at least until I was clear of Brownville. It had looked like the entire citizenry was in attendance as they hauled me out the back door, in cuffs, still screaming my head off. What I had thought was John Peckham, miraculously in two places at once, had turned out to be a goddamned cardboard cutout of him, used as part of his campaign for mayor. Life-sized, his cardboard face leered at you, his hands spread in supplication, fingers in two peace signs displayed in a 'Vee for Victory'. My bag had snagged on his Goddamned 'Vee for Victory' fingers, spinning him around to where he 'assaulted' me. I don't scare easily, but that scared the crap out of me. I reacted in true Sandy Case style, screeching like a wounded cat.

I wasn't the only one scared by it either. Not aware of the hidden aisle behind the shelving, the police force had responded with admirable alacrity. Tables crashed to the floor as guns were pulled, bodies slamming into each other, glass crackling underfoot, with even more evidence destroyed in the melee. By the time they found the space where I lay in a tangle behind the shelving, with the cardboard Mr. Peckham draped across me, the amount of adrenaline and testosterone in the room could have powered a nuclear submarine.

Hanniford's face had been a dangerous shade of red, bordering on purple, when he saw me. For a crazy moment, I pictured Lizzy writing my obituary. I wondered what mundane facts she would dredge up to spice up the fact that I had committed suicide by police while working in a small town in rural Vermont.

To their credit, they hadn't killed me. They tasered me instead, then cuffed me as I lay jerking like a spasmodic fish on the ground. I had passed out cold at that point, probably the only reason I was sitting here instead of in a cell.

Coming to, I found myself looking up into the faces of the EMTs and Chief Hanniford. I mustered as much of a glare as I could and croaked at Hanniford, "You are in deep shit now, Chief! You should never taser a member of the press!"

"You're lucky all I did was taser you! We were ready to shoot you!"

"Never... fuck... with someone who buys ink in 50-gallon barrels!" That line seemed appropriate right then. Panting, I struggled to sit upright.

"You broke into my crime scene, tampered with evidence, and almost caused four officers to shoot each other!"

"Is it MY fault you left the back door open?"

He flushed at that and straightened up without a word. Behind him, Officer Pim seemed to shrink.

Hanniford fixed him with a glare. "No. Actually, it isn't. Get her into a car. We're going to go have a word with your boss."

And here we were. It sounded like he was having more than a word with my boss. It sounded like a LOT more words, more than I was expecting truth be told. I sipped the brew Lizzy had just made. She looked at my wrists, her eyes wide. "Are you OK? What was it like to be tasered?"

I contemplated that for a moment. "You ever had a static electricity shock while you were getting dressed?" She nodded.

"Well, it was like that... if you also stuck a naked wire into an electrical outlet while standing in a bathtub full of water." She blinked and cracked a small smile.

"What about being handcuffed? Was that horrible?"

I shrugged. "That's not so bad. I've done that lots of times."

Her eyes widened. "Were you being oppressed?"

More like undressed, but I wasn't going to tell her that. "Uh, no. There was no oppression involved." Well, maybe just a little, but that came after the handcuffs.

Across the hallway, Officer Pim tried to stifle a yawn. I felt bad for him. If what I was going through was any indication, he was in for far worse. I nudged Lizzy.

"Hey, do me a favor?"

"What do you need?"

I gestured with my chin at him. "Would you get him a cup too?"

"Him? He's one of 'them'!"

"I know. But he looks like he could use it."

She sniffed. "If you insist." She rose and headed for the coffeepot.

"Hey Officer Pim." I was trying for charm.

"I ain't talking to you, ma'am."

"You just did."

"I did not ... ah damn! Stop it! You just keep getting me in trouble!"

"How do you take your coffee?"

He looked over at that, craving in his eyes. "My coffee? I, ah, I can't take no coffee from you, ma'am."

"No, but you can take it from her." I gestured with my head to Lizzy, who stood behind him with a steaming cup.

Pim was caving fast as the aroma hit him. "Well, shoot ..." He cast a nervous glance at the door to Russ' office, where the yelling was curiously absent. "I guess maybe it's OK."

Lizzy handed it to him. "Here. It's black." She marched

past him to sit back down next to me. He looked at it dubiously. I elbowed her as she settled down in her chair. "Lizzy, c'mon. Help me out here. Fix it up for him, would you?"

She looked at me, offended. "So, do you sleep with your enemies, too?"

"Only for about 8 years." I smiled at the puzzled look on her face. "I'll explain to you later... pretty please?"

"Oh, all right." She rose and stomped back over to Pim, who was trying to force down the black brew. "What do you want in it?"

He gave up the cup gratefully. "Some milk and four sugars, please Miss." She snatched the cup and stomped back to the break room.

I gave him a smile. "So, ah, Officer Pim, I'm, uh, sorry about tonight."

He looked away. "I still ain't talking to you, ma'am."

"Even though I'm getting you some coffee?"

He cast a worried look at the closed door to Russ' office. "Ma'am, I gotta say, I ain't never seen my boss as mad as this before. If I were you, I think I would lie low for a while... a long while."

"Do I look like the lying low type?"

He shook his head. "No ma'am, unfortunately you don't."

Lizzy reappeared beside him with the now lighter brew. He took it gratefully, throwing down half the contents in a single gulp. She eyed him disdainfully. "Make it last, because I am NOT getting you more!" She dropped back into the seat next to me, crossing her arms and legs. I sipped my own coffee and eyed the clock. It was 5:12 a.m. "Why are you here so early?" She had arrived about an hour earlier. In my post-tasered state, I hadn't given it much thought.

"Russ called me."

Startled, I looked over at her. "Russ called you? Why?"

She bit her lip and didn't answer for a moment. I leaned over closer to her. "Lizzy? Why did Russ call you?"

She turned large brown eyes up to mine. "He actually wanted to talk to my dad." Suddenly, she looked very young.

"What does your dad have to do with this?"

I earned a "Duh," look from her. "He's the head of the State Police barracks here in the area. Russ was trying to get your ass out of the sling." More yelling erupted from the office. We both looked at the closed door. Lizzy sighed. "Don't worry. Dad's going to call them and tell them to back off. Russ is just having some fun with these morons."

"Fun? Fun? Lizzy, 'fun' is going to the mall, or heading out on a vacation. 'Fun' isn't being closeted in your office with two irate cops for hours at oh dark thirty a.m.! That's not fun!"

She cracked a smile. "Maybe not for you. But Russ actually likes this. Dad says it makes him feel alive and 'relevant'..." she hooked her fingers into quotations, "again. Dad says the paper is on the edge of being closed down for good anyway, so he isn't too worried about what happens tonight."

"What?" My raised voice earned a glare from Pim. He eyed his empty cup before setting it down reluctantly on the receptionist's desk.

"Shh!" Lizzy leaned her head over to me. "You mean you seriously didn't know that?"

"No, I seriously did not!"

"Well, it's true. After 109 years in print, the Brownville Reporter is a few clicks away from being obsolete."

"Wait... what?"

Another 'Duh,' look. "The Internet is killing it Sandy. Don't tell me you didn't know that. It's been happening all over the country. Every day, another small independent paper folds up thanks to the march of modern technology."

I felt like an ass. Thanks to being employed at the

Tribune, I had been insulated from the reality of the effect of the Internet on newspapers. I mean, I knew about it, everyone in the business did, but it had never really affected me before.

The door to Russ's office burst open, disgorging an irate Chief Hanniford and Lieutenant Daven. I earned a scowling glare from Hanniford and an icy ignore from Daven as they marched past. Poor Officer Pim was standing so straight up it looked like he was going to split the buttons on his shirt wide open. In the doorway, Russ White stood glaring after them, hair awry, plaid pajama bottoms puddling over leather slippers. He bellowed one last parting shot at their retreating backs. "And you don't mess with the sanctity of the press! Ha!"

The newsroom door slammed shut in its frame, the ancient glass that still bore the legend, "Utopian Chronicles" in black script on the frosted glass rattling fiercely. Russ bellowed once more, "You break anything, you're PAYING for it!"

He was smiling. I tried and failed to remember the last time I saw him smile. I stood up, touched and heartened by his surprising allegiance. "Give 'em hell, Russ."

He looked over at me, and his smile faltered. "Case! You mind telling me just WHAT the HELL you were THINKING breaking INTO A CRIME SCENE LIKE THAT?"

Oh great. So much for loyalty and standing by your employees. I sighed. This interminable night was about to get longer. Russ threw his office door open. "In my office. NOW!"

I squared my shoulders and stomped past him on quivering, post-tasered legs, shooting him a foul look as I passed. He banged the door shut behind us.

"Sit." He gestured to the chair. I sat.

Glancing towards the newsroom behind me, he asked in a

normal voice, "So Sandy, are you OK? What happened out there? You completely pissed off not one, but both police departments!" he gave a cackling laugh, "So… fill me in! Did they really taser you?"

What the hell? What was this, some sort of split personality here? I stared at him, one eyebrow raised, my jaw partially hanging. He stared at me expectantly.

"So which Russ do I have here? Russ Jekyll or Russ Hyde?"

He laughed softly. "I have to keep up appearances, you know. The walls have ears."

I twisted around in my seat, looking at the closed door. "It's just Lizzy out there."

"I know that, but her father is one of 'them' and we can't be too sure of what gets out of the newsroom now, can we?"

I felt dizzy from the twists and turns the night had already thrown at me. Dead guys, Schweddy Balls, firefights, being tasered, and now Russell White acting like an Honest to God Editor. Behind his glasses, his eyes were alive. "So, what happened over at A Pint of Peck's tonight?"

I brought him up to speed quickly on the events and my subsequent ejection and detainment. He listened raptly, not interrupting. I was winding down when I remembered my phone. "Oh, Russ, I grabbed a couple of photos while I was there too."

"Photos? You got PHOTOS?" I was beginning to wonder if this was going to be his first orgasm of the year.

"Yeah… hang on.." I was rummaging through my bag. I snagged my 'Droid out of the bottom. "Here…" I scrolled through the photos, pulling up the two I had gotten of the very dead Mr. Sebastian O'Nary, the hole like a third eye, stuck in the ice cream case. Russ' mouth dropped as he stared at the photo. "Ho-lee shit."

"So can we use it?" I was already picturing my first

feature story, above the fold, page one, AP picking up on it. Russ stared at the photos, rapt. "Russ? Can we use it?"

"Huh? Oh… I don't know Sandy. This might not be OK to use for our readership."

"What? Russ, c'mon! These are the only known photographs of the crime scene other than what the cops took tonight!"

"I don't know, Sandy.." doubt was in his eyes, "I would like to, but we've never run a photo like that here at the Brownville Reporter. And Sebastian O'Nary's family is among our subscribers. No." he shook his head. "We just can't do it."

Slightly deflated, I took the phone back from him and peered at the photos again. "Well, can we print these out here? I really want to blow them up to see if I can spot any details."

"Oh sure. As soon as Karl gets in, I'll ask him to run these through the computer." Karl Manzi was our staff photographer. A really tall, really skinny guy, he walked like a question mark, a perpetual slouch in his shoulders. Black shaggy hair and a nose stud were the first things you noticed after his height: huge hands were the second thing I noticed when I met him. I had been eyeing those hands speculatively since arriving here.

"Well, we can use the story, right?" I had a moment of faintness wondering if I had been handcuffed and tasered for exactly nothing.

"Oh, absolutely! Page one Sandy. But you have to flesh it out today. We need background on O'Nary and Peckham. We also need to verify if he really did have a kilo of hash and Schweddy Balls. Where the hell did he get Schweddy Balls? That stuff is hard to come by!" Russ' eyes were alight behind his glasses.

I stifled a yawn. "Okay. I have to go home first for a

couple of hours. Hit the shower and drink a pot of coffee." I grimaced as a headache stabbed behind my eyes.

Russ stood up and opened the door. "Well, don't take too long. We have work to do. I'm going to start scouring for background on Peckham and O'Nary. I might run over to O'Nary's business to see what I can find out from his employees."

"Uh Russ?" I stopped, eyeing him.

"What?" He blinked at me.

"Aren't you going home too?"

"Me? Hell no. I have stuff to do."

I looked at his plaid pajama bottoms and leather slippers, gave him a thumbs up. "Okay. See you in a while then."

CHAPTER 5

*N*ews of Sebastian O'Nary's death reached most every man, woman and child in Brownville by 8:00 a.m. Everywhere I looked I saw clumps of people standing on sidewalks, dazed expressions on their faces. A Pint of Pecks was still sealed off, another local cop standing guard in front of the doorway. The yellow tape flapped weakly in the breeze, stretched this time past the alleyway I had used last night.

I slowed as I walked past on the opposite side of the street. Tarps were hung inside the shattered windows to shield the view of the final resting place of Mr. O'Nary, whose semi frozen corpse was being muscled out of there, still wedged inside the ice cream freezer, when I passed at 6:00 a.m.

News of my ejection had also reached a lot of the citizenship as well: I saw more than one person do a double take and point at me as I marched past.

I shoved my wet hair back off my forehead and took another gulp of my industrial sized cup of coffee. My bag rattled and bumped the small of my back. Now that the adrenaline had worn off, I was aware of how sore I was getting from the tasering.

Main Street was busier than usual on this brilliant blue morning. I saw people out in droves; mothers with strollers, groups of teens carrying skateboards, farmers in work clothing. The Brownville Epicure Market's outside tables were all taken as I passed, people rubbernecking over a cup of coffee.

There was a towering beanpole on the sidewalk just ahead of me, tattered red hair in dreadlocks, an old Army coat flapping around his rail thin frame despite the early June sun that baked the cracked concrete sidewalk. Even from here, a full twenty feet away, I could smell sour hair and body punk, although I realized that I was downwind from the Market. That was just as likely the source of the sour smell; most regulars that frequented the establishment leaned towards unshaven legs and monthly showers.

I slowed as I approached him, trying to decide if I should run the gauntlet past him, or cross Main Street. A glance at my watch decided it. Sighing, I squared my shoulders and bulled forward, my goal the pigeon shit stained red brick building half a block up.

He swiveled to turn his eye on me as I approached. And it was an eye, not eyes. Sometime long ago, he had lost one of his eyes to God knows what, embedded chiggers maybe, the result there was one enlarged, watery blue eye like a drunken Cyclops with a sunken socket next to it. I noticed his footwear choice, knee high lace up work boots liberally criss-crossed with duct tape. A grimy hand appeared from under the coat, the fingers surprisingly long. It was turned palm up in supplication, fingers half curled in.

It resembled a dead spider.

Shuddering, I gripped my coffee harder and marched firmly into his space. I realized I was holding my breath. Half a block, only half a block...

His lips moved, spittle flecking his chin. "Lah nagrom! Natas! Natas! Lah nagrom!! Natas!!"

I stared straight ahead, my footfalls a metronome on the sidewalk. He fell silent as I passed, until my back was to him, then clear as a bell: "Beware the Right Wing."

What the hell? Too tired to unravel that little gem, I took another slug of my coffee and marched on. Around me, Main Street in Brownville, VT bustled in its unusual early morning activity, everyone's attention on the scene being played out at A Pint of Pecks.

In the door alcove to the little lunch counter I now was passing, two skinny kids played guitars, sunglasses perched on their faces, the melodies swirling around each other in an intricate ballad. On the little town common that nestled in the square where Route 17 crossed Main Street, I could see placards, carried by a half dozen shuffling people, a commonplace sight during this election season, especially when you had seventeen candidates running for Mayor. A car stereo thumped on a tarted up Honda as traffic idled, waiting at one of the three lights in town. A sagging banner stretched across the street, advertising a mid-summer tractor pull to be held at the fairgrounds on the south side of town. Gently worn-down mountains were visible over the rooftops as I looked north through the center of town; the Green Mountains.

Across the street from where I walked, I could see boarded-up storefronts sprinkled between the tired businesses, blank spaces like empty tooth sockets, looking a little sadder and dingier each day. A few people walked or sat in the sunshine, old men chatting, teens who should have been in school. I noticed the clothing styles on the teens was from 4 years earlier, passé in Chicago, edgy trend here.

The Brownville Reporter building loomed on my left, red brick, white cornices and flat roofed. I reached the doorway just as a rattletrap Volkswagen Beetle cruised past me, an original Beetle, not one of the new ones. Cardboard signs, the kind seen on lawns advertising political candidates, covered every square inch of the car except for the windshield. They were propped upright, sandwich board style on the roof, more covering the doors, hood and rear, held on with copious amounts of duct tape. One even stood upright on the front bumper, waving in the breeze, proclaiming: MOLLY BRUCE FOR MAYOR.

Inside the car, the diminutive figure of the candidate in question could be seen, closely cropped white hair framing her face, carefully creeping her way towards the intersection. A smile, a much needed one, cracked my face.

I clattered up the low stairs into the dim coolness of the reception area. Behind the counter inside, Karry Gorr looked up as I entered, her ready smile absent.

"Oh, hi Sandy... hey, did you really get tasered last night? What was it like?"

"Like going on a blind date with a constipated dwarf to an opera."

"Jesus! That bad?"

"And worse. I gotta get inside, I'll fill you in later." I shifted my bag and headed for the newsroom.

She called after me, "Oh, and... look out." She rolled her eyes.

"What is it?" Thoughts raced through my sleep deprived brain; O'Nary, Hanniford, Pim, Daven, Russ.

She gestured towards the newsroom with her chin. "It's Diane. An entire family of wood ducks this morning."

"Oh, shit." The Diane in question was Diane Collins, a daytime reporter who, until I showed up, usually wrote about human interest events, things like when the oldest citizen received a gold-headed cane (followed almost immediately by their demise), or when the town had events like its Winter Carnival or Soap Box Derby. Since my arrival, they had given her the school beat, covering endless budget meetings and school committee meetings, and human interest interviews with Brownville's notable citizens.

Late 50s, divorced, messy shaggy red hair, Diane had a permanently beaten down air about her. She now lived in the next town north of Brownville, a 10-minute ride on the interstate, 11.4 miles or one exit, to be precise.

Diane marked her commute to work every day by the road kill she saw alongside the road. A bloated raccoon at mile marker 32. The dead squirrel at the bridge crossing the river. A flattened bunny, ears still pointing straight up, on the off ramp. These unfortunate wildlife pancakes could send her into paroxysms of grief and had the power to influence the day's news as distributed from the Brownville Reporter. God help everyone if she saw a dog or cat on her journey.

Karry's report of an entire family of wood ducks spelled a long day for all of us at the paper. I groaned and headed into the newsroom.

I could hear Diane as soon as I entered the newsroom. She was sitting at her desk, her head held in her hands. "Such sweet innocent little things, just turned into splatters! Oh, why do we have highways? I can't take the pain of it all!"

Standing beside her with as sympathetic a look as a sour lemon could have was Dana Oakes, our "Around This Brown Town" columnist. She looked over at me and spied her salvation.

"Uh, uh... no way!" I threw up a hand as she gestured to me. "I've got bigger fish to fry!" She started to advance across the room. Trapped, I spied the open door to Russ's office and darted inside, closing it behind me.

He looked up, distracted, as I closed the door firmly behind me. "Eh, what?"

"Diane and Dana and dead ducks." I slipped my bag off my shoulder onto the floor, massaged my shoulder.

"Oh... that." He removed his glasses and rubbed his eyes. I noticed he still wore the same clothing from earlier, his hair in disarray. I opened my mouth to ask him if he was planning ongoing home to change, when the door behind me was thrown open. Jorge Maxim ducked inside, slamming it behind him.

"Don't you DARE leave me out there with those two!" He shot his right wrist out of his cuff, straightening an invisible wrinkle in his sleeve. Jorge was a goldfinch among grackles in the newsroom. The only African American on the staff, he always looked like he had just stepped off the pages of GQ. Trim, gold-framed glasses and neatly pressed clothing, no matter what time of day or night. I glanced down at my attire out of reflex: crocs, stained jeans and a clean polo shirt. About as good as it gets in my life.

"Good morning to you too, Jorge." I sipped on my cooling coffee.

"Sandy, I need the details of last night so I can follow up." He pulled his notebook out, "Fill me in and leave nothing out."

"Whoa, whoa, whoa Jorge! Uh uh. This is MY story!"

"Like hell it is! I'm the political and legal reporter here, and this is a political and legal story! Give it up!"

Behind the desk, Russ was shrinking down as our voices rose. I appealed to him. "Russ, c'mon! You told me I had anything I caught on the night shift!"

He looked uncomfortable. "You're right, Sandy, I did. I just never dreamed we would have such a bombshell though. And Jorge HAS been here for ten years and knows all the players now..." his voice trailed off.

I stared at Russ, incredulous. "Russell White, there is NO

WAY IN HELL you are going to back down now! So help me God, if you do, I'll… I'll…"

I'll what? I didn't know. Quit? I flashed on my little apartment that was starting to feel just a little bit like home. On Benjamin Morven, stalking me across the country. On what was possibly the biggest story of my career to date. I settled for a glare across the desk at him. Behind me, Jorge wailed, "Russ! You can't do this! It's in my contract! They hired me for these stories!"

Russ straightened up suddenly, his face resolute.

"Shut up, both of you. Sandy.." he looked me in the eye, "I made a deal with you and I am keeping it. You're lead on this one." Behind me, Jorge swore with feeling. "Jorge.." he stared at him until he quieted. "You're working with her on it. You know this town and the players better, you know the nuances. She'll cover the murder and the aftermath, you'll dig for the why and who."

I considered this for a moment. Jorge was good, maybe one of the better investigative reporters I had met. At the larger newspapers, they often had teams assigned on a big story. I turned to face Jorge. He looked at me, the same speculation in his eyes I had. "I can live with that. Jorge? What about you?"

"I get equal billing." He countered.

I shrugged. "That's fine. I just want to be done with stories about the Fireman's Parade." I stuck out my right hand. "Deal?"

"Deal."

Behind the desk, Russ watched, a satisfied look on his face. "All right. That's the kind of spirit I like to see at the paper."

A knock at his door interrupted him. "What is it?" he yelled. Diane stuck her tear-streaked face inside his office.

Beside me, Jorge groaned and put his hand over his face. I braced myself for it.

"I can't take this today! Dead ducks, dead politicians, and now Dana is being a bitch!"

I grabbed my bag. "Gotta go, Russ... talk to you later."

I eased for the door. Jorge called out, "Hey! Wait... I'm coming with you!"

We pushed by Diane, back into the newsroom. Jorge shook his head. "That was a close one."

"Yeah. I don't envy Russ today." Behind us, I could hear weeping coming from his office. "Actually, I don't envy him any day."

Jorge looked over at me as we reached our cubicles. "Why not?"

"Isn't the paper on the edge of shutting down?"

He pulled out his chair and settled into it. "This paper has been on the edge of financial insolvency for the last ten years Case. There's nothing new about that. Why? What have you heard?"

Across the room, Dana saw us and headed our way. I dropped my bag on the floor, murmuring to Jorge as I did so, "Lizzy told me this morning that her dad said the paper was only 'a couple of clicks' away from being shut down."

Jorge spied Dana and sighed. "Huh. I wonder what that is about. Really, it's been nothing new on that end for a long time. The Reporter operates more in the red than the black. Everyone knows the publisher and her family have been supplementing it for years."

Dana reached us, her eyes alight. "What happened in Brown Town last night, Sandy?" She pulled out a small notepad and black and gold pen. I looked up at her dark blue cardigan open at the front, her button-down shirt pulled tight and stuffed into a pair of "mom jeans", the waist line almost up to her sagging breasts, cuffs skimming a solid four inches north of her ankles.

The last time I saw jeans that high, they were in rehab.

Startled, I looked at her, my jaw hanging. "You want to interview me?"

"Well, of course! My readers want to know the inside scoop! So tell me everything! Was it true they found him trussed up and stuffed inside the walk-in freezer with a pint of Ben and Jerry's shoved in his mouth? Was he really wearing nothing but a pair of fishing waders and a hat?" She leaned forward, her pen poised over the paper, dark eyes glittering.

"Where in the world did you get that?"

"Helen Harper called me at home this morning and told me that Sue Gunther had called her and told her that was how he was found." She dropped her voice to a stage whisper, "She also told me he had ties to the mob!"

I looked over at Jorge helplessly. He was studiously ignoring us, a small smile cracking his mouth. I looked back at Dana. "I don't know. You'll have to ask Jorge. He's the legal and political reporter. No comment."

Jorge's head popped up. "Hey!"

I was already heading out of my seat, grabbing my bag. "I have to get over to the police department, Jorge. Be back in a while, partner!"

CHAPTER 6

*I*n the end it didn't take me very long at the Brownville, PD. I went in looking for a status on John Peckhams' detainment, a police report on the scene from last night, and had hoped for an interview or two. I was inside the building all of seven minutes before being ejected unceremoniously back out into the parking lot with exactly no new information. Seems like Chief Hanniford was still a bit annoyed with me. Talk about holding a grudge.

No worries. I'd sic Jorge on them.

I leaned against the rust-pitted fender of my trusty old car, a tired looking but reliable gray 1999 Volvo v70. Purchased new on the wave of optimism I felt when I graduated from college, it had been packed full numerous times as my life changed. It had been my back road tryst spot during Benjamin's and my honeymoon days, had carried me from California to Chicago, and was faithful to me throughout my marriage to Benjamin Morven even when he wasn't.

Later on, it creaked and thumped across the country to Vermont, packed with the remnants of my life as I fled

Chicago. Lately, it had developed some mysterious warning lights and noises, things I couldn't take care of yet.

Besides revenge, Benjamin was proving to be adept at avoiding making a single payment on his divorce settlement. He skated on the ragged edge of contempt, his lawyer bills likely higher than the judgment's total. And there didn't seem to be a damn thing I could do to speed things up. So, until the day my ship came in, my rusty, pollutant leaking PCB laden barge, carrying Benjamin's tainted money, I avoided driving old Peggy (short for Pegasus) as much as possible. But the new police and safety complex, Brownville's pride and joy, was a couple of miles outside of downtown, further than I was going to walk.

Chewing on the top of my pen, I pondered the murder and wondered what pieces were there that I needed to make sense of it all. From all accounts, Sebastian O'Nary was a gentleman, and a good businessman, well regarded around town. His reputation had helped catapult him into the forefront of the crazy Mayor's race that was taking place in Brownville.

I wondered if that might have played into his death, especially since one of his major rivals was in custody for his death. Why would John Peckham kill him, and in such a clumsy, public fashion? None of it made sense. Of course, the entire political process in Brownville didn't make sense either.

Since arriving in town, I had watched the mayoral primary race with a sense of growing bewilderment and amusement. I was used to more mainstream political battles, with clearly defined parties and candidates, you know, like maybe a Democrat and a Republican, with an Independent or two thrown in for good measure. Never had I seen so many grass roots entrants, with such diverse platforms to run on.

When it was announced that the current Mayor, The Honorable Donald Silva announced he was stepping down after a 12-year run for health reasons, the resulting free for all was nothing shy of incredible.

Well, at least to me it was incredible. The locals regarded it like it was business as usual.

For weeks, candidate after candidate was photographed walking down the granite steps of the old Town Hall, papers clutched firmly in hand. There were housewives, businessmen, and even a couple of unemployed people who spoke openly of the salary being the drawing factor. We had people like Molly Bruce, whose heart was in the right place even if her experience ran more towards gardening, running a one-woman campaign, her platform to bring transparency to the office (for reasons that were as muddy and unclear), and to return benches to Main Street.

We had John Peckham, whose "Free Ice Cream and Lower Taxes for All!" messages were on the damned life sized cardboard cutouts of himself. In such a chaotic mess of candidates, he had appeared to have as much chance as anyone.

Also in this crazy race was Jeannette Perkins, whose platform was to create a business center in town, for what businesses neither she nor anyone else knew. When pressed for details of how she would pay for such an expenditure, her reply had been, "We could hold a series of town wide tag sales, one that all the merchants can donate to, with all proceeds donated to the project."

There were people still on probation for domestic violence, people who had lost their licenses to DUI, and people who were just the other side of the Alzheimer's line. But out of this pile of people, two clearly credentialed leaders in the race had emerged; Sebastian O'Nary and Hal Morgan.

O'Nary was beating the drum of pro-growth, pro-business, and was actively championing bringing industry to the town. He spoke tirelessly of his dreams of bringing the Lucky Plucker chicken plant to town, utilizing the brownfields that stretched to the north too toxic from years of paper mill chemicals to farm or develop.

The town of Brownville proper sat on the edges of the Connecticut River as it meandered south through Vermont on its march to the ocean. Massive flooding had already occurred in 1890, 1932 and 1955. The last one had ripped apart the area north of town, once a forest of factories and mills. The resulting pollution had left the area virtually uninhabitable for the past 57 years. Local legend had it that it was seven years before the grass could even grow there again. News that a chicken processing plant could and would spend the millions to clean up the brownfields had been met with incredulity and guarded optimism.

I wondered if that plan had died with O'Nary.

Meanwhile, Morgan was actively anti-business, endlessly harping on providing more green spaces, parks, dog parks, riverside parks, shuffleboard courts, community gardens; his list of non-tax paying plots of land was endless. What he wasn't as forthcoming with was how the town would pay for all this green space, preferring to allude to "donors" who would make the vision a reality. He had a sizable backing; Brownville had been long divided by the tree hugging, Birkenstock wearing liberals, who now supported Morgan, while the dyed-in-the-wool pragmatic Yankee farmers, who had thrown in with O'Nary.

Until last night, O'Nary was looking like a shoo-in for the primary election. Morgan a lock for the other top spot. Vitriol had been spiking on both sides of the political line in the sand. I, along with the rest of the town, had been looking forward to the debate scheduled for next week between Morgan and O'Nary.

I chewed on my pen cap some more and pondered my next move. I still had nothing on John Peckham's status, or why he was detained. I had to get Jorge going on that angle. Obviously, Hanniford woke up on the wrong side of the bed this morning. And why such a huge firefight? Was it a drug angle? You didn't often hear about hashish in the area. Run of the mill stuff, marijuana, some cocaine, or mostly kids huffing aerosol cans, a habit that gave me a headache just thinking about it. But hashish? A kilo? That was some serious dope.

Behind me, two officers sprinted from the building and jumped into a car. Lights flashing, they hit the siren and screamed out of the lot, turning left towards town. I looked up as the car bumped out of the driveway, suspension bottoming out for a moment. What the hell? Why not?

I jumped in Peggy and hauled ass after them.

CHAPTER 7

*C*yrus Morton farmed a large, rambling family tract north of Brownville, carrying on a family tradition that had been in place for over a century now. Once sprawling into the region of the brownfields, the family farm, while smaller now than it was 100 years ago, still covered an impressive 600 acres or so. Much of it was patchwork plots and fields, dimpled with rocks that sprouted up out of the ground.

They tapped maple trees in the spring, boiling up the sap into syrup that sold in the Brownville Epicure Market. In winter, a field of Christmas trees, Morton's Tag N' Cut, saw a brisk business. Here and there, rag tag beef steers dotted the fields, bordered by cornfields planted for silage. Hay, firewood, compost; like all New England farmers, they survived by diversity and thousands of hours of back-breaking work.

The Mortons were well known and well respected around town, and with the exception of Ephraim C. Morton's memorable arrest for debauchery back in 1919, they generally kept to themselves, causing no problems.

Right now, however, Cyrus was sitting in the cab of his

41

John Deere 5203, smack in the middle of the intersection of Main and Maple streets, at one of the three traffic lights in town and at one of the most major intersections. Cars jammed both sides of the intersection, doors flung open, left randomly in the roadway, their drivers having fled.

I came squealing in behind the cops, throwing old Peggy into the gas station parking lot at the corner, while grabbing for my pad and camera.

Cyrus was sitting there with the tractor cab door open, casually plinking the traffic lights with a handgun. And damn; he was a pretty good shot, too. The lights swayed in the breeze, plastic littering the ground as he carefully took aim at the yellow lens on the light facing him. Pop! A spray of yellow plastic rained down on the pavement.

The two cops I had chased piled out of their car, throwing the doors open and taking up a shooting stance behind it. They yelled at Cyrus to stop. He calmly flipped them the bird and took out the green arrow in a shower of green shards. Bewildered, the cops conferred through the body of the car.

I snapped a couple quick shots of Cyrus as I crouched behind my car and started jotting notes. From the other side of the intersection another police car rolled in from the south, moving at a leisurely pace, weaving around stopped cars until he was pulling right up to Cyrus's tractor. I held my breath. In the silence that descended across the intersection, you could have heard a pin drop.

Officer Pim got out of the car and walked right up to the cab.

"Aw, Cyrus, what the hell are you doing?"

"This goldurned light ain't working again. I been settin' here twenty minutes while it keeps changing for the other side, but not for us! I tole you the last time it happened that I wasn't gunna put up with that shit again!"

Officer Pim pushed his hat off his forehead and rubbed his face. He looked weary, having been up all night like I had.

"Cyrus, you cain't do that. I told you, it happens again, you just go and tell us about it, we'll fix it. Now you done made a mess."

The old farmer spat over the wheel onto the ground, and looked at Pim. "Jimmy, you should know me by now. I ain't waitin' on nothin'. I got field over that way I gotta get to and sitting here while a bunch of Masshole yokels clogs up the intersection ain't getting' my work done."

Pim sighed. I jotted notes. Jimmy? So his name was Jim Pim? His parents must have enjoyed alliteration.

In the cop car in front of me, one of the officers was slowly standing up. He yelled over the door at Cyrus and 'Jimmy' "Hey, Cyrus, can you git on out of that intersection? We got traffic backed up all the way to the highway now!"

Cyrus leaned out and yelled back at him. "Jason Hole! You shut up before I take out your tires! I told you two weeks ago this light was a problem! Guess you didn't believe me!"

"I told the DPW about it! What more can I do?" he threw his arms out in frustration.

"The DPW... Ha! That's rich! Buncha lazy, good for nothing.." his voice dropped off as he sat back into the cab of his tractor. Beside him, Officer Pim put a foot up on the step of the tractor, leaning on it with familiarity. "C'mon Cyrus. You made your point. And now we'll get new lights here. I agree, these are a pain in the ass. But you cain't stay here shooting them, that's gonna make a huge mess with the paperwork and stuff. Why doncha follow me over to the station and we'll fill out the paperwork so you can get on your way over to the Meadows?"

'The Meadows' was a local term for a network of fields and small clusters of houses that stretched to the east of town along the river's edge. Morton farmed a fairly large section of it.

I held my breath. He was basically inviting Cyrus to come get arrested.

Inside the tractor cab, I could see Cyrus shaking his head. "Jimmy, I been settin' here for pert near half an hour now, and you want me to come down to the station and waste MORE time? Son, your daddy didn't raise no fools, but I'm beginning to wonder if hanging around with people like JASON AND ROBERT," this bellowed out the cab towards the other car, "are turning your brains to mush!"

Pim, still leaning with one foot resting on the tractor's step, shook his head. Amazingly, a small smile was visible. "Cyrus…. come on now. You're tired, we're tired, I been up all night and now I'm pulling a double, and the Captain, well he's fit to be tied right now, what with the murder that happened last night. Cain't we.."

"Murder? What murder?"

Living on the outskirts of town and being at work since before dawn, Cyrus was one of the few people left in the township that hadn't heard about Sebastian O'Nary's death.

Officer Pim looked up at Cyrus. "Shit, Sebastian O'Nary got himself killed last night down to a Pint of Peck's on Main Street. We been working the scene all night."

"What?! Sebastian? You're shitting me, son!"

Pim shook his head. "Nah, I wish I was, but I ain't. He's dead alright. And the Chief ain't in too good a mood today neither." He dropped his voice, barely audible to where I crouched. "If'n I were you, Cyrus, I'd just sign the complaint and get on over to the Meadows. Chief gets involved, he's gonna take a chunk of your ass out."

Silence for a long minute. Then Cyrus banged on the wheel in frustration. "Well, they gunna fix these goldurned lights this time? I'm not the only one sick of 'em, you know."

"I know, I know." Pim raised his hands in surrender. "I hate 'em too. But we ain't had the budget for new ones, Cyrus." He glanced up at them, his face falling, "In fact, now they gunna have to put someone here to work traffic for a few days."

Cyrus grinned widely, gaped teeth visible through the Lexan cab windows. "Use Jason or Robert. That's about all they're good for anyway. So what happened to Sebastian?"

Pim nodded towards the police station. "Tell you what, you come on over to the station and I'll fill you in, ok?"

"Alright." Cyrus reached down and fired up the tractor again, the diesel roaring and belching black smoke. Pim gestured to the two officers who were still crouched down behind their car doors. I slowly stood up, putting my notebook on the hood of my car. Pim caught sight of me and flushed red. He looked away.

My cellphone buzzed in my bag, felt more than heard over the blatting diesel. I fished it out and flipped it open. It was Jorge.

"Case here."

"And where the hell is here, Sandy? What were you thinking, leaving me with Dana like that? You just wait until the next time you need something..." His voice carried on, tinny through the phone's speaker. I was semi-ignoring him, looking instead at the pair who had emerged from the gas station behind me.

Frick and Frack, Ying and Yang, Beavis and Butthead, these two were an odd pair. I could see them being named Igor and Ivan. "Igor" was tall, hunched slightly, with a thickened face and forehead. He sported one eyebrow across sloping forehead, his hairline receding back already. His chin was following his hairline, making for a face shaped like a pointy boulder. He wore dusty looking jeans, black work boots, and a wife beater tee shirt. His arms were massive.

Beside him, "Ivan" was a small, darty eyed rat like man, black hair pulled back in a greasy short ponytail, a silver ring in one ear. He wore a leather vest with no shirt, his little pot belly protruding, crusty jeans over boots. He was tapping a new pack of cigarettes against his hand as he watched the scene at the intersection. They both looked Eastern European to me, unremarkable in Chicago, but out-of-place here in Brownville, VT.

I shifted the phone to my other ear as Jorge ranted, watching them from one eye. My inner sense was tingling.

"Well? Are you even listening to me?"

"Huh? Oh sure, Jorge. Listen, I need you to find out what is going on with John Peckham. Hanniford still has his knickers in a knot at me."

"Where are you now?"

"Over at the BP station. Cyrus Morton just took out the traffic lights with a handgun."

Jorge's laugh traveled through the phone. "Right on Cyrus! That intersection is a pain in the ass."

"Well, it's about to become even more of a pain now. The lights are in pieces all over the ground."

"Hey, Case, I almost forgot, there's a press conference today at the auditorium at the Town Hall, 4 p.m. sharp."

"Mmm?" I was watching Igor and Ivan again. They had sauntered towards a sagging, flaking Olds 98 parked along the edge of the lot, eyes still on the confusion in the intersection. Ivan was sneering as he looked at the police cars. Igor was gnawing on a Kit Kat bar, chocolate crumbs smearing his mouth. In my ear, Jorge droned on; something about the press conference. I tuned back in. "Jorge, why are they holding this conference again?"

"Jesus Case! I just spent ten minutes telling you why!"

"Well, Maxim, I happen to be on the scene of an event, so excuse ME if I seem distracted by blathering!"

A muttered curse through the phone line, then, "Will you just get your ass back here then? I gotta go... Dana is heading my way again... thank you very much!"

I barked a laugh. "Ask her when the flood is coming!"

"Flood?" Jorge was bewildered.

"Yeah... she's wearing her highwater jeans today."

"Jesus Case! Sometimes I can't believe how bitter you can be. No wonder you got divorced and fired!"

"What? Maxim, you rotten..." The words stuttered out of my mouth.

He clicked off.

I stood still, holding the phone, shock tingling through my spine. How the hell did Jorge know that!? I had taken my maiden name back after the debacle and had taken pains to erase everything and anything connected to my life with Benjamin. The last thing I needed in my new life was the weight of failure from my old one.

And now, with Benjamin's latest poison pen rantings being broadcast across the country in high speed, I sure as hell didn't want anyone connecting me with him. Freaking Jorge! He must have researched me. The only question was, how many other people in the newsroom had he shared that with?

Fuming, I clambered into Peggy's sagging front seat and fired her up. Jorge was screwing with the wrong reporter here. My hand trembled as I stabbed the key at the ignition.

I seesawed around in the lot to get room to pull away from the snarl of cars the officers were trying to sort out. In my rear-view mirror, I saw Officer Pim standing next to his car; door open, one foot in, ready to climb in and head back over to the cop shop to process Cyrus Morton.

He was staring after me.

47

CHAPTER 8

*B*rownville's Town Hall was a ubiquitous New England rambling white clapboard structure located kitty corner to the town common. It occupied one side of the triangle the common occupied: Route 17, aka Elm Street and Main Street formed the other two boundaries. The Town Hall had an old auditorium located on the lower floor, used for events such as the recently canceled debate. It could hold up to 250 people.

I could see the green was teeming with people as I briskly strode up the sidewalk, still fuming at Jorge. As I drew nearer, I saw that there were rows of chairs placed in the front of the Town Hall, and that most of the Mayoral Candidates already occupied them. What the hey...?

Stopping, I looked closely at the scene in front of me. It looked like 500 people or more were at the press conference. Holy crap! That was a huge turnout for a last minute, late afternoon gig.

I saw Molly Bruce's car parked in the driveway to the Town Hall, her "MOLLY BRUCE FOR MAYOR" signs visible above the heads of the throngs. Looking at the candidates already in attendance, I spied Hal Morgan, in the place of honor right next to the current Mayor, Donald Silva. Molly Bruce was sitting a couple of seats down from him, her lips pressed in a thin line. I saw Jeannette Perkins, the let's- have-tag -sales- to- pay- for- things lady, John Hennly, an unemployed contractor who wanted a job, and holy crap, David Gilson, the candidate most recently arrested for wanton destruction of property, violation of a protective order and disturbing the peace. He was out already? He sat slouched in his chair, lips pursed petulantly, a baseball cap pulled low over his forehead.

There was a single folding chair with black bunting draped over it, to Don Silva's left, presumably for Sebastian O'Nary. I noted Hal Morgan's expression, suitably grave with a smattering of self- satisfaction tossed in. I started pushing my way closer to the front.

"Case. You made it." Jorge's voice in my ear. I turned and leveled flinty eyes on him, the eyes that made men far stronger than him quake in their shoes.

He ignored it.

"What's with all of this?" I waved at the crowd. "I thought it was going to be held inside?"

"It was. They had to move it out here because so many people showed up." He turned, looking towards the front of the building. "Come on. This way." He angled to the right, cutting through a sea of denim, Carhartt, Birkenstocks, caftans and office wear. I followed in his wake.

It looked like half the Hill Towns, the little towns that speckled the flanks of the surrounding hillsides, had come down to the valley for the entertainment. Voices babbled in a dull roar around us, random phrases audible here and there.

"You bent over and caught your WHAT in the door?"

"They traced my genealogy all the way back to Henry the VIII. I'm fucking ROYALTY, I tell ya!"

"So I said to her, I said, 'Martha, I'd rather have tulips on my organ than roses on my piano'. She didn't appreciate that much."

I ducked and weaved, keeping Jorge's blue linen shirt in sight. We popped out at a yellow taped line in front of the Town Hall that Jorge lifted and held up for me. Ducking, I followed him through.

To one side of the clearing, several more chairs had been set up, the hastily computer generated sign saying; PRESS flapping in the breeze. I noted about half the seats had already taken, the local radio station, the paper from over in New Hampshire, and holy crap! There was even a Boston reporter with camera man.

Next to her, I spied a reporter and photographer from a larger paper from Bennington. Little Brownville, VT had never had such a big press coverage for anything before. Jorge and I took two seats and settled in. I looked around behind us. "Where's Karl?" I was hoping to catch a glimpse of our photographer's huge hands again, and to fantasize about the rest of his appendages. Jorge shrugged.

I leaned over and spoke sotto voice in his ear, "You mind telling me just HOW you managed to dig up that little piece of info about me, Jorge?"

"It wasn't hard, Sandy. Ben Morven is pretty famous, so there's a lot out there about him. The question begs itself to ask: How in the WORLD did someone like YOU hook up with someone like HIM?"

Stung, I stared at him, my jaw sagging. He looked impatient with me. "Come on, Sandy. That's not how I meant it. He's one perverted mother. So how the hell did Miss All American White Bread Sandra Case end up with Mr. Sadistic?"

Wait! What? Perverted? More than I knew about? "Miss

All American White Bread...... Maxim, what the hell are you talking about?"

Up on stage, the microphone let out a feedback whistle as Connor Murphy, the town's press officer/administrative assistant, pulled it to his lips. He smiled an apology as the electronic shriek cut the roar of voices off mid stride.

I winced, rubbing my ears. I shot a glare at Jorge, hissing, "This conversation isn't over Jorge!"

He rolled his eyes impatiently.

Over the screech of feedback, Connor tried again. "Thank you all for coming today. Could you please take your seats? The press conference is ready to start."

The noise subsided a few decibels. I craned to see who else was on the makeshift staging in front of the town hall. I spied Chief Hanniford seated to one side of Silva. My eyes narrowed; I elbowed Jorge. He grunted and looked at me impatiently. "WHAT is it Case? And do you MIND not jabbing me in the ribs?" I did it again for good measure. "Jorge, did you get ahold of Hanniford today? What's up with John Peckham?"

"I wasn't able to and they aren't saying. Perhaps they will release a statement here." He looked over at me, saw my expression. "Oh, no Case... what are you thinking here?"

I turned guileless eyes to him. "Nothing, Jorge."

The squeal of the PA cut me off again, Don Silva was at the podium. He looked dazed, his hair uncombed, shirt buttoned crookedly under a worn suit coat. He stood frozen, peering out over the throng of people. The noise dropped off abruptly, five hundred pairs of eyes trained on him.

The silence stretched out. Behind him, his press officer cleared his throat and whispered something. He jumped visibly, his reverie broken. Looking down at his papers, he took a breath and leaned into the microphone.

"Ladies and Gentleman, thank you for joining us on this

solemn occasion. On this day, we honor the men and women who went to war in far-off countries, some never to return. They sacrificed their all for our freedom..."

The microphone was abruptly muffled as Connor covered it with his hand. He bent his head over next to Don's, his lips moving fiercely. Don looked blank. Connor pocketed the speech he had in front of him and thumbed through a wad of papers.

Around us, the noise began to rise again. Jorge leaned over and whispered to me, "And there you see why Don Silva is being forced to step down after so many glorious terms. They really should have made him do it last year and let Randy," Randy Hall was the town's administrator, "hold a special election. But they decided to save the money and wait for the regular election instead."

"What's wrong with him?"

Jorge shrugged. "They won't say, but I would guess dementia or Alzheimers. Rumor has it the PD has picked him up a number of times now, walking around wearing nothing but a pair of sneakers. Good thing he lives over towards the Meadows and not in town."

Oh. That would make for some copy. "Jorge, why has none of this ever made the paper? People should know he's a few neurons short of a synapse."

"Sandy, in small towns like this, there's no need to broadcast everything. For one thing, most people know, and for another, everyone knows everyone else. Russ and Don go way back. How would his family like it if Russ let us humiliate him? It really isn't in anyone's best interest. It's gossip, not news. So we kill those reports and focus on other matters."

What? "Jorge... the mayor is batshit crazy, and that's NOT NEWS?"

The PA squealed again, drowning Jorge's reply. Don stood

in front of it, a piece of paper in his hand, Connor at his shoulder. Taking a deep breath, Don leaned into the microphone once more. His voice rang out clear and steady.

"Ladies and Gentlemen, thank you all for coming today. Surely this is a sad, momentous day in Brownville, and I am sure you have many questions and concerns. We will address all the questions we can at this time."

He paused, cleared his throat, Connor poised tensely behind him.

"Without further ado, may I introduce Connor Murphy, my Mick press liaison." I heard shouts of laughter at that as Connor's face burned red. He grabbed the microphone. "Always a kidder, huh Don?"

Don stared back at him, blank eyed, a bit bewildered. Behind him, Randy Hall rose and tapped him on his shoulder, directing him to sit down. Connor turned to the crowd, gathered a breath, and leaned into the microphone.

"I know you have many questions, so we will try to answer them all for you, as best we can. For those of you just joining us today, last night we lost a good friend to many of us, Mr. Sebastian O'Nary, to a heinous act of violence, violence that Brownville isn't used to seeing in its storied streets. At the same time, another candidate, Mr. John Peckham, has been detained as 'a person of interest'. He has not been charged with anything, and at this time, is merely being held to facilitate the investigation."

He paused as the voices rose in excited chatter again. "Chief Hanniford of the Brownville Police Department is with us today to give an update on that situation. I also know that many of you are anxious about the mayoral debate that was scheduled to take place. We have decided that for right now it is in our best interest to postpone that debate indefinitely."

I heard muttering from the crowd at that. I looked at

Jorge. His eyebrows were raised. Leaning over, I hissed in his ear, "Why in the world would they shitcan the debate? What about the other sixteen candidates?"

He shook his head. "It was supposed to be between O'Nary, Peckham, Morgan and Bruce. I guess with two out of four unavailable, they are going to hold off."

"And no one else has anything of value to add to it?"

He shrugged impatiently.

On the stage, Connor was turned around, hand covering the mic, talking to Chief Hanniford. I noticed that Hanniford looked annoyed. He rose and stepped up to the podium, still talking to Connor.

The roar of the surrounding crowd steadily rose. I glanced over my shoulder, towards the street, and saw two familiar faces at the tape holding the crowd back from the press box. "Ivan" and "Igor". I nudged Jorge. "Hey, who are those two clowns, Jorge?"

He looked over in the direction I pointed. "Where?"

I leaned around him. "Those two. In front. Skinny dude with greasy hair, big lunk beside him."

Jorge looked at them a moment. "I don't know. I don't think I've ever seen them before."

"Ivan" noticed me looking at him and gave me a leering smile. I saw black holes where teeth had resided at some distant point in his life. Jorge saw the smile. "Hey Case, I think you have an admirer."

"Piss off Jorge."

On stage, Hanniford cleared his throat. The PA squealed again, cutting off the rising babble.

"Ladies and Gentlemen, may I please have some quiet?" He paused as the noise dipped.

"Last night, we responded to a call from the area of 232 Main Street for a report of shots fired. Upon arrival, we found a deceased male and evidence of a massive firefight.

The male, Mr. Sebastian O'Nary, was dispatched with a single gunshot wound to the forehead. As part of our own ongoing investigation, we have taken the owner of the storefront where Mr. O'Nary was found, a Mr. John Peckham, into the station for questioning. He has not been charged with any crime, and I cannot comment any further on an investigation that is underway. At this time, we have sealed the crime scene to prevent any further tampering," his cold grey eyes sought mine at that, "and will keep it sealed until further notice. Please use the pedestrian walkway around that area until then. We will keep the public informed if there is any further development. We do not believe that this crime was random, so there is no need for alarm. I ask that any citizens who see anything suspicious report it to us immediately at 802-33….."

"Suspicious like the cops detaining an innocent citizen for political reasons?"

The yell came from our right, at the edge of the crowd. Jorge and I craned around to see the speaker. Holy shit! John Peckham, pissed off, disheveled and baggy eyed, pushed his way to the tape and ducked underneath, followed closely by his lawyer, William 'Bilkem' Chem. I felt my jaw drop. Beside me, Jorge sucked his breath in sharply. "Oh, this is going to be good!" he hissed gleefully.

On the stage, the candidates gaped and sat up sharply. The noise rose to a roar around us as the crowd realized who was yelling. I noticed "Ivan" and "Igor" frowning at him. My curiosity tweaked at that. Why would they care?

On the stage, Hannifords' eyes were glacial. I saw him cover the microphone as John Peckham reached the stage. Connor Murphy pushed his way up next to Hanniford at the podium, sweat beading his face.

Jorge was on the edge of his seat, eyes dancing. I strained to hear.

Hanniford shook his head savagely, his mouth a grim line, Connor's hands flew in the air as he hissed something at John. 'Bilkem', his lawyer, stepped forward and shook a finger under Connors' nose. Screw this. Freedom of the Press, my ass.

I jumped up and ducked under the line of tape in front of me.

"Case! What the hell are you doing? Get back here!"

I ignored Jorge and strode up to the lectern. Hanniford's expression darkened further when he saw me; I was glad to have over 500 witnesses. John Peckham looked around as I reached him, anger in his face. I could smell the sour, unwashed smell of him.

"What? Who the hell are you?" John barked.

I stuck my press pass in his face. "Sandra Case, The Brownville Reporter, Mr. Peckham, I'd like a moment with you, sir. Seems that information about last night has been less than forthcoming and I would like a chance to get the facts about what happened."

I was gambling on the body language the men had been displaying, that they weren't about to allow Peckham his moment at the mic.

Hanniford exploded. "Get the hell out of here right now before I arrest your ass and lock you up until the sun doesn't shine anymore!"

"On what charges?" I bellowed back.

"I don't know and I don't care! I'll find some, lady!" In his anger, Hanniford had taken his hand off the microphone. Our shouting match was being transmitted across the entire town common now. Out of the corner of my eye, I saw Jorge ducking under the tape to join me.

John drew himself up as tall as he could and yelled back at Hanniford. "How dare you threaten someone for trying to ask MY side of the story? You can't silence me!" He turned to me, "Ms. Case, I will be HAPPY to grant you an exclusive interview about the horrendous treatment I received at the hands of our so-called law enforcers last night!!"

Hot damn!

Jorge reached my side just then, dark eyes glittering. He placed a hand on my arm, his gaze locked on Hanniford. "Chief, I understand your predicament, but Ms. Case isn't breaking any laws here."

Hanniford's breathing was rapid, his eyes gray icicles. Through clenched teeth he hissed, "Get. Her. OFF. This. Stage. Right. NOW!"

Jorge tightened his grip on my upper arm, trying to guide me back. I wasn't having any of that. "Why shouldn't I be able to ask questions? That's my job, mister! And I have a lot of questions about what went on last night, as I am sure everyone out there does too!" I waved at the crowd, staring dumbstruck at us.

Hanniford struggled to maintain control. I saw his right hand twitching near his belt. Oh, how he probably wanted to taser me again. The memory pissed me off more.

Raising my voice to my best stage projecting one, I bellowed. "For instance, I would be REALLY interested to know exactly WHY the Brownville Police Department felt the need to TASER me last night!" I heard gasps from the edge of the crowd, along with some laughter.

Hanniford arched an eyebrow. "I would think the reason is self- evident."

Beside me, Peckham frowned and tugged on his coat cuffs. "They tasered you? Why?" His lawyer, 'Bilkem', stepped up next to me and handed me a card. "Here. I specialize in police brutality."

Hanniford glared at him. "I thought it was car crashes and divorces." 'Bilkem' shrugged, "That too."

I drew myself up to my full 5'5" and yelled at Hanniford.

"I want to know why there was a firefight! And why there was a kilo of hash in the freezer under John's Schweddy Balls!" I heard more gasps and laughter. Jorge hissed in my ear, "Case! Shut up!"

I was never good with that directive.

John Peckham gaped at me. "Hash? Like hashish? In MY freezer? What the hell?" His bewilderment was evident. From his lawyer, I heard, "Sweaty balls? What the hell?"

Hanniford realized at that moment that the microphone was open, the crowd rapt, hanging on every word. With a curse, he savagely yanked the plug out of the back, producing another electronic scream.

Behind us, Molly Bruce stood up and yelled, "William Hanniford! You put that plug back in that mic right now! You can't censor everything in this town, you know!"

He flicked her a withering glare and said nothing. Incensed, she stomped up to the podium, her finger wagging. "You better pray that I don't become mayor, mister, because one of the first things I will do is call for a reform of the entire police department, from the TOP DOWN!" That produced a smattering of cheers from the edge of the crowd. Heady with excitement, she launched into it. "I will also ask for FULL ACCOUNTABILITY from ALL DEPARTMENTS and strive for COMPLETE TRANSPARENCY in all governmental matters!" She waved her arms wide, her white helmet hair shining in the sun.

Beside her, John Peckham gaped at her, stunned into silence. I heard muttering from the other candidates as she faced the crowd and launched into her political rhetoric.

"Hey! Why is she getting time? I want equal time!"

"Wait a minute! She can't do that!"

"I want some time too! You can't give it to one person only!"

I heard a chair fall over backwards as Hal Morgan jumped to his feet. "This is a travesty! Get her off the stage!"

I wasn't sure if he was referring to Molly or me. I took advantage of the pandemonium to grab Peckham's arm, getting his attention. "Here." I handed him my card, "I really want to talk to you and get the straight skinny."

He looked at me bewildered. "I think I should be asking YOU what happened last night. Really? There was hash in my freezer?" I nodded solemnly. Beside me, Jorge was pulling on me as the yelling from the candidates rose. "Case, get the hell off of here before Hanniford tasers you again." He tugged me towards the chairs.

"He wouldn't dare."

"Don't make any bets on that."

The candidates were in full song now, pushing each other and shouting towards the crowd. I saw Hanniford's glare over the heads of Molly and Hal as they went nose to nose, shouting at each other. His eyes were glacial. I gave him a little half smile and a wave as Jorge pulled me down the steps to the lawn again.

Across the stage, I saw "Ivan" glaring at me too, his expression unexpectedly murderous. Beside me, Jorge's body convulsed in silent laughter.

"Jesus Case! I can't believe you just did that!"

"Why not? You think you wouldn't have?"

"I KNOW I wouldn't have! Hanniford will hold a grudge forever now!"

Behind us, the yelling rose from the stage. Glancing over my shoulder, I saw Molly Bruce being pulled back from the edge by David Gilson, the out-on-his-own-recognizance candidate. Behind him, Jeanette Perkins, the let's-have-tag-sales proponent was pounding on his back with her fist shouting, "Leave her alone!" Hal Morgan's face was beet red, his arms waving wildly as he shouted at Connor Murphy and Don Silva. Oddly, Don was grinning from ear to ear.

Hanniford was already off the stage.

The noise was a roar around us. Jorge glanced back and shook his head. "We need to get out of here before we get caught in the middle of a full scale riot."

I looked around. The crowd was animated, with hands waving and people yelling at each other. I saw two old ladies shoving each other, shouting something unintelligible as we passed.

I leaned over next to Jorge as we hustled back through the throng and asked, "Are politics always like this in this town?"

He shrugged. "Not always. Sometimes it's worse."

CHAPTER 9

*D*ana Oakes was perched like a beady-eyed bird on her chair when we arrived back at the office. I spied her swooping towards us as I dropped my bag under my desk.

"Mayday! Check six!" I hissed at Jorge before I followed my bag under the desk.

"Whaa..?" He turned around and looked up into her bright eyes as I crawled through the tangle of wires under the cubicles and desks.

"Jorge!" Her voice was falsely bright. "Where's Sandy? I just saw her here."

"I... I have no idea where Case got to." His polished shoes shifted as he craned around, looking for me. I crawled under two more unoccupied desks, resurfacing next to a pair of knee high suede purple boots with red stockings above them. Lizzy was opting for color today, full on primary colors. I emerged next to her elbow.

"Hi Lizzy."

She glanced down at me, her brown eyes round in astonishment. One eyebrow raised slowly. "Um... hi?"

I gestured across the cubicles with my head. "Dana."

"Oh." A smirk flickered across her lips.

"Whacha doing?" I pulled the unoccupied chair over and sat next to her, crouched down so Dana wouldn't spy me. Lizzy's fingers were dancing over the keyboard of the laptop.

"I'm doing Diane's column."

"What? Where's Diane?"

"She had to go home."

"Over a bunch of dead ducks?"

Lizzy nodded and rolled her eyes. "Yeah." She leaned forward, scanning her page, a slight frown on her face. "Honestly, I can see why she's so batty though. This town will make you nuts."

"Why? What are you writing about?"

"Some dude has a new business in town, called 'Virgin Whoopee Pies'. Said he's going to go around selling them at church fairs."

"Virgin Whoopee Pies..? What the heck is that?"

She rolled her eyes, spinning the laptop around to me. "Here. Read this paragraph. I got to interview this nutbag, thank you very much."

I started scanning where her long fingernail pointed (painted primary blue):

'Johnson is enthusiastic about his new business venture. He explained his business model to us, "I have a recipe that is slap-your-grandmother-good for Whoopee Pies. I'm going to make up a bunch of them, stick a cherry in the middle and call them 'Virgin Whoopee Pies'. I'll go around to church fairs and county fairs and sell them out of my camper. I am estimating I can make 20 to 30 thousand a year my first year selling these pies!" '

"Virgin Whoopee Pies?" I looked at Lizzy, my eyebrows raised." Doesn't this clown know the only virgins around here are the fast sheep?"

Lizzy stifled a laugh, her brown eyes twinkling. Looking at me, she reached out and carefully plucked a dust bunny off my head with her cobalt blue nails.

"So, um, how was the press conference?"

Behind me, I heard Jorge's voice raising as he tried vainly to get Dana to leave him alone. I shrugged at her question. "It was... interesting. They canceled the mayoral debate."

"What? Why?"

I shook my head. "We aren't sure on that yet. The candidates are pissed off about it, though."

"I bet. That's like the highlight of the primary. What's going on with the murder?"

"John Peckham's out and I scored an exclusive interview with him."

"What?" Her exclamation made Dana and Jorge go silent. I saw Dana's head pop up over the cubicle tops, looking at Lizzy. "Shit!" I muttered, doubling over and peered through the cubicle crack at her. Lizzy grabbed the telephone receiver and held it to her head, straightening up enough so they could see the phone at her ear. With a sour glare, she turned back to continue her harangue on Jorge.

"Thanks, Lizzy. I really don't want to deal with her right now."

"Da nada. But how in the world did you land an exclusive with John Peckham?"

I shrugged. "Right place right time?"

Behind me, I heard Dana muttering curses as she stomped away from Jorge's desk, empty-handed again. I slid down into the knee well of Lizzy's desk as she stormed past. She strode straight out the front door of the newsroom without slowing. I released a sigh of relief.

"She's annoying, yes?" Lizzy remarked.

"Yes. She is. Why in the world do they run her column? It's pure gossip."

"She's married to the second cousin of the publisher. I heard she really wanted to be the political reporter, but they kiboshed that. They gave her a column instead. She's been doing it for ten years now, and frankly, Russ is afraid to let her go."

I climbed stiffly to my feet, brushing my knees off from dust collected on my journey. "Well, thanks for the refuge, Lizzy. Better get back to Jorge now."

"Anytime." She bent her head back over her laptop. "I simply have to finish this AMAZING story about the latest entrepreneur to pop up in Brownville, anyway."

Her sarcasm made a smile crease my mouth.

Craning over the cubicle tops, I spied Jorge peering back at me. He raised an eyebrow at my appearance. "Later, Liz." I strode around the desks to reach him.

"Where the hell did you go? And thanks a bunch for leaving me with that woman again!" His righteous indignation made me smile briefly. I dropped into my chair and wheeled it across the walkway at him.

"Never mind Dana. You haven't told me yet what you meant before that crack about 'Miss All American Whitebread'! Who else have you told, Jorge?" I hissed at him.

Drawing back slightly, he eyed me warily. "Well Jesus, Case, it's public record you know."

"Only if you're looking for it. Why were you looking for it?" I felt a fluttering in my chest.

He raised one shoulder in a shrug. "When Russ hired you, I was curious why a city slicker like you would come out here, so I checked you out. What's the big deal?"

I drew a ragged breath, my temper barely in check. "Maybe I don't like people researching me? It smacks of invasion of privacy, Jorge."

A wry smile creased the corner of his mouth. "Says the woman who was hired as an investigative reporter!"

"That's different!"

"How?"

"Well… it just is! And what do you mean, my ex was a perverted son of a bitch? I mean, I know he is, but what are you talking about?"

Jorge stilled, wary eyes on mine. "Have you looked him up online, Case?"

"Uh..no. Should I?"

He frowned. "I don't know. Maybe not. Maybe you should just leave well enough alone. You're divorced, that says it all."

"Who else knows?" I cast a glance around the newsroom, the late day sun bathing the drab interior with gold streaks of light.

Jorge shook his head. "No one knows from me. I can't say they haven't researched for themselves, but I doubt they would find much."

My eyes narrowed. "And you would find more than anyone else?"

"Case, if you had a pimple on your ass lasered off, I would find it."

"Well, I guess you did, because you found out about Ben."

"I'd say he was a classic ass pimple." Jorge shook his head.

I took a deep breath. "What… what did you dig up about my… my… last job?"

Jorge looked at me for a moment. "That you were with the Chronicle for only ten months. It sounded like you had a promising future when you were suddenly released from your contract. Is there something you want to talk about?"

I shook my head, not trusting my voice. "No, no… I just don't like finding out that people are going behind my back trying to dig shit up on me, that's all."

"Look, as exciting as your life is, can we get on with the

business at hand? Holy shit, I couldn't believe you pulled that stunt today!"

I felt smug satisfaction. "Worked, didn't it?"

He shook his head. "It worked, but there's going to be fall-out, mark my words."

Russ banged the door to his office open, his hair still awry, still in pajama bottoms. He glared across the news-room at me. "Case! Maxim! Get in here!"

"Let the fallout begin." Jorge muttered.

CHAPTER 10

This time Russ wasn't amused. He paced around his office, rubbing his face. Jorge and I sat in the rickety wooden chairs, watching him silently.

"Jorge, how the hell could you let her DO that? You know as well as I do that we need Hanniford's support to keep on top of this investigation! Now he's telling me that all information will be disseminated through the Burlington Journal from now on! He's setting them up for exclusives! Do you know how the publisher is going to take that? She's already been on the phone. She didn't just chew on my ass, she gnawed around the edges until it fell out!"

I shifted uneasily on the chair. Jorge shot me a warning look. I ignored him.

"Come on, Russ! I got us an exclusive with John Peckham!"

Russ stopped and stared at me. "Oh, really? Well, where is it?"

"He's got my card! He said he's going to call me!"

"Sandy, until he calls you, IF he even does, you have exactly NOTHING to show for this afternoon except a huge rift between us and the police department, a rift I don't know if I can mend! You gave him your card.... big honking deal! You really think he's going to call you?"

I opened my mouth... and nothing came out. Holy shit, Russ was right. I had nothing from Peckham, no phone number, no information, hell I didn't even know where he lived. I squirmed in the hard chair.

Jorge spoke up, "Russ, don't get too bent about it. She did what any good investigative reporter would have done. There was a lot of bullshit happening, and she uncovered it. They were trying to quash John from speaking. Why? Why won't they let him talk? And why was he ranting about being held illegally, for political reasons?"

I was thinking frantically as he spoke. Jorge had to know where he lived. I could head over and speak to him sooner than later. Russ's next words interrupted my train of thought.

"Jorge, it's obvious you are better versed in the workings of this town than Sandy, so from here on, you are the lead on the story. Sandy, you work under Jorge now, you got it? No more kiting off on your own, pissing people off. One more screw up like this, and you are off this story completely!"

Stunned, I gaped at him with my best dead-fish face. Jorge put a warning hand on mine briefly.

"Got it, Russ. Sandy, come on, we have work to do." He hauled me to my feet. A strangled sound like I was gargling with motor oil came from my throat. Jorge two stepped me out the door.

"Jorge...!"

"Don't!" he muttered in my ear. "Not here. Walk with me."

He steered me out the newsroom door and out into the lobby. The sun had finally set, the streetlamps outside the ornate old front doors flickering on as we faced each other. I felt blood burning in my face. Jorge put a hand on my shoulder.

"Sandy… I've known Russ for quite a while now, and I know when to hold 'em and when to fold 'em. Tonight is not the time to challenge him. Believe me when I tell you, he would have you out on your ass in a nanosecond the mood he's in."

"But… but…" my motor skills in my mouth failed me, leaving me sputtering like a car running on three of four cylinders. Jorge shook me gently. "Case. Get a grip! Nothing is changing except for how Russ perceives it, got it? All this means is you have to pull your horns in a bit… if you can." He eyed me dubiously.

My verbal skills came back to me with a bang. "Jorge! What the hell? I know he's pissed, but geez! Come on, man! I have an exclusive with Peckham! I know he'll call me! I know it!"

Doubt crossed Jorge's face. "I don't know about that Case. It's one thing in the heat of the moment to say you will, but quite another when a day goes by and you've cooled off. Plus, I would be surprised if 'Bilkem' lets him speak to anyone right away."

Shit. The lawyer. "Well, where does John live? If I go to his house, he'll have to say something to me, even if it's get the hell out of here."

Jorge shook his head before I was even finished speaking. "Uh uh, I wouldn't go there, Sandy. Not to his house. He says one word in complaint, and Russ will bag you."

"But why!? Why was he so supportive last night and ready to fire me tonight?"

Jorge simply said, "Jan Petersen."

"Oh.." Jan Petersen was the publisher of the paper, the last member of the founding family, the woman rumored to be financing the operation out of family pockets. I had long heard of her, but had never seen her. Her name was spoken with reverence bordering on awe around the newsroom. I recalled then that Russ had told me she was pissed... mega pissed. My heart sank.

"Look Case, this is what we will do. I'm not booting you off the story. Hell, where would I get my comic relief if you weren't working with me?" I snapped my head up at that, my eyes narrowed. Jorge grinned widely. "Life would be boring without you here, Case. So let's figure out a game plan, ok?"

I looked up at him and sighed in resignation. "All right, Maxim. You got it. Now what should we do first?"

CHAPTER 11

I opened the Burlington paper warily the next morning as I sat in front of the Brownville Epicurean Market. The sun scorched my cheeks, even at this early hour, promising another toasty June day. A baggy clothed teen on a skateboard rumbled past on the sidewalk, his shirt flapping in his wake. I took a sip of my coffee, steeling myself for the story.

The story was about what I expected.

What I wasn't prepared for were the photos.

There I was, in full living color, on the stage, my finger in Chief Hanniford's face, my face bright red, Jorge vainly trying to stop me. I looked at the caption, then realized the photo credit had the photographer's name and AP after it.

Shit! The photo was released for nationwide use! I felt panic fluttering in my throat. Benjamin Morven knew I was on the East Coast, but as far as I knew, he didn't know with which paper. I felt the sidewalk falling out from under me.

A million years ago, when I was young and dumb, I had done something incredibly stupid. I had further compounded that initial stupidity twice over, once when I let

Ben know about it, and twice when I went for blood in the divorce settlement. I can still remember the day the judge finally handed down his decision.

Because of his OCD, Ben hadn't hidden his assets in time, assets that despite his penchant for fine wines and clothing by Yoshi Yoshi, were far larger than even I knew.

The blood had drained from his face when the Judge told him he would be paying me over $250,000 for the privilege of being married to me. I vividly remembered leaving the courtroom when he pushed up next to me, the smell of his cologne triggering my gag reflex.

"You talentless bitch. You never learned that you shouldn't fuck with someone who buys ink in 50-gallon barrels, have you? Mark my words; You will regret this."

Truer words were never spoken. And now, he knew exactly where I was and where I was working. It was going to be The Chronicle all over again.

Morosely, I read the accompanying unflattering commentary about me, and about my paper. Russ was going to go batshit about this. Groaning, I set down my coffee and rubbed my face. It was too late to unring this bell.

My cellphone went off.

"Oh, crap..." it had to be the paper. Steeling myself, I picked it up and looked at the display. PRIVATE came up in the caller ID window. I hesitated, my finger hovering over the button. Taking a deep breath, I stabbed it, making the connection.

"Sandra Case."

"Oh, um... hello, good morning, Ms. Case. This is John Peckham calling."

Holy shit! He called!

"Oh, er, hello Mr. Peckham. And how are you this fine morning?"

"Well, I've been better Ms. Case, I've been better. Look, I

72

wanted to get in touch with you about our conversation yesterday. I'd like to get some time to speak to you this morning if I may."

If I may? You bet your ass you may. You might be the only thing that keeps my current job for me.

"Oh, um, this morning? Well, let me check my schedule, Mr. Peckham, hold on.." I made a show of flipping through an appointment book by rustling a paper napkin near the mouthpiece of my phone. "I think I could fit you in about ten o'clock. Would that work for you?"

I heard an answering rustle from the earpiece. I suppressed a smile; it sounded like newspaper to me.

"Oh, er, ten? Could we do ten thirty instead?"

"Uh, sure. Let me write this in." I paused, "Okay, would you be willing to come in to the paper to meet me?" thinking of what a coupe it would be for Russ, Jorge and everyone else to see him there.

"Oh, I really would prefer to not come into town, Ms. Case. How about we meet at my house instead?"

Case... don't go there... Jorge's voice rattled in my head. I pushed it aside. "Oh, certainly Mr. Peckham. I can do that. Where is your home?"

"It's over near the Meadows, Dunbarton Lane, number 71. It's a white colonial with a stone wall out front. You need directions?"

"No, I can find it okay. 10:30 it is then."

"I'll see you then, Ms. Case."

He broke the connection. Shit! I still didn't have his phone number. I kicked myself mentally about it. Oh well, in about two hours, I would be face to face with him, anyway. I looked at the Burlington paper once more with a heavy sigh, hoping that Jan Petersen was a late riser.

Apparently she wasn't. Russ's door was closed tight when I arrived twenty minutes later. Jorge was already at his desk, typing furiously. He glanced up at me, gestured with his head towards the closed door. "Make yourself scarce today, Case."

I looked over at the mute wooden door. 'What happened?"

"Ms. Petersen herself just left ten minutes ago. She didn't look pleased."

Oh crud. I thought about telling Jorge about John Peckham's call, decided to wait until after I spoke to him. Slowly, I tugged my laptop out of my bag, plugged it in and connected it to the ethernet cable. A giggle cut through my dour thoughts. Glancing up, I saw Diane and Dana staring raptly at a computer screen, hands at their mouths to suppress the giggles that were escaping. I frowned over at them. "Hey Jorge, what's up with those two?"

He glanced up at them, brow furrowed. "I don't know. Dana said something about an AP article about funny blogs on the web. She and Diane have been over there giggling and screeching for the past half hour."

A new burst of laughter cut through his last words. Diane gasped, "A vulva in a Volvo? Oh my God, Dana! This guy is killing me!"

My blood froze in my veins, stilling my hands. I heard another burst of barely suppressed laughter. Glancing over at Jorge, I hissed, "Why is Dana leaving us alone this morning? Last night, I was crawling under desks to get away!"

"That's how you got over there? Christ on a crutch, Case! I thought you levitated or something." He looked up at them again, lips twisted in a wry smile. "I told her we were off the case completely. That Russ was covering it himself. They won't dare go to him."

Another round of giggling came from the two shriveled hens. I hastily typed in my password. With clumsy fingers, I typed in the address of the blog from hell... my ex-husband's blog, fortunately written under a pen name. What was unfortunate were the devastatingly detailed descriptions of me he gave me in every blistering paragraph.

Skating on the thin line of slander, he was systemically chopping me to bits in a blog that was reaching every corner of the United States and Europe. Online Monthly had named his blog one of the top ten adult humor sites last month, with daily views numbering in the hundreds of thousands.

My heart sank when I read the phrase, 'a vulva in a Volvo' against the backdrop of a new burst of cackles across the newsroom. I felt the coffee and bagel in my belly turning to bitter acid. My eyes flew across the withering text on the screen.

"Divorce isn't something you do lightly. It wasn't because I was an award-winning journalist and she was a talentless hack. No, I could forgive her those faults. The day I decided it was truly time to dump that hag was the day I looked at her standing there stirring a pot of soup like she had Hansel and Gretel in it and realized that she had more chins than a Hong Kong phonebook."

"Case... are you okay?"

"Making love to her had developed into the distinct sensation of sinking into the long dead and dehydrated bunghole of a camel, the shock of it akin to going to a feast and being served a can of past date, putrefying oysters, the texture and smell of which reminded me of her..."

"Case! What's wrong?"

Startled, I shut the blog down. "Noth..nothing. I, uh, just am tired I guess. Hey, I think I'll head out for a while, stay low for a bit, okay?"

I didn't look at him as I said this. I felt his eyes on me. Striving for nonchalance, I closed my computer lid and went to stuff it back in the bag.

"Case... don't you think you should unplug your computer before walking away with it?"

Damn it all…. I fumbled for the cords. "Yeah, yeah. Uh, call my cell if you need me, okay?"

I heard concern in his voice. "Hey Sandy, you okay?"

I waved vaguely at him and escaped without a word. Dana looked up at me as I passed, her eyes speculative. "Good morning, Sandy. Are you off to cover the Garden Club's dedication this morning?" I heard the bile in the tone. Beside her, Diane gasped, and said, "Oh my God Dana! Listen to this line! 'Making love to her had developed into the distinct sensation of sinking into the long dead and dehydrated bunghole of a camel, the shock of it akin to going to a feast and being served a can of past date, putrefying oysters…'" She dissolved into ferocious giggles. I passed without a word. Bitch.

I pushed through the doors into the lobby just as Lizzy was entering. Vaguely I noticed she was in a short leather skirt, ankle high black boots, and a black leather vest over a white mesh top. Steampunk meets Goth. Her hair was done up in a twist, with a black ribbon woven through it, sparkling eye shadow at the corners of her eyes and blood red lipstick completed the look. She raised an eyebrow at me as I charged past her blindly, concern evident in her cocoa colored eyes. "Sandy?" she called after me.

I raised a hand in a halfhearted wave and pushed through the outer door to the sidewalk beyond. Acid churned in my belly, my breath ragged like I had been running. I felt the familiar fluttering in my throat of a full-fledged panic attack coming on. Shit! I hadn't had one of those in months! The sunlight blinded me as I stood on the sidewalk for a moment. Turning mindlessly, I left and started walking; the sun baking my right cheek.

The blog was the beginning of the end. Next would come a message to everyone in the newsroom detailing my indiscretion. Without having truly established myself here as someone of value, the only end I could see would be being told I was no longer needed. Ben wasn't going to rest until he had driven me completely into the ground.

Main Street Brownville was in full summer mode. I looked around as I walked, trying to ignore the tightening sensation in my chest, my coping method to derail the attack before it became medication worthy. I never used to have these before Ben. I should have known by the way he screwed up my health that he was about as good for me as eating an asbestos sandwich. I also should have known that he would find me wherever I ran to. There was no doubt in my mind where the article about the blogs had originated. No doubt a copy of it sat in the inbox of every person at the paper today. It wouldn't be long before the inevitable comparisons to me began. Dana would be the first with Diane in her wake. Diane by herself wasn't all that bad, but expose her to Dana and the claws came out in force. I wondered if I could find some roadkill to leave at her desk.

I stopped when I reached the sidewalk across from A Pint of Pecks and stood staring at the storefront. The windows were covered in plywood now, as was the door. Yellow tape still hung desultorily in the morning heat, limp in the still air. The temporary pedestrian walkway around it was still in place, movable metal gates that curved out into the street a few feet, designed to keep people from stopping in front of the store. A couple of teenagers loitered in the walkway, craning to see any signs of the violence that happened.

My mind moved away from Ben and began chewing over the events in the store, wondering how all the pieces fit together. The problem was, they didn't. Which meant an even larger piece was missing. I wondered if John Peckham would be able to shed any light on it for me.

From up the street, motion caught my eye. A bicycle wobbled down the street, going the wrong way on Main

Street, the rider a white-shirted police officer with a shiny blue department bike helmet on. Black shorts, utility belt with gun and flashlight clanking against his fish belly white thighs, he made his way towards the kids. Idly, I watched him. Brownville had an officer assigned to ride a bike up and down Main and Elm streets all day. Usually it was a trim, birdlike man who buzzed and weaved through traffic, at times pulling cars over from his bike. I hadn't seen this officer before….or had I? Damn… I most certainly had seen him before. It was Officer Pim.

My discomfort was forgotten as I watched him roll to a stop near the kids in the walkway. I couldn't hear his words, but I could see him point to the sidewalk as he moved them along. I glanced either direction and darted across the street just as he shifted his butt back up onto the bicycle seat.

"Good morning, Jim!" I tried for nonchalance.

He looked up at me and groaned. "You again!" He squirmed and reached vainly for a pedal. I pushed my body in front of his bike.

"Yes, me again. What are you doing out on bike patrol? I thought you were a patrol officer."

His face flamed red. He muttered something. I leaned forward so that my forehead almost touched his. "What? I couldn't hear you."

He still smelled like laundry soap.

He jerked back from me, clearly discomfited. Interesting.

"Ma'am…. I got nothing to say to you." His cheeks were flushed a dark red.

I cocked my head at him, eyeing him. "Officer Pim, or Jim, I should say, why are you being so rude to me?"

He stared at me incredulously. "Rude? Rude? Lady, you don't know what rude is! Rude is shoving your way into a crime scene! Rude is jumping up on stage and causing a melee with the entire group of mayoral candidates! Rude is getting my boss so p'o-d that he stuck me out on a goddamned bicycle, all because I talked to you. Rude was tricking Timmy making it so I had to talk to you in the first place! You want rude? I'll give you rude! Leave me the hell alone, lady!"

He pushed the bike forward, intent on riding past me. I grabbed his handlebars, determined to stop him so we could get to the bottom of this. The front wheel rode up and over my right foot, propelled by his considerable weight. I had a flash of blue helmet, black shorts and then the sky as he catapulted over the handlebars right into me. We crashed down onto the pavement in a tangle of arms, legs and bike. The air whooshed out of my lungs as his weight crashed down on me. Dimly, I heard giggles coming from the sidewalk.

I lay like a gutted fish, gasping for air, the bulk of Officer Pim draped across my already stressed body. The handlebar of the bike dug into my ribcage, my right leg was twisted underneath me, and my bag was jammed up around my neck. I stared up at the whirling sky for a moment, the upper stories of A Pint of Pecks and clouds lazily swinging circles overhead. I felt Pim push himself upright off of me, swearing under his breath. Even with the weight gone, I still couldn't breathe. My panic attack had emerged in full force.

A shadow fell over my face, Officer Pim leaning into my line of sight. His helmet sat crookedly on his head, a scuff mark visible on the front of it.

"Hey... Sandy... you okay?"

I focused watery eyes on him silently, unable to speak.

"Shit!" He fumbled for his radio.

No, no, no, no! I grabbed his ankle and shook my head. His forehead creased. I patted my chest, shook my head again. I heard him mutter shit again as he crouched down. I noticed blood on his knee.

"Listen, are you okay or not?"

My voice squeaked as I forced words out. "I'm fine. Just help me up, okay?"

"You sure?"

"Help me up, dammit!" I found more volume as air returned to my lungs.

More giggling came from the sidewalk. Pim pivoted and glared at the two kids, who were avidly watching the show. One of them held a smartphone pointed at us.

"Hey! Move along you two or I'm calling your parents!"

The bigger kid stuck his tongue out at him. "Nice way to hit on someone!" The smaller boy dissolved into giggles.

Pim shot them a withering glare and reached for my arm, hauling me unceremoniously to my feet. The world spun again, and I staggered. He caught my elbow and steadied me.

"Whoa, whoa, whoa... Are you sure you're okay?"

"Got the... wind... knocked out..of me. I'm... okay..."

He eyed me dubiously. "Maybe you ought to sit down for a minute."

Yes. Sit down and get him on his way so I could grab a pill out of my bag. I hated taking them; they made me slow witted, but damn, right now I really needed one. To my horror, I felt tears prickling my eyes.

Officer Pim escorted me carefully to the sidewalk, to the bench that sat just down from A Pint of Pecks. I sat gratefully, gasping for lungfuls of air. He returned to his bike in the street and I snuck a peek in my bag for my pills.

I dug down through layers of debris, looking for them. I heard his footsteps as he returned to where I sat. Two large, black shod feet appeared in my vision, standing right in front of me. I didn't look up at him.

"Uh... Ms. Case... what's the matter?"

I kept my head down, gave a shake. "Nothing. I'm okay. Just leave me alone now, all right?"

His black clad feet stayed in my line of sight.

I heard him sigh, then a foot moved to put the kickstand down. I tensed.

He sat down next to me. The bench creaked under him.

"Look. I cain't go anyplace until I know you're okay. Now do you need medical attention?"

I felt a tear escape my left eye. Crap! I'd rather cut my arms off than cry in public. I shook my head, then gestured at my bag. "I'm having a panic attack... I need to get my medication, then I'll be fine."

It mortified me to say it, but it was the lesser of two evils. I needed to be alone, and I needed to get myself together to leave for John Peckham's house, and having Pim hovering over me wasn't going to work.

He jumped up. "A panic attack?! Let me call an EMT!"

I was shaking my head before the words were out of his mouth. "No, no! I just need to get my medication out of my bag! I'll be fine!"

"Can I get you anything? Some water maybe?"

"Water would be great, thank you." I dove back into my bag, sifting through the layers. The familiar brown bottle peeked up at me from the bottom. Gratefully, I popped the cap and threw one in my mouth. Hesitating, I threw a second one in for good measure. It was already that kind of day.

Pim had pulled a water bottle from the bag on the back of his bike. He thrust it in front of me now. I took a couple of swigs, felt the panic that tore at my throat starting to subside. Damn that Benjamin! How I wished we had never crossed paths.

I offered the water back to Officer Pim. He shook his head. "Keep it. You might need more." I took another swig. He sat down next to me again. Shit. He wasn't leaving.

I looked over at him without raising my head, noticing again the blood from his scraped knee. A variety of places on my body began to hurt as I looked at the scraped flesh. Tomorrow was going to be rough.

"I'm sorry about your knee." I muttered.

"My... wha... oh! I hadn't even noticed it." He flicked a finger across it, wincing as he did so.

He looked over at me. "Ma'am, why do you have to be so darn contrary all the time? I surely didn't want to run over you like that, but I didn't expect you to grab my bike either!"

I kept my head down, raising one shoulder in a shrug. "I was just trying to talk to you for a minute."

I felt him still next to me. "Talk to me? Why?"

"Just... I don't know, to apologize I guess for getting you in trouble." And to see if I could get you to spill any more about what is going on.

He sat in silence, idly rubbing his knee. Across the street, I saw the familiar rag tag shape of the demented beanpole, the gibberish muttering man who stalked Main Street. I noticed he was wearing woman's sandals today. I also noticed he was staring with an almost feverish intensity at us from across the street. I frowned at him, nudged Officer Pim.

"Hey, what's up with him?"

He looked over at me, then across the street. "You mean Joe?" confusion in his voice.

"If you mean that Cyclops over there, then yeah, Joe."

"That's Joe Donahue, although most everyone calls him One Eyed Joe now."

"What's up with him?" I felt the Alprazolam kicking in, the tightness leaving my throat.

Jim shrugged. "It's sad to see him now. Just too much partying when he was younger. A real shame because he was brilliant. And he's got a weird medical condition too, speech dyps... dis... uh, dips-a-for-e-a or something. He talks backwards most of the time."

Whoa. Backwards? I looked across Main Street at him again. He still stared back at me with an unblinking focus.

"So it's not all gibberish when he talks?"

Jim shook his head. "Far from it. If you can figure out the backwards and forwards stuff he throws in, he's got times when he's still pretty with it. He's on Main Street and Elm streets all day; there isn't much that escapes his notice."

Really... now that was something to remember. I felt the sun on my head, noticed that it felt good. Some drowsiness peeked in around the edges. I thought briefly about my ex and his blog, deciding it wasn't worth worrying about at the moment. Thought about the paper and...

Shit! My interview with John Peckham! I jumped in my seat, my mouth suddenly dry. Jim looked at me in alarm. "You okay ma'am?"

I was whipping my arm up to check my watch. 10:12. Shit, shit, shit! It was at least a fifteen minute drive just to get to the Meadows. And I still had to hike up to where I kept my car parked. I bounced to my feet, and the world tilted left. Whoa, baby.

Jim scrambled to his feet as well, wincing as his weight hit his leg. He grabbed my arm, steadying me again. I shook him off with a glazed smile. He looked at me with a tight expression.

"I gotta go... I have an interview in twelve minutsh." Shit, my tongue was feeling thick. Maybe I shouldn't have taken that second pill.

Jim just nodded, his face closed. I thought I should say something more, but couldn't find the words. Turning on a wobbly heel, I left him on the sidewalk and sprinted back across Main Street.

Peggy sat forlornly in the weedy lot next to Sam's Squids and Fine Cuisine, a seafood market where I had permission to park long term, a fine coating of yellow pollen covering her once sparkling gray exterior. Fumbling with my bag, I tugged keys loose and opened the door, dropping into the front seat. The time read 10:20 now. I went to fire her up and paused, my sluggish mind working.

Cyrus Morton had been heading to the Meadows when he shot out the lights. He had been heading east instead of north, the usual route that dog legged off the main road and hooked around, bumping over the railroad tracks before meandering alongside the river for a couple of miles. A jog around an oxbow it then reached the cluster of houses in the Old Village, a tiny settlement that remained from the 1700s, before Brownville itself came to be. Dunbarton Lane was right in the middle of that cluster of houses.

Why was Cyrus heading in a different direction then?

I fumbled my Android out of my bag and thumbed open the map program. It loaded across the 3x3 screen in glowing colors. Flicking it in, I zoomed in until I found the detail I needed; the Meadows.

The road meandered down from the north to a cross street that street bisected by another cross street, a dead end I thought…. except…. there was a dotted line from the western end of it, a dotted line that crossed the tracks and came out at the edge of Brownville itself, over by the dump… about a minute from where I was now parked.

Screw it. I fired up the old Vulva, er, Volvo and pointed it out of the parking lot.

CHAPTER 12

*D*ust boiled up around Peggy's undercarriage as I creaked and thumped down the narrow, rutted lane, fields stretching off to my left, the train tracks and river to my right, visible intermittently through the trees. I noted the number of dirt pull offs along the banks, beer cans and used condoms littering the ground. Looked like I'd found the local Lover's Lane.

I noticed the back end of a freight train through the trees, chugging along at the sedate 30 mph they were limited to on these tracks. The rattle and clatter of the steel wheels and hissing of the engine rose to a roar as I pulled alongside.

Freight boxes stained with graffiti, open cars stacked with lumber, and at last, two engines hooked together pulling the whole shebang.

I pressed harder on the accelerator, the clock on the dash reading 10:26 now. Damn it all... why didn't I get Peckham's number when he called?

I could feel the fuzz wrapping around the edges of my brain. I could breathe now... but my thought process was glacially slow. I goosed the throttle again. The train dropped back behind me, the roar and metallic clanging growing fainter.

Rocks pinged off the underside, the front end thumped through the potholes with jarring thuds. I snuck a peek at my phone; the map showed the road would be swinging to the right, crossing the tracks, and coming out in the heart of the Meadows, specifically Old Brownville as the area was referred to.

A glance in my mirror revealed clouds of dust, and a faint spark of light from the train's headlight. It was far enough back that I could pop over the tracks and not have to worry about it.

Ahead of me, the road curved into the woods to the right; the fields falling away. I swung the wheel and slewed around the turn. Peggy's undercarriage protested as I bounced through a swale before climbing a short, steep rise to cross the tracks, where crossing lights blinked at me, warning me of the oncoming train. Glancing to my right, I could see the train was still a good quarter mile away.

I nailed the gas, Peggy lurching up the dusty slope. The front wheels thumped over the rails, then off the edge... and the entire car lurched to a halt as the undercarriage high centered on the steel rails.

My mouth went dry.

I slammed the gas pedal, wheels spinning uselessly. A mournful wail filled my ears as I frantically hit the throttle over and over, full panic mode kicking in, tearing through the layers of the sedative that sang in my bloodstream.

A glance to the right showed the train much closer now, looming, the light blinding, sparks flying from the wheels as they locked, horn wailing nonstop....

I grabbed my bag and bailed out the driver's side door, stumbled on the ties and fell heavily to my knees. The horn blast sent me scrambling up as the sound of screeching metal filled the air around me. I dove down the side of the rail bed, my bag banging hard into my legs, before falling again onto the rough gravel road where I rolled over and onto my feet in one adrenaline born move.

I watched helplessly as the massive locomotives slid down the rails, propelled by the weight of the cargo behind them, the scream of tortured metal almost unbearable to hear. With only scant yards to go, the engineer finally let go of the horn, his eyes locking onto mine for a moment. I raised my hands in a "sorry man" supplication as his locomotive slammed into Peggy, shoving her sideways in a new scream of metal, glass exploding under the impact.

I'm not a lip reader, nor did I stay in a Holiday Inn Express last night, but I could see the engineer's mouth moving as he yelled one word over and over again… the same word I was repeating endlessly as Peggy was swept away on a current of steel.

Shit! Shit! Shit!

CHAPTER 13

*W*hoo WHO whoo WHO whoo WHOOO! I grimaced into my pillow as the noise outside my apartment window pierced my uneasy sleep. From the enormous maple tree at the edge of the yard, two owls bellowed into the night, their voices booming in my tiny bedroom. Blearily, I raised my head, peering at the stand. 2:12 a.m. Great. I had only been asleep, if you could call it that, for about an hour. Groaning, I pulled the pillow over my head, trying to block the noise.

My body throbbed in multiple places, and none of them were good throbs or good places either. Freed from sleep, my brain ticked into overdrive again, a hamster in a wheel, running as hard as it could. The Reporter, the murder, Officer Pim crashing into me, my ex and his frigging blog, poor Peggy dying in a squeal of steel on the tracks… a huge sigh escaped me.

I twisted over to one side; the sheet tangled around one leg in a sweaty mess. It wasn't like me to destroy a bed when I was in it alone, but this one would need stripping in the morning.

Whoo WHO whoo WHO whoo WHOO!

"Freaking birds…" I'm city raised. I can sleep through a traffic jam outside my window. These country nights were hard to take, most of the time because they were too quiet, and when they were noisy, it was from birds, bugs or frogs. The idea of some minute reptile or exo-skeleton'd creature making enough noise to be heard throughout the valley was a bit on the creepy side to me. I was used to city reptiles, the kind with baggy pants, flashing gang signs.

I twisted back over to my other side as various places on me started protesting in pain. Usually I slept like a dead person after taking meds for a panic attack, but this day had been too adrenaline fueled for that.

The aftermath of losing Peggy on the tracks hadn't been pretty. Good old Chief Hanniford himself had come out to the scene upon hearing who was involved. His sole reason for appearing had been his intent to arrest me on a variety of charges related to getting my car destroyed. They ranged from littering and improper disposal of a vehicle to deliberately obstructing the rail bed, some federal offense he pulled out of his ass. The timely arrival of Jorge Maxim was the only reason I was now home instead of being incarcerated at the Women's Correctional Center.

I rolled over again as both owls hooted in unison. God! I thought I was noisy during sex… I had nothing on the common barn owl. Stretching my arms over my head, I stared at the ceiling. The worst aftermath of all had been John Peckham. He hadn't called me back, nor had he answered when I finally finagled his number out of Jorge. I had left three messages on his machine, explaining I had run into some difficulties on my trip over there.

So here I was with exactly nothing more for all my efforts and with exactly one less car to boot. I wasn't sure how I would replace Peggy either. I only had the minimum insurance on it, with no replacement value included. A new car was out of the question, at least until my lawyer ran down Mr. Shithead Ex-husband Benjamin and relieved him of my settlement money. I wasn't going to hold my breath about that one either. I had exactly $5,614 in my savings account. I was loath to take all of it out for a car though. Which left me with either using a couple grand of it for some deathtrap, or taking a loan on a used one.

My father's voice rang in my ears: 'Never finance something that does nothing but depreciate'. "Okay dad, maybe you want to send me some money from wherever you are then?" I muttered into the darkened room. My father had passed away almost ten years ago now. I doubted he was going to help me out in this case.

Outside my bedroom, the owls started up with their hooting again. Whoo WHO whoo WHO whoo WHO-awk! The noise abruptly ceased, like something had startled them. I lay still, listening to the night that was suddenly quiet. Too quiet.

It's your nerves. Calm down and go back to sleep. I punched the pillow up and settled back into it. Click. A frown creased my forehead at the noise.

Scrape... splat... 'shhhhhh.'

What the hell was that? I sat up, staring at the window. It stared mutely back at me, a lighter rectangle of grey against the darkened room. I heard another stealthy noise from outside.

My apartment was located off of Elm Street, about two blocks down, on Walnut Street. It was a neighborhood of working folks, old houses turned into apartments and condos. Most had lawns of some sort, a variety of old-growth trees punctuating the green rectangles. It was a place where old people sat on the porches and young children rode their bicycles in the driveways.

My humble abode was a duplex, a 70-year-old stucco sided house that the owner had turned into a home with a rental. The owner lived next to me, my apartment a mirror image of hers. My bedroom was over my kitchen, looking out onto the front yard with the street scant yards away. A small porch was built off the kitchen, just the right size for sitting and drinking a late day beer.

We had had problems in the past with raccoons getting into the garbage, which was located between the two front porches. I wondered if that was the case now.

SPLAT... "Ow! Дерьмо!"

"Заткнись!"

THAT was no goddamned raccoon!

I kicked the covers off, hesitated, then grabbed my top left dresser drawer. Rummaging under my socks, I pulled out my gun. Living in Chicago for all those years had taught me the value of being prepared. The cops could take twenty minutes to get to you. I could end the problem in twenty seconds. Racking the slide back, I popped a round in and checked the safety. Carefully, I slid over to the window.

The owls were silent, probably long gone by now. The streetlight up the road from us cast shadows through the leaves of the maple tree at the sidewalk.

Moving slowly, I slid the screen up in its track, grateful that the house had vinyl replacement windows with lovely, smooth vinyl screens and tracks. I craned forward carefully, peering down at the porch roof, straining to see any movement...

SPLAT!

I jumped at the noise. What the hell??

A shadow flickered at the edge of my porch, an arm drawing back, something dark in the hand, ready to throw at the house. Squinting at the edge of the porch, I quietly flicked the safety off.

SPLAT!

I carefully aimed up into the crown of the tree as the arm reappeared, dipping into what looked like a bucket. The arm drew back again....SPLAT!

CRACK! The gunshot boomed through the still night, leaves crackling as the bullet passed through the crown of the maple tree.

"Святое дерьмо! ЗАПУСТИТЕ!"

Two man sized shapes barreled off the porch and onto the lawn, arms flailing wildly. The larger one tripped and did an admirable yard dart imitation into the grass of the front lawn as lights flicked on across the street and beside my apartment. Rolling back to his feet, he staggered up as the security light finally blinked on, illuminating him momentarily.

I tracked him as he bolted for the street, my finger squeezing down on the trigger....before finally relaxing again. I just couldn't bring myself to shoot at a person, even if they desperately needed it.

Quickly, I racked the round out, and wrapped the gun back up to hide it again. I knew I wouldn't fare very well in an inquisition from Chief Hanniford if he was to find out I was the one who fired the shot. As I stashed the gun back under the socks, I pondered what I had seen when the light had come on.

The big man sure looked an awful lot like "Igor".

CHAPTER 14

*T*here's nothing like a 2:00 a.m. gunshot to bring the neighbors out in force. Many of the folks who were peering out of screen doors were people I had never seen before despite having been in residence here for the past few months. My bunny slippers nodded on my feet as I made my way across the kitchen to my back door, pausing to peer outside before flipping the porch light on. Some sort of goo smeared my window, making line of sight outside tough.

Frowning, I flipped the porch light on.

From the lawn I heard a gasp and a shriek as the light blazed on, oddly red tinted through the goop. What the hell was that? With a last tug on the belt of my robe, I popped the locks and opened my back door.

Oh, for Pete's sake....

I gagged as the smell hit me, the smell that came from the bloody lumps that dotted my porch. Blood was splashed all over the wall of the house, dripping down in crimson streaks that were rapidly turning black. I blinked at the piles of bloody flesh in bewilderment. What the hell were those?

On the lawn, my landlady was staring at me, aghast, her

hand over her mouth, plaid robe dragging in the wet grass. She pointed at the wall beside my door, swallowing heavily. Behind her, I heard voices as some of the neighbors ventured over for a closer look.

I looked vainly for a clean spot on the porch to step on; finding none, I settled for grabbing the door jamb and leaning out to see what had horrified her so.

Written on the wall to the left of the door, in dripping block letters was, "Dye Beech" I felt a laugh bubbling up in my throat, I struggled to quash it. English as your not-so-second-language, eh?

The voices on the lawn were turning into a babble as more neighbors arrived at the scene. My landlady, Mrs. Kahn, took her hand away from her mouth finally, her throat working as she struggled to keep from bringing up the contents of her dinner. Her mouth moved soundlessly for a moment, then, 'Sand… Sandy..are you all right?"

"Yeah, yeah, I'm okay. I'm sorry about this, though. I have no idea why anyone would do this to me."

I heard tires crunching on the street as a sedan pulled over under the maple tree, the Brownville Police sign reflecting in the lights from the house. Shit. I was hoping they wouldn't get called. Sighing, I steeled myself for the inquisition.

Two doors slammed as the two officers exited the car, putting hats on and adjusting belts. I squinted to see who would have been sent to the scene, praying it wasn't Hanniford.

It wasn't. One of the officers was Officer Pim.

I blinked in surprise. What the hell? Did the man never go home and sleep? A memory of how I had left him on the sidewalk this morning, er, yesterday morning hit me. I felt a flush in my cheeks. "Smooth Case, just smooth."

His face was tired and unreadable as he arrived at the

edge of the porch, although I noted that his eyes widened at the carnage. His partner, a chunky middle-aged man I had seen at the murder scene, was in the lead, hoisting his belt up self-importantly as he arrived at the steps.

He stopped, frowning as he surveyed the mess, his gaze swiveling up to find me. His rather unfriendly gaze, I might add.

"We had a report of a shot fired over here. What's going on?"

I did my best to appear bewildered, gesturing at the mess on my porch.

"I don't know, Officer. I was sound asleep when I heard it. I thought it was a firecracker. I heard my neighbors outside, so I came down to investigate and found this." I shrugged.

His frown deepened as he surveyed me suspiciously. Hanniford must have been telling them all during roll call to watch out for me. Officer Pim looked at the mess, at the overturned bucket lying on the grass, at the words, "Dye Beech", at anyplace but at me.

Trying for friendliness, I called out to him, "Hey Jim. What 'cha doing on the night shift? I just saw you working days. Don't you ever sleep?"

He jumped, his cheeks flushing, flicking a glance at his partner, who laid an unfriendly stare...at him. Geez. Talk about having some sand in your mangina.

Screw this. I went on the offensive at the first patrolman. "Officer! I want to know what the heck all this is! And I want you to find this creep right now, because none of us are safe as long as he is on the loose! Also, I want to file a citizen's complaint against this perp for the threat they left on my wall!"

He turned and glared at me. "Threat? What threat?"

I waved at the writing. "Right there! They tell me to die!"

He made a show of reading the words. "Well, I hate to

burst your bubble ma'am, but that says, "Dye beech", which COULD refer to coloring a tree."

"Oh, puleeze!" I couldn't help myself; I rolled my eyes. "What did I get for my police protection tonight? Fisher Price's 'My First Police Officer'?"

He narrowed his eyes at me. "Lady, you better not start disrespecting the Law here." He slapped his hand on his holster, "Because I got the Law right here. See this gun? It's an extension of me, in fact it's JUST LIKE me, so you better not forget that!"

I put my hands on my hips, glaring back at him. "Really? Well, I guess I can see the resemblance…it's a snub nose that fires blanks…. JUST LIKE YOU!"

His jaw dropped. "Why you miserable bitch!"

On the lawn, Mrs. Kahn had dropped her hands, her discomfort at the smell forgotten. "Timothy Butler!" she yelled at the police officer, "I can't believe you just said that! Don't you forget for one red hot minute that this is MY tenant and MY house these creeps threw this… this… what the hell is this?" She pointed at a bloody chunk.

"It's decapitated chickens, ma'am." Officer Pim finally spoke up.

"Decapitated chickens..?" I stared at him, frowning. He wouldn't look at me. "Where the hell does anyone get this many headless chickens?"

Officer Pim finally looked up at me, albeit a bit reluctantly. "They're all the same size, so I'd say they're from a commercial operation."

Officer Butler drew himself up. "Well, as fascinating as this is, there's no threat here. This is a simple case of vandalism, hardly worth worrying about. We will submit a report to the Chief."

My landlady made a strangled sound in her throat. "Vandalism? Vandalism! You call a bunch of blood and headless chickens vandalism?"

Officer Butler was already heading for the car, leaving Officer Pim shifting his feet nervously in the wet grass. He finally looked up at me. "Ma'am. It may be nothing, but I suggest you file a complaint in the morning about it." He called to me softly. "In the meantime, keep your doors and windows locked, okay?"

I stared across the gulf at him, noting the concern in his eyes. Slowly, I nodded. "Okay... and Jim?" he paused as he turned away from me, still refusing to look back at me. "Thanks... for everything." He nodded once. From the street, Officer Butler yelled, "Come on Pim! Move it!"

He walked away without another word.

CHAPTER 15

"The mayoral candidates have petitioned for a public meeting and friendly 'informational discussion' on the Town Common." The paper rustled as Jorge flattened it out with his hand. "The purpose of such a meeting is to meet on a common ground to answer questions from the public before the primary election. The candidates feel that being deprived of the chance to have a debate has needlessly hindered their campaigning ability. The candidates respectfully request that such a meeting take place one week prior to the primary election, namely this coming Tuesday, at 5 p.m."

Hal Mulville, our managing editor, sat across from Jorge, his face, as usual, revealing, well, nothing at all. Like a single-celled amoeba that slid across a microscope slide, Hal was singularly unresponsive to stimuli. We were divided about whether he was real or a cyber-borg.

We sat in the newsroom on this rainy Wednesday morning, my mood as colorful as the gray clouds that scudded across the horizon. Jorge was his usual dapper self, all pressed slacks and crisp shirts. And Hal....well, I wasn't sure

Hal was even in the newsroom with us. In body maybe, spiritually, he was someplace in Key West right now.

I shifted in my seat, kicking my bag morosely with my foot. Without looking up, I asked Jorge, "Who signed off on this petition?"

He scanned the names. "Looks like most of the candidates, with the exception of Hal Morgan, John Peckham, and John Roth."

Hal finally spoke up. "Has Roth campaigned at all?"

Jorge shook his head. "No, he's managed to avoid talking to anyone about this. He won't even come out of his house if you go over there to try to get his input."

"Then why the hell is he even running?" I scowled at Jorge, my mind elsewhere even as I asked the question. Jorge shrugged. "Same reason that everyone else is running? $85,000 a year to start?"

My mind hopped subjects. "Any word from John Peckham yet?" In the almost 24 hours since my disastrous attempt to go see him, John Peckham had fallen off the face of the earth. No callbacks, no sign of him anyplace, and most troubling, his lawyer had called me wanting to know if I knew where he was. Every hour since the murder, the clock ticked harder and louder, giving me the distinct feeling I was falling behind the pace. Now I sat here, sleep deprived, borderline PMS, and seriously pissed over losing my car and waking up to find a bunch of chicken guts strewn around my front yard. I wished I had given in to my impulses last night and taken out the big man's leg. Maybe then we could start unraveling who he was and why they seemed to have a hard on for me.

Jorge's voice cut through my reverie. "Case? Hello Case….are you with us?"

"Huh? What? Yeah… what is it?" I glanced at him then back down at my bag, half my brain worrying over the puzzle of Igor and Ivan. I looked up again as the silence stretched out. Jorge was still staring at me, concern evident. "Hey Sandy… do you want to go get a coffee or something?"

Across the walkway, Hal sat expressionless. I heard Diane's voice in the lobby.

"Yeah… that would be good. I'm a little low on juice this morning."

He nodded at Hal. "You want anything?" Hal blinked a slow blink, then shook his head no. Our chairs creaked as we both stood up, me grabbing my bag, Jorge his coat.

Diane came bustling through the lobby doors as we exited, her red hair every which way. I couldn't decide if it was a new style, or if she slept wrong last night. She looked at us with narrowed eyes, her lips pursed. Jorge raised one brow at her. "Good morning Diane!"

"Good morning my ass." She sniffed and hustled past us, a disdainful flick of her hair.

Jorge pivoted around to look after her. "Jesus! What crawled up her butt?"

I shrugged and kept walking. I guessed that perhaps her current foul mood maybe had something to do with the flattened squirrel I had found on my walk in to work, his physiology rearranged by 4,000 pounds of motor vehicle. The same flat squirrel that now resided in Diane's parking space, laid neatly across her stenciled name on the pavement.

With an exasperated head shake, Jorge turned away from the red-headed barge and held the outer door open for me. We emerged into gray drizzle, the granite steps slick with water.

"Where to?" I pulled my collar up. Jorge looked up Main Street and replied, "Let's take my car and head over to the coffee shop on Elm. I don't feel like sitting under an umbrella today."

I didn't feel like dealing with Main Street at all, truth be told. I trailed along behind Jorge as we made our way to his car, a silver Ford Focus. Popping the locks, we ducked inside out of the rain.

I sat in silence as he fired up the car and swung out onto Main Street. I noted that the common was deserted this morning, empty of the usual assortment of ragtag people who normally frequented the benches. As he made the turn onto Elm Street, I spotted a reedy beanpole bobbing down the sidewalk, his gait exaggerated by the pair of women's ice skates he wore on his feet. Today he also wore a hat, an old fedora, crumbled and misshapen, his long trench coat flapping around his stork like knees, his one blue eye open wide and staring. I swiveled around in my seat to look at him as we passed.

Jorge snuck a look at me. "What are you looking at, Case?"

I swiveled back around and sank down in the seat, still not feeling like talking much. I jerked a thumb over my shoulder. "One Eyed Joe."

"What about him?"

"Is it true he speaks backwards? Some kind of weird speech problem?"

"So I've heard. They say he has Dyslexic Dysphonia, which is a pretty unusual condition. Who told you about it?"

"One of the cops."

He glanced at me again. "I didn't know any of them were still speaking to you."

I scowled. "Most of them aren't. And it seems like I'm spending an awful lot of time having to talk to them for one reason or another."

He nodded as he slowed, looking for a parking spot near Home Grown Roasters. "I know they gave you a hard time over the car."

I snorted, mumbling, "And that isn't even the half of it." I hadn't told anyone about the incident at home last night, er, this morning. That was striking too close to home, something I needed to chew on, or maybe even brood over.

But Jorge Maxim wasn't the kind to let anything by him, especially when it came to police news in Brownville, VT. I should have known that.

"You mean this morning, at your place?"

My head swiveled around in an admirable Linda Blair in the Exorcist impression. "Dammit Jorge! You're doing it again! How'd you hear about that?"

He shrugged with exaggerated nonchalance. "Part of my job is to call the PD every day and get the police log emailed over to me. I saw the report and recognized the address."

He skillfully slotted the car in at the curb and killed the motor. Turning to face me, he asked, "Care to talk about it?"

I sighed, blowing out my cheeks, sinking down into the seat a bit more. Rain ran in streaks down the windshield, drumming off the hood. A wave of exhaustion hit me; days of running full bore coupled with nights with limited sleep. Last night, I had passed off the pager to Kyle Giard to cover for me so I could try to get a full night's sleep after the trauma of the wreck. Tonight I would have it back, and I still had little to no sleep under my belt. I felt about as warm and fuzzy as a basket of angry blue crabs.

Get it over with, Case, my brain told me. You know Maxim won't quit until he knows the entire scoop.

I shifted in my seat again and gave Jorge the short version of what happened last night. He listened in silence until I reached the part about recognizing the big guy in the lawn. His eyes went on full alert.

"Describe him to me again." He jotted notes on his pad. Stopping, he tapped the pen against his front teeth before turning a speculative eye on me again.

"The language you heard... what language do you think it was?"

I frowned a bit. "Geez, I don't know. It was guttural, European sounding, maybe Polish? Lithuanian? Russian?" I stopped when I saw the look in Jorge's eye. "What? What is it?"

"Sandy, the drugs they found in A Pint of Peck's?"

"Yeah? It was hash, right?"

"Yes. It was hash. An odd thing to find even on its own, but doubly suspicious when you realize that it was imported hash." He stared at me, waiting for me to make a connection. I tried and failed. My drug knowledge is generally limited to products containing fiber and promoting regularity.

"So why is that significant, Jorge?"

His eyes glittered behind his glasses, a bloodhound on a scent. "For one, imported hash is virtually nonexistent in this country. It was big back in the 50s, 60s, 70s. But once medical marijuana came onto the scene, all the so-called hash produced now is simply a by-product of that." He flipped back through his notebook, looking for a particular page of notes. Finding it, he regarded me again. "My local source tells me the last time anything resembling imported hash was found in the immediate area, it was over in Bennington, and it was a small amount, like a couple of grams, this was back in the late 80s. There hasn't been a full kilo of imported hash recorded in this county for about 42 years now. And for a total kick in the teeth, this particular block was wrapped in the classic linen wrapping, with lettering stamped on it, lettering in a foreign language. Bonus points of you can guess what language it was, Case."

I stared at Jorge, my mind slowly clicking through the possibilities. Without waiting for my answer, he looked me in the eye and said, "If you chose 'Russian', you would be a winner."

"Russ… what the hell, Jorge? You think those two clowns have something to do with the murder?"

He shrugged. "Who knows? But if it looks like a duck and quacks like a duck…"

"Then in this town, it's probably a chicken." I finished for him. Staring out the windshield, I asked the question that had been bothering me. "Why chickens, Jorge? Who would be screwed up enough to have a big, honking pail of decapitated chickens to throw at someone's house?"

He was silent for a long minute, staring out at the rain-slicked pavement. Cars hissed past, throwing little sprays of water up off the wheels. With a shake of his head, he stuffed the notebook in his inside pocket. "Come on. Let's get inside and get some java. We can finish this discussion over breakfast"

CHAPTER 16

The bell over the door jingled merrily as we made our way into the heavenly scented interior. My stomach came alive with a gurgle, reminding me that I never ate lunch or dinner last night. I felt suddenly faint with lack of food. The counter swam before my eyes for a moment.

"Whoa there, Case! Don't nosedive into the goods, now!" Jorge's hand was on my upper arm, steadying me. I flashed on yesterday morning, Officer Pim doing the same thing to me as I staggered off the street after our crash. I pushed the thought away. Saliva pooled in my mouth as I surveyed the case.

The blonde behind the counter sported a nose stud, an eyebrow ring and multiple piercings in each ear. I could see the lace of a tattoo crawling up under her shirt collar too. Vaguely I wondered how she would look in the nursing home in sixty years. She looked at me expectantly. I pointed at the plates of food lined up under glass.

"I'll take one of those Danish, a bagel, toasted with butter; oh can you put sausage and egg on it too? And a blueberry muffin. Um, oh yeah, a large coffee with a shot of espresso, extra light, extra sweet." I surreptitiously felt the waistline of my jeans; I think they felt a bit looser after not eating for a day.

Jorge looked at me with ill-disguised shock. "Jesus, Case! Where the hell are you going to put all that food? You have a tapeworm to feed, too?"

I shrugged, suddenly craving chocolate and eyeing the chocolate croissants that I hadn't seen before. "I didn't eat much yesterday, okay?" I snapped at him.

Wisely, he dropped the subject.

Taking our drinks, we found a table in the window to sit at to continue our conversation. I slurped my really hot coffee carefully, eyeing Jorge over the rim.

"So Maxim, what's the Russian connection then? And how do dead chickens play into it?"

He stirred his own coffee, black, no sugar, soon to be accompanied by a side of wheat toast, dry, and a fruit cup.

"I'm not sure yet, Case. But I think that perhaps you and I should try to find our friends and see if we can get an ID on them."

I gestured behind me with my head. "I saw them up to the intersection, the day Cyrus was taking the lights out. They were in an old car, a... shit... what was that thing... some kind of Oldsmobile, maybe?"

"Where were they?"

"In the Mini Market. They must have been getting stuff inside, because the car was parked off to one side, away from the gas pumps." I slurped my coffee as my food arrived. Hungrily, I tore into the bagel with egg and sausage. Butter oozed over my lips and chin. I felt positively orgasmic with delight.

Jorge stared at me, dumbfounded, as I inhaled the bagel in three large gulps, then pulled the Danish to me. Pausing to take a drink of my coffee, I noticed his expression.

"What?"

He slowly shook his head, a small smile on his lips. "Case… I'd rather have to clothe you than feed you."

"Piss off Jorge." I tore into the Danish. "I was hungry." crumbs flew out of my mouth onto the table.

He fastidiously picked fruit out of the cup, ignoring my glutton fest across the table. Laying his notebook out on the tabletop beside him, he picked up the conversation we had been having earlier.

"You asked about commercially prepared chicken chunks. There's only one place that is close to here that process-es chicken commercially. That would be over towards Boston, the Acme Poultry Plant. It's a small one, producing only about 100,000 birds a quarter."

I paused, my cup halfway to my mouth. "Someone actu-ally named a plant 'Acme'? I thought that was all from Wile E. Coyote cartoons."

A small smile creased Jorge's mouth. "Actually, Case, there are a lot of companies named 'Acme'."

I shook my head. "That's not the one Sebastian was trying to bring in here, was it?"

"No. That's a big company, the 'Lucky Plucker Poultry Producers'. They have their main plant out in Pennsylvania and are trying to expand into New England."

The Lucky Plucker Poultry Producer… I tried to wrap my mouth around that, failed. I took another slurp of my coffee, eyeing my blueberry muffin.

"Any idea what the status of that plan is now that Sebast-ian's headed for Boot Hill?"

Jorge shook his head no.

"And you think the chunks of dead flesh found on my porch this morning came from Acme?"

"I didn't say that, I merely pointed out that was the closest place, and even then, it's at least 150 miles from here."

I frowned at him. "No one is going to drive that far with buckets of dead chickens in their car just to throw them at me."

"I would say you are probably correct, Case. So that begs the question: who is doing chicken processing locally?"

"You just said the closest place was 150 miles away."

"No, I said the closest commercial place was 150 miles away. There's probably someone doing processing in their backyard."

My bagel turned over in my stomach.

"Wait a minute… you mean people would hack apart live chickens as a home hobby?"

"People process meats all the time, Case. Goats, chickens, steers, you name it. There's probably someone in the area who butchers chickens. I know some of the ethnic groups do it regularly."

"You mean like the Birkenstock wearing crowd at the Brownville Epicurean Market?"

Jorge stared at me across the table. "Actually, I've seen it most with the Russian immigrants."

Oh… I stared back at him. "This Russian connection just keeps coming up, doesn't it?"

"Very much so." He took a sip of his coffee. "I say we find your two friends first and follow the trail back from there."

I frowned as I pushed my muffin around on my plate. "How the hell are we going to do that? I've seen them a couple of times, but where do you go to track them down? This town sprawls off in all directions."

Jorge smiled at me. "You start with your local resources."

CHAPTER 17

*R*ain was still drumming on the sidewalks as we approached the Brownville Epicurean Market, where One Eyed Joe stood, huddled out of the weather under the awning of the market. He swiveled his head around to stare at us, his expression unnerving. I leaned closer to Jorge and muttered, "What the hell happened to his eyes?"

"I heard that was a result of a bad car wreck some years ago, rumored to be the same reason he has this speech disorder. Apparently he was shitfaced and tried to jump his car over a gully with less than stellar results. He almost died."

"Oh.." I searched for sympathy, came up empty. I just have a problem with people drinking and driving. It's one of my quirks.

"Good morning Joe." Jorge strode right up to him, a big smile on his face. "How are you this fine morning?"

Eyeing me warily, Joe shrugged. Jorge pressed on. "Have you eaten yet today?" Joe's head swiveled back to him, hunger evident in his eye. Jorge gestured to me. "Sandy brought you a blueberry muffin."

Wait… what? The hell I did! That muffin was earmarked for my lunch! I glared at Jorge. He ignored me.

"Sandy, give Joe your muffin." He cast a sharp look at me. Leaning forward, I hissed at him, "The hell I will! Go buy him one!"

"Case, will you just shut up and do as you are told for once? Give it to him. It's important that it comes from you. I'll buy you a goddamned muffin later, okay?"

With a last foul look at Jorge, I fished my muffin out of my bag and gave it to the odiferous beanstalk. He took it from my palm, mumbling, "sknaht" in a raspy, breathy voice. I glanced at Jorge. He was leaning against the building front, looking like he stepped out of an issue of GQ. He waited as One Eyed Joe wolfed down the muffin at a speed that made me envious before he spoke again.

"It's been pretty exciting down here on Main Street lately, hasn't it Joe?"

Wiping his mouth, he nodded. "Yob, ll'I yas. Sereht neeb a hcnub fo sodriew dnuora yletal." He eyed me a moment, "S'tahw reh yrots? S'ehs tog a ecin ssa."

Jorge smiled at that. "Now, now, let's stay focused for a moment here, okay? In your travels have you seen any new faces around? Specifically two men, one small and dark ponytail, kind of greasy, hanging out with a big lunk, heavy, tall, one eyebrow? Also kind of swarthy?"

Joe turned, balancing on his skates deftly, pointing down Main Street, out towards the interstate that hissed in the distance. "Heay. Yeht dewohs pu a keew oga, gnimoc mrof eht yawhgih ni a yarg elibomsdlO 89."

"Yes! Those are the ones! Have you seen them since?"

"Yreve yad."

"Where? Are they around Main Street a lot?"

He shrugged. "Yltsom revo ot mle teerts dna eht nwot llah. Yeht osla neeb dnuora eht nommoc."

110

Joe stopped talking, staring at me with a look I couldn't fathom.

"Ehs elgnis? S'ehs ton yrev thgirb. Ve'I neeb gniyrt ot llet reh tuoba laH nagroM tub ehs serongi em. Dumbass."

I jumped at the word emitted clear as a bell from his mouth. It was like having a pet Pomeranian suddenly stand up and start reciting the State of the Union Address to you. Flustered, I shot a look at Jorge. He was regarding One Eyed Joe with a look of puzzlement on his face.

"What do you mean by that?"

Joe scowled, folding his arms across his chest. Mutely, he stared at Jorge. Jorge stared back.

I watched the silent contest in growing bewilderment. At last Joe shook his head and began to sing in a reedy, soprano voice. "First of May, first of May, outdoor fucking starts today..." he flapped his arms, shuffling around in a circle, clomping on his white skates. I noticed pom-poms dangling off the tops of them.

Jorge pushed himself off the wall. "Come on Case. We're done here for now."

As we walked away, I could hear the clack clack clack of the skates on the ground, with his high-pitched voice trembling in and out. I looked over at Jorge, still pissed that I had lost my muffin and had to stand in the rain for twenty minutes for nothing. "Well? Did you understand any of that gibberish?"

"Some of it. We'll get it all when we get inside."

I raised an eyebrow as we clattered up the steps. "How do you plan on that?"

He pulled his tape recorder out of his pocket as we entered the lobby, rain sparkling on the floor around us. "This is how I always talk to Joe. Just put it in reverse mode for the playback."

Oh....

He paused at the newsroom door, peering in at who was inside. I skidded to a halt behind him. "Who's in there, Maxim?" He was already turning, pushing me towards the small room the photographers used as a portrait room. "Looks like Jan Petersen. I think we should be elsewhere for a few minutes."

"Shit! I wonder if I'm going to have a place here much longer."

Jorge shrugged. "I wouldn't worry too much about it. You were only doing your job."

The door to the so-called studio room pushed open, revealing the little eight by twelve space they used, walls covered with background on one end, lights with white umbrellas positioned here and there. A Nikon sat mounted on a tripod at one side of the room. I walked over and started fiddling with it as Maxim emptied his pockets onto the counter. He punched the controls, and the warble of rewinding tape filled the room. I peered through the lens at the background, picturing a photo shoot with myself in various stages of undress, and Karl Manz, he of the huge hands, shooting.

Maxim set the player down. "Ready, Case?"

Reluctantly, I moved away to listen to the tape.

"s'ti neeb ytterp gniticxe nowd ereh no niam seerts ylelal, t'nsah tie o?"

"Boy, I'll say. There's been a bunch of weirdos around lately. What's her story? She's got a nice ass."

I jumped at the statement, looking at Jorge incredulously. He threw his head back and bellowed with laughter. "Oh, fuck off Maxim!" I couldn't believe what I was hearing.

"Won s'tel yats desucof rof a tnemom ereh, yako? Ni ruoy slevart evah uoy ness yny wen secaf dnuora? Yllacificeps owt nem, eno llams dan krad, liatynop, dnik fo ysearg, gnignah tou htiw a gib knul, yvaeh, llat, eno worbeye? Osla dnik fo yhtraws?"

"Yeah. They showed up a week ago, coming from the highway in a gray Oldsmobile 98."

Sey! Esoht era eht seno! Evah uoy nees meht ecnis?"

"Every day."

Erehw? Era yeht dnuora niam teerts a tol?"

"Mostly over to Elm Street, and the Town Hall. They also been around the common."

I felt excitement at the lucid statements the beanpole was making! I turned and gave Jorge a high 5.

The raspy voice continued on: "She single? She's not very bright. I've been trying to tell her about Hal Morgan, but she ignores me. Ssabmud."

I gaped at the recorder like a piked fish as Maxim bellowed with laughter. "Oh, now THAT is RICH!"

He wiped his eyes as he paused the tape. I punched him in the arm. "Shut up, Maxim! What does he mean about Hal Morgan?"

"He says he was trying to tell you about him. So what did he say?"

"How the hell would I know? I don't think I've ever spoken to him before!"

A memory surfaced, one of walking down Main Street one afternoon, and having to push by him as he spoke in gibberish, fingers curled up like a dead insect. And the intense staring across the street at me while I sat with Officer Pim.

I felt a guilty stab at thinking of Officer Pim. I pushed it away hurriedly.

Jorge was struggling to regain his composure, still giggling softly as he rewound the tape again. We listened to it a second time. This time he was more focused. "So..." he held up a finger, "Number one, those two clowns arrived in town right before the murder. Number two, they were at the press conference, front and center to boot. Number three, they, or at least one of them apparently had a vendetta against you, and number four, they very well may be Russian, and the Russian connection keeps popping up, over and over. I can believe in some coincidences, but this is getting way past the coincidental stage for me."

"But, why me? What in the world would make them go after me?"

Jorge stared at me for a moment, his eyes looking through me. "It could be that they see you as a threat of sorts. And the only reason I could see you as a threat to them would be because you keep appearing front and center in the murder investigation, at least publicly anyway. Let's face it Case, you weren't exactly shy and retiring at the press conference. And you let on that you had knowledge of what had happened inside the ice cream shop." He paused a moment, rubbing his nose thoughtfully. "And I would say it really wasn't a case of 'going after you' so much as it was warning you off."

"Well, that's just fine and dandy for you to say! You weren't the one scrubbing rancid chicken blood off your porch at 5:00 a.m. either!" I fisted my hands, placing them on my hips. I could feel my blood pressure rising again. Part of me wondered how many calories these regular adrenaline dumps were burning off. Probably at least enough to justify a piece of chocolate cake later on.

"Case, if they had wanted to, really wanted to, they could have simply offed you last night instead of going through all the trouble to throw guts at your house. It wouldn't have been all that hard."

I didn't like that thought, not one bit. Christ, as if having Ben Morven on my trail wasn't bad enough.

Agitated, I paced around the tiny studio, rubbing my

arms, my thoughts chaotic. Dammit, I had enough in my life with my disastrous divorce. I wasn't going to just stand by and let some two-bit clowns screw with me on top of it, no, sir. Maybe it was time to go on the offensive. Jorge watched me warily. "Case, I don't like the look in your eye. What's going on in that brain of yours?"

I glanced at him sideways. "Nothing."

"With you, 'nothing' is always 'something'. Give it up Case."

I heard the newsroom door slam open and heard heels clacking down the hallway. Jorge and I stopped talking, listening as Jan Petersen made her way down the hall, heading towards the accounting offices in the rear. We let out a collective sigh.

Jorge pocketed the recorder. 'Come on. Let's go see if you still have a job."

"I thought you told me not to worry about it!"

He shrugged. "No point in getting worked up ahead of time. You're probably fine."

Probably? Probably? My mouth flapped wordlessly as Jorge pushed open the door and headed towards the newsroom. With a savage yank on the handle, I grabbed my bag and followed him.

CHAPTER 18

*L*izzy Burnitis was standing at the copy machine as we entered the newsroom. She made eye contact with me as we threaded our way through the maze, her eyebrow raised questioningly. I noticed she was decked out in Classic Goth today, shades of black with black eye shadow, her face as drawn as a vampire's. She left the machine, moving to intercept me as I headed to my desk.

"Hey Sandy... are you okay? My dad told me what happened to you yesterday." Her brown eyes were concerned. I felt a prickle in the back of my eyes at her concern, unexpected on this dreary, stressful morning. I nodded, not sure I could trust my voice.

She cocked her head at me. "I guess you found out that you can't really use that road as a shortcut if you don't have a sport ute or truck, something with high wheels."

"I guess not. Why the hell don't they close it or mark it or something?"

She shrugged. "People do use it all the time, but every year some moron takes a car down there and gets it stuck on the tracks. Normally, they get it off in time, but once in a while, they don't. Yours is the first one I've heard of that happened right as the train got there."

Moron? My eyes dried up.

"Why were you over there in the first place?" She was frowning at me, apparently oblivious to the moron remark. I sighed internally. She's just a kid, Case.

"I was trying to make it to John Peckham's house in time for our interview."

"Oh. But you left here way early..." her voice trailed off. "Say, what was wrong yesterday? You looked like you had seen a ghost."

I remembered shoving by her in the lobby, intent on escaping Diane and Dana and the blog from Hell. I glanced quickly around, looking for my two female nemeses. The newsroom was blissfully quiet.

I looked back, spied Jorge on his phone at his desk. The door to Russ's office was closed. Changing the subject, I asked Lizzy, "Why was Jan here?"

She looked uncomfortable for a moment. "She was in with Russ."

"Any idea what's up?"

She shook her head. "They had the door closed." Her face belied her words. I eyed her for a moment. "Come on, Lizzy. You know more than you are letting on here."

She shook her head stubbornly. "No.. I don't.. not really... I mean, she was yelling and stuff, but we couldn't hear what she was saying."

I knew she was lying. I also knew I couldn't grill her any further.

"Hey Case, come here." Jorge had hung up the phone and was looking across the cubicles at me. I left Lizzy to her copy machine and made my way to him.

"What is it?" I dropped my bag under my desk.

"I had a message from one of my last remaining friends in

the PD. They told me there's been a missing person report filed for John Peckham. He's been missing for 24 hours now."

"I thought they had to wait 48 hours in a missing person case?"

Jorge leaned against his desk. "They do... normally. But don't forget, he's also a 'person of interest' due to the carnage in A Pint of Peck's. The police aren't terribly amused that he's gone. They also aren't all that impressed with the fact that the last person he spoke to was you."

"Yeah? So? What's that have to do with anything? He blew me off."

"How do you know that? YOU never made it to his house."

I stopped. Jorge was right. I frowned, wondering what might have happened if I had made it out there.

As usual, Maxim read my mind. "Maybe it's a good thing you didn't make it, Sandy. If something happened to him, you might have been right in the middle of it."

He folded his arms, eyeing me. "Case, I would advise you tread lightly for a while. My source also told me the police are going to be watching for you, with instructions that if you so much as drop a candy wrapper on the ground they are to bring you in and not let you out."

"Jesus! What century is this town from, anyway?"

"Last century, Case. And don't you forget it."

"Sandy! Jorge!" We looked across the newsroom where Russ stood in his open door. He was grim faced, waving us in to see him. We glanced at each other.

"Uh oh.." Jorge muttered.

"Well, let's get it over with then." I stood up, squaring my shoulders. "Maybe if they bag me, my problems in this town will be over with anyway."

Jorge shot me a look. "And you think everything will be magically better then? That Morven will just disappear?"

Damn him. Why was it Maxim always had a way of dragging me back down to earth?

We filed into Russ's office. Today he was dressed in prim editor mode, button-down shirt, brown lace-up shoes, pressed slacks. He was pushing papers around on his desk, avoiding eye contact as we came in, closing the door behind us. Jorge and I glanced at each other as we sat down. Mentally, I girded my loins.

Silence stretched out, the only noise the sound of papers being pushed around on Russ's desk. Finally he looked up at us.

"Sandy, Jorge.....I've been here for thirty-two years now, and I fully expected to be here maybe another three or four years at most. I also expected that in a paper this small, in this day and age that I would be dealing primarily with small time stories, staff conflicts, budgeting issues, things like that. I never dreamed that I would have a full-blown, national story on my hands complete with all the threats, intrigue and issues that go along with it." He fell silent for a moment, still fiddling with the papers on his desk. "I also never thought that our own police department would be capable of such dirty dealings as they are doing now." He raised his eyes, staring at us both. For once, I felt no desire to speak. "Well, they made a classic mistake this time. A mistake beneficial to you, Sandy, being as Jan was ready to terminate you this morning." I swallowed dryly. Beside me, Jorge spoke up. "Russ, what's going on? And why would Jan want to terminate Sandy? She was doing what any good investigative reporter would do, getting into the story and digging."

I felt a flush of gratitude at his words.

Russ looked at Jorge, then me. "You see, for decades now, we have rolled along, using the same formula that thousands of small papers across the country have always used. Local news first, use broad ranging stories, such as ones about the school system, local politics, sports, human interest, that sort of thing. Stay away from contention, unless someone else has already reported it. Use AP as filler for more 'hard' news and stay away from lightning rod issues. The town is too small to have the paper be divisive. We have to play to the broadest range possible to keep our circulation numbers up. Let's face it, outside of our county, who is going to care about news from Brownville, VT?"

He shifted forward in his chair, folding his hands. "So we have followed this formula religiously, Apple Festivals front page above the fold, the new roof on the Town Hall taking up months of front page local news, Diane and Dana filling entire sections inside, and our numbers slowly dropped. Not a lot each month, but steadily, an erosion of customers we may never get back. And now... now we have the biggest story I've seen in my thirty-two years, and it's opening up this town in ways I never dreamed." He looked me in the eye. "For one, when you took the night shift, I never, ever dreamed you would be right in the middle of something this big. I thought it would be the usual car crashes, house fires, petty burglary, things like that. I never would have knowingly put you into something like this." He paused again, lost in thought. I opened my mouth to ask a question that was bothering me; Jorge's hand grabbed my knee, squeezing. I glanced at him; he shook his head minutely. Fuming, I waited impatiently for the ax to fall.

Drawing a deep breath, Russ sat back and looked at us both. "Here's the situation. By getting into the story yourself, you violated the operating principals we have for our reporters. It made the Brownville Reporter look foolish... at first. As you two may or may not know, we have been on pretty shaky ground as a newspaper for some years now. Jan and her family have been actively supplementing the books to keep us going. The Reporter has actually been operating in the red for almost six years now. After the photo and story from the press conference hit the wire, Jan was fielding calls all day from other publishers around the country about it. Suddenly this story is becoming hot, and I mean red hot. For the first time in a decade, the number of issues sold in a day actually rose, and our website hits doubled. So needless to say, Jan's ill humor had become a bit tempered. But not so much that she was willing to keep you on, Sandy. The police department was all kinds of angry over what happened, angry enough that they were telling us that we no longer had any access to them for information. Now losing your police as information is devastating and sets you up to look foolish. So Jan met with Captain Hanniford this morning to try to mend some fences." He stopped again, shaking his head. "He basically threatened her. He told her that unless you were removed from the staff that neither he nor his officers would be terribly concerned about any issues that may occur with any employee of the paper, that they would get help to us when they were good and ready… if at all. Jan Petersen is not a woman to be trifled with. You get her back up, and she will stick the course, even if there's nothing but fire and brimstone along the way. She got her back up over that one."

Jorge spoke up, "Jesus Russ! That's so many kinds of illegal, it isn't even funny! She can file a complaint about it with the State's A.G. and Ethic's Commission!"

Russ shook his head. "We already had that conversation. She was alone with him when he made the statement and unfortunately didn't have any recording of it. Which is maybe just as well, because she threw her own threat into the fray back at him."

Uh oh. I didn't like the sound of that. Finding my voice finally, I asked, "What did she threaten him with Russ?"

He glared at me. "You."

Me? I gaped at him. Jorge gave an incredulous laugh,

looking askance at me. "I would say that was a threat with some teeth in it!"

"Shut up, Maxim." I smacked him in the ribs. "How am I being used as a threat here, Russ?"

Russ shifted in his chair, chewing on the arm of his glasses. "She told them she would make you lead on the story and give you carte blanche on resources. She also said she would see to it that everything you produce is picked up by AP."

AP? Holy shit! I'd been trying to get picked up as an AP stringer for years! I felt a flush in my cheeks.

Russ stared at me intently. "Sandy, I have to warn you, I'm not on board with this 100% yet. And I told Jan this too. Everything you do, and everything you produce passes through me first, okay? I mean, EVERYTHING! Not so much as one red hot word sees publication unless I've had my eyes on it too."

"Oh, absolutely Russ. No problem."

He glared at me, not fooled by my meek acquiescence. "That goes for actions too. You don't so much as initiate a walk down Main Street without my approval."

Now that was going to be a problem...or was it? I looked over at Jorge, our eyes meeting in perfect communication. The corners of Jorge's mouth twitched a smile suppressed with effort.

"Okay Russ. I can do that."

CHAPTER 19

"*He* said if I initiate things I have to get approval first, not if YOU did!"

We clattered down the granite steps of the Reporter, spilling out onto Main Street. The rain had stopped, patches of blue appearing in the gray sky. Cars hissed by on the soaked street; I smelled wet pavement, flowers and grass, a heady smell I hadn't experienced since living in Virginia. I inhaled deeply.

Jorge glanced up at the sky, then hooked left, heading up the street at a fast clip. I trotted to catch up with him. Ahead of us, a ray of sunlight hit the town common, making droplets of water on the leaves of the trees sparkle like diamonds.

Jorge smiled, a bit grimly. "Well then, I say that we take a walk in the Common and see if your two friends are in evidence today." He glanced over at me. "I take it you aren't going to tell Russ about last night?"

I shook my head. "Oh, hell no! If he heard that, I think that would mean the end of me being involved in this story at all."

"I would say that is correct, Case. So let's see if our fine friends are out and about."

We entered the common through the Main Street side, wet grass swishing against our ankles. I saw candy wrappers, a couple of piles of dog poop, but no sign of Joe and his friends. Wet benches gleamed in the strengthening sun, devoid of people. We exited on Route 17, aka Elm Street, with nothing except wet ankles, and one of my shoe cleats filled with dog poo. Jorge waited as I swore and scraped it out on the granite curbing.

He leaned against an ornamental lamp post, the gas light style ones the town had installed a few years back in a street beautification program, hands in his pocket, looking around as I jabbed at my right shoe with a stick. "You know, Case, being seen in public with you is bad for my image. It's hard to look cool and contemporary when your co-worker is digging feces out of her shoe with a twig."

"If these pinhead dog owners would stop using the Common as a bathroom for their four-legged shit machines, I wouldn't be standing here digging crap out! Jesus, this is disgusting!"

"It's life, Case. Sometimes you walk in a rose garden, sometimes you step in the fertilizer."

"Well, aren't you Mr. Philosopher today? I'd like to see how philosophical you would be with a shoe full of dog turds…"

"Hey Case! Look!"

I glanced up in time to see a battered gray Oldsmobile 98 making the turn off of Main Street onto Elm Street, two heads visible in the front seat. Unfortunately, it was also going north…away from where we stood.

"That's them! That's the car!"

Jorge swore as the car trundled north in light traffic. "I

can't see the plate from here, and my car is parked by the Reporter. We'll never get to it in time."

We watched traffic move away from the intersection, the gray roof of the Oldsmobile visible among the more brightly colored cars it moved with. Just before it crested the low hill that would put it out of sight, we saw it swing left, cutting across oncoming traffic onto a side street.

"Hey!" Jorge was peering intently after it. "I think they turned onto Victoria Street! Come on, Case!"

He took off in a fast jog.

I scrambled to my feet, my bag hanging lopsided off one arm, a feces covered stick in my right hand, my shoe tread still half full of crap. "Jor... shit!" I hitched my bag and took off after him, feet thump-slapping as I ran. Make that thump-slap-squish.

Glancing at traffic, he darted across the intersection as they were rolling, deftly avoiding a Subaru and a mini-van. Hesitating momentarily, I plunged into the roadway behind him, triggering an angry cacophony of horns from a laden dump truck, and a Mercedes with Connecticut plates. I sped up past the dump truck, and flipped off the Mercedes, twice actually, once for being from Connecticut, and once for being in a Mercedes.

Jorge was 50 feet in front of me, moving quickly, feet rhythmically slapping the pavement. I turned up the speed, ignoring the burn in my lungs, and slowly drew up to him. We thudded off the sidewalk across Maple Street and sprinted down the next block. The burn in my lungs was turning into a full out shortness of breath. Dots speckled my vision as the street sign for Victoria Street loomed.

"Jor... stop... I.. can't..."

He looked over at me and stopped. I doubled over, hands on my knees, heaving for air. Frowning, he glanced back at how far we had run.

"Case… we only ran for less than a ¼ mile. You really can't breathe?"

"You… do… that… carrying a pack… and… tell me… how well… you… are breathing."

He reached out and took the strap of my bag in his hand. His eyes widened when he felt the weight. "Jesus, Sandy! What the hell is in there? Concrete blocks?"

I straightened up, went to wipe the hair out of my eyes, realizing belatedly that I still had my shit covered stick in my hand. I threw it down on the sidewalk.

Jorge looked impatiently at the street in front of us. "Come on. You want me to carry that?" He held out a hand for my bag. I shook my head, hugging it closer to me. Among other things, I had my gun in there, wrapped in a pair of underwear. I felt uncomfortable not having it close to me. We walked the last ten feet to the intersection where a large, old brick apartment building with tired storefronts on the first floor stood on the corner.

Every town has a Victoria Street, the street where the stores that sell novelties and the low-rent bars are. Above these businesses were a number of run -down apartment houses, the kind that rent by the week. The police spent many of their working hours here, quashing fights or looking for people. Our Victoria Street was a block long and dead ended at a derelict warehouse, the entrance chain link fenced off. 'Millers Goods and Sundries' could still be seen in black and white paint along the top of the building, a reminder of Brownville's boom time at the turn of the century. Both sides of the street were lined cheek to cheek with brick buildings, sharing common walls for the most part, the odd alley here and there, an open area where a building had burned many years ago now a parking lot. I saw 'The Love Box' across the street diagonally from us, windows covered with newspapers, advertising novelties for adults. Just up the street was a honky-tonk bar, the Headroom, open even at this early hour, a few smokers clustered in front of the doorway. Past that, was 'Madam Lourdes Fortunes', who had been short sighted enough to not realize she would be going out of business, leaving an empty store front with soaped over windows. Another bar was across the street further down, on the opposite side. A liquor store completed the sad medley of businesses.

We stood on the corner; me catching my breath and Jorge looking intently at the street. I didn't see the Oldsmobile. What I did see was motion as a large man exited the last apartment building on the right, walking briskly down the street to his waiting Lexus.

It was Hal Morgan.

Jorge and I shared a look, raised eyebrows, silent communication. He leaned back away from Victoria Street as taillights flared on the car. Gesturing to the recessed doorway of the television repair shop that was behind us, we moved into the depths of it, and waited as Morgan got himself turned around and exited Victoria Street. I could see him looking at traffic as he eased out and turned northbound on Elm Street. He never looked our way.

"Well. Isn't that interesting?" Jorge said as we re-emerged onto the sidewalk.

"What would he be doing down here?" I looked at the sad storefronts on Victoria, finding the building he had come out of. My eyes tracked up over the front of it; two stories topped with a flat roof, the windows decorated with ornate millwork from a bygone era.

"I don't know. But I will be finding out. As far as I know, he doesn't have any holdings down here." He moved out from the corner. "Come on. And keep a sharp eye out."

He was telling me? I wanted the jump on these two clowns. "Wait, a moment..." I rummaged in my bag. I donned a scarf, tying it around my head like a movie star, then put on my oversized sunglasses. Jorge rolled his eyes. "Jesus, Case. You look like you're trying to channel Jacki-O."

"I don't want them to see me!"

"Oh... sure... like they're going to miss someone in a hot pink scarf and huge shades, carrying a pack on her back. Yup, you're undercover all right."

"Piss off, Maxim." My nerves were jangling.

We stepped off down Victoria Street together, eyes tracking everything around us. The on-street parking was about half full at this hour; I craned to scan the cars all the way to the chain-link fence; no Oldsmobile. The smokers in front of the Headroom fell silent as we approached, wary gazes watching our progress. I drew myself up straighter, looking ahead through my Hollywood shades. Beside me, Jorge sauntered casually, hands in his pocket, only his eyes belying his watchfulness. I blinked and coughed as the smoke hit my lungs from the group, saw a fat man in a stained tee shirt purse his lips and blow a stream of smoke straight at us. My eyes stung as the bad breath and burning tobacco hit me. I stifled a cough, felt Jorge tugging my arm, pulling me through the group. I heard a mumbled remark behind us as we moved away, someone muttering, "Looks like someone got hisself some white meat."

I tensed, rage blossoming in my belly. Jorge tugged me again, muttering, "Case... don't."

"Jesus... If that redneck fell in a pond, they'd be skimming stupid off the surface for a week." I didn't bother dropping my voice.

Jorge's lips were a thin line. "Case. Leave it. We have other things to do."

I glanced back over my shoulder at the group. The fat

man was grinning widely, gaps showing where teeth used to be. I narrowed my eyes at him.

"Come on." He cut diagonally across the street towards the parking lot, with me trailing in his wake. I was aware of eyes on our backs.

The parking lot was small; holding no more than 15 cars when at capacity. Like the street, it too was about half full. I spied gray metal over in the back corner.

"There!" Jorge said as I saw the car. I glanced up at the buildings towering over the lot, two and three stories of brick and windows. I saw plants in some, curtains billowing out in others. On a couple of windows, air conditioners leaned crookedly, water dripping down the façade. Moving along the edge of the lot, we cautiously approached the car.

It sat empty, sagging on the right front corner, windows rolled down. Moving closer, I spied candy bar wrappers littering the front seat and Budweiser cans on the rear floor. Jorge moved behind the car, writing something down.

He rejoined me, putting his notebook in his pocket. "Come on Case. Let's get out of here."

"Leave? I want to find these assholes!"

He pushed me towards the street. "How the hell are you going to do that? They could be in any of these buildings. I have the plate, let me see if that gives us anything. Besides.." he was looking towards the group that still watched us, "We have an audience."

"Well, let's give them a show then!" I marched out into the street, retracing our steps back to the other side of the street. I heard Jorge hiss, "Sandy! Sandy... Goddamit! Where the hell are you going?" I kept walking, a smile plastered on my face. Jorge caught up with me as I reached the sidewalk. "Case, I swear, I'm going to kill you before this story is over with!"

Smiling broadly, I grabbed his upper arm, pulling him

closer to my left side, my right burdened with my bag. I felt him stiffen with surprise. I tilted my face at him, a genuine smile on it now. He was scowling.

"Oh, honey..." I cooed as we reached the edge of the sullen group. They weren't smiling now. The fat man was standing on the edge of the group, to my right, arms planted belligerently on his flabby hips. "What's with the lib-tards in this town?" he stated as we drew abreast of them. I recognized the voice as the one I heard earlier.

My bag accidentally swung off my shoulder, slamming the fat man's legs sideways, buckling his knees the wrong way from how they were supposed to work. I heard a pop as he hit the sidewalk with a muffled yell. Someone in the group snorted with laughter.

"Oh, sorry!" I gave him my best contrite smile. "Here, can I help you up?"

He rolled on his back, holding his knee, a lit cigarette rolling away from him on the concrete. "You fucking bitch!"

Jorge was tensed beside me, his hand on my arm. "Hey, it was an accident, and she said she was sorry."

"Come on, dear... he can get his own ass off the sidewalk." I pushed away, Jorge in my wake. I saw incredulous expressions on the others as we pushed our way through them. They stayed silent. I could hear the fat man still swearing as we reached Elm Street again. Jorge let his breath out finally. "Goddamn you Case!"

I was ignoring him, my attention focused across Elm Street. "You know, I could really use a sandwich right about now." Jorge looked at the clapboarded, one story saggy little sandwich shop that sat across from the entrance to Victoria Street, then back at me with ill-concealed surprise. "Food? You're thinking about food again? What the hell, Case! Your metabolism must be in permanent overdrive!?"

I twisted around to look at him. "Actually, I'm thinking a nice, leisurely meal seated right....there." I pointed at the empty table that sat in the window... the one that faced right down Victoria Street.

"Ah..." Jorge said thoughtfully.

CHAPTER 20

There's something intrinsically gross about fly speckles all over a plate-glass window, especially when that window is in a restaurant. I glanced up at the expanse of glass, noting the black constellation that swooped across it, then down at the yellowing plastic table cover, the dull silverware laid out next to the paper placemat.

Across from me, Jorge wiped the table surface for the tenth time with a balled up napkin. We sat in silence as we watched Victoria Street. My fat redneck friend had finally been helped upright off the sidewalk, his arm draped over the necks of two equally fat redneck friends, one a muffin topped woman. He disappeared back inside for another drink to kill the pain.

I ignored the menu as the sullen brunette deposited two glasses of tepid tap water at our places, her pad clenched under her arm. At noon on a Wednesday, I was proud to say we were fifty percent of the clientele. A radio thumped in the back; two construction workers sat at the counter grimly polishing off plates heaped high with greasy fries.

Across the street, Victoria Street drowsed in the full sun,

the morning's rain long blown out to the coast. Smokers came and went from in front of the Headroom. A few cars made their way down to the liquor store, and one middle-aged man furtively made his way into the Love Box. Otherwise, all was still. 'Igor' and 'Ivan' remained absent.

Jorge attacked the table again after our waitress left with our orders (two burgers, hold the e coli), swearing under his breath. I rolled my eyes as he grabbed my napkin to replace the white sodden shreds he had left from his.

"Come on Jorge! Now you're just getting OCD!" I swiveled around looking for another napkin. Overhead, a fly buzzed loudly in the window.

"How the hell does the Health Inspector allow this place to stay open?" He rubbed harder at a particularly sticky spot.

I ignored him, choosing to stare down Victoria Street instead. I could be dropped into a Third World country and be okay as long as my food was served to me already dead. I suspected Jorge would have an issue with the hygiene; he was already fretting about botulism and salmonella right here in the USA. Christ, sometimes it was like being with Ben all over again. I grimaced at that thought.

"What is it, Case?"

How the hell did he always catch me in moments I thought were private? I fiddled with a fork, not looking at him. "I was just thinking about my ex, and about what you said the other day." I raised my head and looked at Jorge. "I've never looked him up. What do you mean when you tell me he's twisted?"

Jorge stared at me silently for a moment, then sighed. "Look, Sandy... he's a brilliant writer, and prolific too. But he's also not wrapped very tightly. Look at that blog he's spending all that time and energy on."

I scowled. I didn't want to look at that freaking blog; I spent too much time trying to pretend it didn't exist. Jorge continued, "I read back through that the other night. There's some seriously twisted stuff in there. At the bare minimum, I would advise you to consider getting legal counsel and protection from this guy. And I would strongly urge you to consider a protective order against him and possibly a lawsuit. Guys like him don't stop on their own, particularly if they feel that they have a weak victim." He picked up the glass of water, eyed it, reconsidered and set it back down.

"But Jorge, what is out there that makes you say he's twisted? I know he is, but you've never met the man and yet you formed a pretty strong opinion about him."

He was looking out at Victoria Street again as he answered. "Sandy… some of it you just don't want to get into. But I will tell you that he uses screen names for various forums, and sometimes he uses the same names for vastly different forums. For example, he used the same name on a journalist forum and then on a bondage one." His eyes met mine. "The man has some serious kink fetishes."

I stammered, realizing that Jorge was wondering about me. "I know we, um, used some props in our marriage, but nothing I would call kinky." Well, if you excluded the hand-cuffs. And the dog collars. I felt my cheeks flame.

A smile surfaced at the edge of Jorge's mouth. "Case, I don't want to know what's making you blush." I felt my cheeks flame hotter. Damn it, Maxim!

He glanced back out the window as our burgers arrived, grease pooling on the surface of them. I remained silent as she deposited our plates and iced teas, leaving without a word.

"Jorge, we were, um, a little adventurous in our marriage, but nothing full out kinky. Certainly nothing that would shock you." I squashed the bun down on my burger, trying to not notice the wet noise it made. "You and Melody, you guys must have some fun from time to time."

Jorge had been married to Melody for a dozen years now. She was a brilliant, ferocious woman, a corporate lawyer. I pitied anyone across the table from her in a courtroom. I took a bite of my soggy burger, ignoring the old bacon flavor it came with.

"Case, we have 'fun', most certainly we do, but our 'fun' generally doesn't involve flogging or tying blindfolded women up and pouring hot wax all over them either."

My burger flipped over in my belly and turned to pre-vomit.

"What are you talking about?" I felt my pulse pounding in my ears.

Jorge shifted uncomfortably. "Look, you divorced the guy and moved on. All I'm saying is keep your distance and maybe think about getting some protection from him if he keeps this up. He has other blogs you know, blogs where he just spews hatred of everything you can think of. Blacks, gays, women, men, children, Christ, even puppies. He's not wrapped tightly, Case."

"Where did you find the bit about tying up women and dumping hot wax on them?" Jesus Christ... my mind flashed back to moments over the years when Ben had 'accidentally' hurt me during sex. I dropped the half-eaten burger on the plate, my appetite gone.

We had been so intent on our conversation Victoria Street had been forgotten. Motion out of the corner of my eye directed my attention back to it. 'Igor' and 'Ivan' were exiting one of the buildings along the row, heading towards the parking lot at a rolling walk. It was the same building Hal Morgan had come out of earlier.

I stiffened in my seat. "Jorge." I said quietly. He was peering through the fly crap at them. "I see them." They walked up the street, 'Ivan' with a rapid, scurrying stride, 'Igor' in an odd rolling gait. I watched as they hooked left, into the parking lot and disappeared from view. I looked across the table at Jorge. "Now what?"

"We wait. And we see which way they go. Then we get my car and go for a cruise."

The minutes ticked past. No Oldsmobile. Our burgers sat in a cooling pool of grease, forgotten. The waitress came by, frowned at us and left us alone. Flies hummed and mated in the window. I couldn't stand it any longer.

"I'm going back down there." The chair skidded back as I stood. Jorge looked at me with alarm. "Case, just cool your heels for a few minutes." He looked over at the group in front of The Headroom. "I don't think it's wise to go back down there on foot."

I shook my head. "I wasn't going to go back down Victoria Street." Jorge looked up at me with a frown. I gestured up the road. "I was going to go down Sycamore Street." Sycamore ran the next block over from Victoria, the buildings that fronted Victoria had buildings backed up to them that fronted Sycamore on the other side. "I'm sure there's an alley or two we can wander down."

Jorge tossed a couple of bills on the table next to our uneaten lunch. "Let's roll."

The gray Oldsmobile still sat in the back corner of the lot, visible through the garbage tattered chain-link fence we were pressed up against. Jorge batted a spider off his left ear, muttering a heartfelt curse. Some sort of amorphous gray blob stained the cuff of his trousers. Wisely, I decided not to point that out.

Across the lot, the smokers still milled around in front of the bar, everything looking slow and beaten down on this brilliant June afternoon. I eyed the car and the surrounding buildings, wondering where our friends could have gotten to. Old mill era brick apartment buildings towered overhead, behind us and on both sides of the lot. On Victoria Street, I could see the fence that blocked the road from the old ware-house. Frowning, I craned to see the lot as best I could from my awkward vantage point, somewhat kitty corner away from it, between two buildings.

"I don't see them anyplace." Jorge was also craning and frowning.

"How many places could they have gone from where we saw them last?"

"I suppose they could have doubled back already, while we were crawling through that roach-infested heaven here." Jorge shot a foul look at the alleyway we had come down.

"You know Maxim, sometimes you're just a big pussy." I wasn't impressed with his whining. "They walked back to this lot like they were on a mission. So why would they turn around and walk away again?"

He shook his head. "I don't know, Case. But I also don't see many likely places they could have gone from here, either."

It had been at least twenty minutes since we had seen our friends leaving the apartment building. I sighed, and shifted impatiently, thinking that this was a waste of time.

Motion caught my eye in the back corner of the lot. Beside me, Jorge hissed, pulling on me to signal me to get down. We sank down behind the scraggle of weeds that lined the fence. 'Ivan' appeared first, wiping dead leaves off his head, followed by 'Igor', who was moving slower, still with that odd rolling walk I had noticed. I wondered if last night's escapades had injured him. God, I hoped so! 'Ivan' gestured impatiently to 'Igor', who was lugging a large, dirt stained box. With 'Ivan' still harrying at him, they hustled across the parking lot to the car. I shared a look with Jorge. Where the hell had they come from?

We held our breath and crouched as low as we could behind our meager concealment in the weeds as they reached the car, 'Igor' dropping the box into the trunk with a thud, all the while 'Ivan' looking around nervously, agitating at 'Igor'. They didn't look in our direction.

The motor turned over slowly, oil smoke belching out of the exhaust. I could see 'Igor' stuffing what looked like a candy bar in his mouth as they rolled out the exit of the parking lot. Across the street, the smokers watched desultorily.

"Well." Jorge straightened up, grimacing as he wiped his head, "That was interesting. Come on, Case. Let's go get my car and take a ride."

I shook my head. "No, I'm going to check out the lot and see where they came from first."

"Oh come on Case, we can do that when I get my car!"

I was already working my way down the fence. I knew a fence located at the back of a lot like this would have at least one place where I could get through.

I was right. Four posts down, the chain link billowed loose, weeds worn to dirt below it from constant knees scraping underneath it. I ducked, wiggled, caught my bag momentarily, and popped free mid lot. I could hear Jorge cursing again as he started crawling behind me. He certainly was well read; he had quite the interesting vocabulary.

We stood for a moment in the lot getting our bearings, looking around to where we had seen our buddies. There was a two story flat roofed brick building on that side of the lot, the warehouse behind it. I thought that maybe they had gone under the same fence we had just crawled under, but the fence ended at the edge of the building, away from where we had seen them. I craned up, looking at windows and doors on this side, Jorge doing the same next to me. He gestured with his chin. "I wonder… the bulkhead?" A cellar bulkhead sat on this side of the building, metal doors streaked with rust. We crossed the lot, eyeing it carefully. A rusted chain with a padlock looped through the handles, looking like it was untouched for decades, weeds growing unchecked around it. I twisted around, my bag a lead weight in the small of my back, scanning the edge of the building. Bent and broken weeds caught my eye. "Jorge... over here." A small cellar window was missing, leaving a black rectangle to the interior. The dirt was freshly disturbed in front of it, the vegetation trampled. Jorge looked at the small opening with surprise. "That big lout actually fit through that?"

I was already crouching down, swinging my legs through the hole.

"Case! What the hell are you doing?"

I dropped into the cellar with a thud.

CHAPTER 21

J stood still as my eyes slowly adjusted from the brilliant June day to the dim half night of the cellar. Jorge's head popped in the window behind me.

He was not amused.

"God damn it, Sandy! Get your ass out here! You're trespassing! Russ will send us both packing if he finds out!"

I ignored him, moving slowly into the space, aware of the fact that my gun was in my bag. I heard Jorge fuming outside, then a scraping sound as he levered his legs inside behind me. Truth be told, I was counting on him following me, and glad I was right. I was pissed… but not so pissed that I could have searched this entire place myself. He appeared at my right shoulder, brushing more dirt off his head. He no longer looked like a GQ centerfold.

We scanned the cellar in silence. Low ceiling, exposed piping snaking everywhere, piles of dirt over the broken cement floor. The entire thing smelled of decay and mold. I looked for signs of travel, recent occupation, saw empty beer cars near where we had entered, a condom lying on the floor like a flattened earthworm, numerous cigarette butts.

Jorge hissed in my ear, "Looks like we found a local hangout spot."

"Yeah, a regular Redneck Fuck Hut by the looks of it." I muttered back.

Further in, I spotted scuff marks in the dirt, heading towards the window on the far wall. Ducking under hanging pipes, I followed it, wondering if I should get my gun out now, then decided that Jorge might not handle that well.

He was silent behind me as we followed the marks across the basement, small shadows scurrying in the corner of my eye. I stopped short when I realized the marks had ended.

Right in front of a cellar window on the other side of the building.

We shared a look. Jorge stepped forward cautiously, peering through the window.

The ground was at eye level, more broken weeds drooping into the hole, leaning against the window. I found myself looking out at the old warehouse. Reaching out, I touched the frame to see if the window was loose. It fell forward at my touch. I jumped as the wooden frame tumbled onto the ground outside.

We shared another look. "Jorge, what's the story on this place?" gesturing with my chin at the warehouse.

He shook his head. "Not much of one. Closed back in the early '80's and has been like this ever since. They keep the taxes up and the perimeter intact. I have never heard of kids partying in there, or any problems. There was some angst about it being a fire hazard, but there's been no reason to worry other than its age."

'Who owns it?"

"It's a corporation. They bought out Millers and closed less than 5 years later."

"And it's been unused since?"

"That's my understanding, yes."

Well, that was strange. Why would a company leave a large facility like this untouched, but keep up taxes and the security for twenty-five years or more?

I cast around for a place to step up onto, spied a black pipe running along the wall about a foot up. Swinging my bag out ahead of me, I stuck my toe on the pipe and shimmied through. I heard Jorge sigh. "Case. You're going to be the death of me yet."

Little did we know I would almost fulfill that prediction that afternoon.

CHAPTER 22

*M*iller's Feed looked remarkably unmolested for having been vacant for 25 years. No graffiti stained the walls, no broken glass, the roof still true and somewhat square. The gravel lot in front of it was spattered with debris and knee deep weeds, looking like it was truly deserted. But staring at the exterior, I had my doubts about whether it really was unused. Beside me, Jorge surveyed the surroundings with the same speculative look I was feeling.

Something was off here.

Sharing a look, we cautiously moved forward, scanning the ground for signs of where anyone else might have already passed through here. I saw some trampled grass and piles of dog poop. Even here, the neighborhood dogs were using this as a dumping ground. Scowling, I carefully watched my step.

Loading docks protruded from one wall, the wooden doors padlocked tightly. In the front, where the retail portion of the warehouse would have been, sheets of plywood covered every door. They too were intact. A long-abandoned rail spur curved into the yard and ran parallel to the building; they would have off loaded feed and grain from there and trundled it into the building through the large barn doors at the end of it, doors that sported heavy, shiny padlocks on them now. The chain-link fence crawled up and over the train tracks, sealing entry from that direction.

We made our way around the back of the building. The Mill River gurgled at the bottom of a steep rock and sumac covered bank, bits of trash glinting in the sun. I scanned the backside of the building, tilting my head up to see the roof that towered three stories high. A fat pigeon waddled on the edge, peering back down at me. My foot hit something wet and slippery, momentarily throwing me off balance. I skidded sideways, towards the drop off into the river, my arms flailing. Jorge lunged, catching me by my bag strap, halting my plunge over the lip.

"Damn it all!" I looked around to see what had been so slippery and spotted the huge pile of flattened dog feces. "Oh, you have GOT to be shitting me!"

I lifted my left foot; it was packed full of brown goo. "Oh, for Christ's sake!"

Jorge's hand tightened on my arm. "Sandy..." his voice was quiet.

"What?" I was pissed now, big time. This was simply turning out to be too much of a day.

"So far we haven't seen any place to get in here except where we came through... yet there are cubic yards of dog waste everyplace."

I was scraping my foot against a sumac trunk, balancing precariously on one foot, my bag dragging me off balance. "Yeah? So? Those damn shit machines are everywhere."

"But how did they get in here? Or are they already in here?"

I froze as we both heard the rustle at the same time, and the low growl.

We made eye contact with each other as the weeds parted to reveal a stocky brown and white dog with a massive head and jaw. Now I don't know much about dogs, but I had seen these in the news more than once, enough to recognize a pit bull when I saw it.

Oh shit….

Jorge had gone stock still next to me, still holding my upper arm. I eyed the dog and scanned our surroundings quickly. Not good. The back of the building was flat, meandering clapboard with windows climbing to the top floor, unbroken save for an old back entry on a porch that stood about twenty yards from us. I eyed it, wondering if there would be any salvation from the dog there. The steps were rotted and sagging off the frame, leaving a five-foot jump to the deck. The dog would be on us before we could even get halfway there. Getting back to where we came in wasn't going to happen without a fight; the dog was between us and where we had come in. The side of the building stretched away an impossible distance, with the added bonus of the unknown once you reached the corner. I could see chain-link fence coming up from the ravine and disappearing. The piece of land we stood on was maybe twenty feet wide, backed by the building and fronted by the steep drop off into the ravine. There wasn't a fence here; the steep slope provided its own barrier.

Porch… run… or ravine.

I thought about my gun; as much as I didn't want to be renamed Alpo, I also hated the thought of shooting an animal.

The dog growled again but didn't advance. I whispered to Jorge, "What the hell should we do now?"

His face was tight. "I don't know Sandy. I don't know a lot about animals."

"Can you call someone?"

His head whipped around towards me. "Who?" he hissed, tension audible. The dog growled again, head lowering, back prickling with hair. I noticed the hair was also standing up around his neck. He advanced a stiff step.

"Jorge! Shut up!"

"Shut up? You're the one talking to me!"

The dog growled, louder this time, and in stereo. What the hell?

More rustling as a second dog appeared, this one white with black markings, longer legs, some sort of bull dog cross. My heart sank. Beside me, Jorge stiffened. "Oh, boy... we are in deep shit now."

Porch... not an option.

Run... also not an option.

That left the ravine. Or my gun.

I leaned over and whispered to Jorge, "I need to get into my bag. You have to let go of my arm."

"Your bag? What's in your bag?"

"My gun."

"Your... WHAT?!"

Growling in stereo again.

"Shh... let go of me. And when I start moving to the right, stay with me."

"Jesus Christ, Sandy..." he released my arm. The brown dog took a stiff step towards us, then another, followed by the white one. I noticed the white one was starting to move to the right of the brown dog, moving to where it could circle around behind us. I slowly swung my bag forward, sliding a step sideways, Jorge mirroring my movement. Both dogs tensed. I fumbled with the strap. The white dog was moving now, slinking around between us and the building as we slid another step in unison towards the ravine. The brown dog lowered his head, keeping his eyes firmly on us.

And they were not friendly eyes either.

My fingers were stiff, clumsy as I struggled to open the top of my bag. Human threats were something I could deal with; animal ones were from the unknown to me. The white dog stopped and snarled, stubby white teeth glinting. All the hair on it stood straight up. I didn't have to know anything about dogs to know that wasn't a good sign.

We had made it to within five feet of the edge of the ravine when all hell broke loose. I expected the white dog to be the first aggressor; instead it was the brown one who suddenly snarled and launched himself at us, stubby legs churning with impossible speed as we ran backwards from him in synchronized panic, his mouth open showing massive jaws and teeth. I caught a glimpse of a collar on him as he launched at me; from behind I heard more commotion as the white dog launched its attack too.

I threw my bag up in front of me, knocking the brown dog off balance as Jorge and I tumbled over the edge into the ravine, suddenly falling and bouncing down the steep lip towards the water.

Scrubby trees flashed by my vision, rocks slammed into my back, my legs flung up over my head, somersaulting, Jorge crashing and rolling next to me, another blow to my back, crazy whirl of green and brown, then…… blackness.

CHAPTER 23

Water gurgled and bubbled as I lay on the blanket, during one of the picnics I used to take with Ben down at the park. We would roll out a blanket, break out a bottle of wine, and enjoy a selection of nibble food. Following that we would nibble on each other until we were so steamed up we could barely wait to throw the blanket in the car where we would run home and screw like rabbits. Sometimes, we didn't even make it home, but instead did the nasty in the car, the threat of being caught adding spice to the experience. I sighed with the memory of warm sun on my face, like now, of lust and love, before everything was tainted and gone. Ben smiled at me, his hair college long and unkempt, then frowned as a shadow fell over his face.

"Sandy."

I looked up from where I was lying on the blanket to see a man standing over us, the sun behind him so I couldn't see his features.

"Sandy... wake up."

I didn't want to wake up. I wanted to see who this man was. Something about him looked familiar. I heard dogs barking frantically. People always brought dogs to this park. They were little shit machines as far as I was concerned.

"Damn it Sandy... come on... wake up."

He moved, allowing sunlight to hit the side of his face. I frowned trying to see him. Was it Officer Pim? What was he doing here?

"Sandy... Sandy... come on Sandy. Wake up."

Officer Pim wasn't in my past, he was in my future... or my present I meant. What was going on? Where was I? I opened my eyes; the park was gone, replaced by red-tinted weeds and scraggly sumac. Boulders stuck up randomly, water gurgled by my face. I felt wetness under my cheek. I heard the voice again, concern evident. "Sandy? Sandy? Come on... wake up, hon."

Everything hurt. The shadow fell over me again as the person shifted. The dogs continued to bark frantically.

My eyes slowly focused on Jorge.

Jorge. The warehouse. The dogs. Shit...

I reached around, clamping onto Jorges' arm. "Jorge... what... what?"

"Take it easy. Take it easy." He sounded like he was talking more to himself than me. "I've got to call an ambulance for you."

An ambulance? Why? I was battered and woozy, but nothing I couldn't handle. "Jorge, just wait a moment on that... oww!" My arm protested as I slowly pushed myself up from the ground. Mud coated my face, my hair flattened against my head with it. The world swam for a moment, then righted itself. I finally looked at Jorge.

He was just as battered as me, his glasses gone. He reached out and wiped my forehead, his hand coming away crimson. I reached up, found a cut at the hairline that was bleeding like crazy. Above us, the dogs continued to bark frantically.

149

"Shit!" I wiped blood away, reached for a handful of water to splash on it. Blood and mud splashed down my face. "Jorge... are you okay?"

"Yeah... I guess. Sandy, we need help getting out of here."

"Well, we can't call authorities or we are going to end up in jail, especially me. Help me up." I reached up to him as more blood ran down my face. He hauled me upright. The world tilted. "Whoa.." I grabbed his shoulder for support. "Where's my bag?"

"Your bag?" he frowned a moment, then spied it stuck on a tree trunk about ten feet up from us. "Can you stand?"

"Yeah." I didn't dare move my head much. Nausea was already rolling through my belly. I would bet I had a concussion going on from this deal.

Jorge scrambled up the steep slope and snagged my bag off the tree, then skidded back down on his rump in a shower of leaf debris. I swayed a moment, then sank back down on my haunches as I opened the top and pawed through the contents. Pulling out my spare underwear, I used them to soak in the water and wipe the blood off again. Jorge knelt in front of me. "Here. Give me those." He looked at the fabric, realizing belatedly it was a thong. "What the hell Case?"

"Hey, I'm prepared for all eventualities, okay? In my bag are some bandaids too, can you dig one out?"

He eyed the contents of the bag dubiously. The barking had finally stopped, although I was willing to bet they hadn't left the area yet.

Jorge fished a battered bandaid out and wiped my forehead again. I winced as he rubbed the torn flesh. Clumsily, he tore it open and pasted it across my head.

"Anything else hurting?"

"A lot of things, but nothing I can't handle. Jorge, how the hell are we going to get out of here?"

He looked up at the embankment we had just hurtled down, then down at the river rushing past, then back up at me.

"Not a lot of choices here, Case. How well can you swim?"

Oh, sweet Jesus in a tuxedo shirt.

I looked at the water dubiously. Where we knelt across from us was a retaining wall that rose some thirty feet up over our head. No way to climb that. Downstream from us, the river was channeled into a huge culvert that carried the rail bed over the water. I could see sunlight through it on the other side.

I looked upstream. Vegetation hid our bank from view, the wall stretched out of sight.

Behind us, the embankment rose jaggedly, years of being undercut during spring storms having made it too steep to navigate easily... even if there weren't two four-legged piranhas on top of it. I heaved a sigh that made specks float across my vision. Jorge was on his feet, considering our options as well. I called out to him, "Are you going to be able to see without your glasses?"

He shrugged. "I can, just not that great. God only knows where they are."

I slapped at a crow-sized mosquito that had purchased the blood buffet on my arm, leaving a smear of red cells across my bicep. Another two promptly honed in on me. "We gotta get moving, Jorge. We'll be exsanguinated if we stay here." Jorge was waving his hand at the cloud that was forming around his head. "Jesus!"

"They're the state bird of Vermont." I muttered as I rose to my feet unsteadily. "How deep do you think this is here?"

"I don't know. One way to find out I guess." Holding onto a sumac on the bank, he gingerly stepped into the current, one step, two... then he disappeared under the surface.

"JORGE!" Panic welled in my throat. The sumac he was

hanging onto was bent over the tip beneath the surface. I scrambled to grab it, intent on pulling him up when he resurfaced, sputtering and spitting water. I flailed on the bank, grabbing the back of his shirt. Leaves stuck to his head, mud smeared his face. Impossibly, he started to laugh. "There's a hole right there." He rose out of the water until he was waist deep. "A fucking hole, beautiful!" He started laughing again. I realized he was unraveling. He pushed my hand off his shoulder and started slogging his way down the edge of the bank slowly, heading away from me, still chortling. "Jorge, JORGE!" He waved a hand at me dismissively and kept going. Great, now my coworker was chugging around the bend and I didn't have a ticket on the crazy train with him. With a last sigh, I slowly slid my feet into the water, clutching my bag to my chest.

Holy mother, it was cold! Jesus, it was June and yet this felt like it had come straight off the side of a glacier that morning. The earlier rain had swollen it, creating muddy brown swirls that obscured any hope of seeing more than four inches under the surface. I tensed as something brushed my leg. God, I hoped that was a branch!

Ahead of me, Jorge had made his way laboriously into the tunnel that straddled the river. He clutched the smooth iron sides momentarily as the current deepened and strengthened, then let go, allowing it to carry him on the surface. I hesitated at the entrance, my bag clutched at my shoulder. Jorge yelled back over his shoulder, his voice ponging off the steel, "Come on Case! Last one in is a rotten egg!"

I could see him emerging into the sunlight on the other side. Taking a deep breath, I lowered myself into the water and let it carry me into the blackness of the tunnel.

Reflections of the water danced on the ceiling of the arch as it swept me into it, struggling to keep my bag in my hands and above water. I saw black shapes clustered on the very top; one of them moved, unfolding leathery wings. Holy shit! It was an entire colony of bats! The top of the tunnel was a carpet of them, shifting and moving. I thought I could hear squeaking as the current carried me through. I yelped loudly as one of them fluttered loose and took flight, my voice magnified by the metal tunnel. The noise disturbed the colony, sending more wings loose. Panic-stricken, I started flailing. Unfortunately, my movements pushed me away from the edge of the tunnel and put me further out into the current. I popped out the other side in the middle of the stream... too away far to grab Jorge's outstretched hand. I caught a glimpse of his mouth in an 'O' of astonishment before I was pulled away from him at an ever-increasing speed.

CHAPTER 24

"*Y*ou're in the middle of Brownville, Sandy. You can't possibly drown in the middle of town. No one dies like this... this is too incredibly stupid for words."

I kept telling myself this over and over as I was helplessly pulled down the middle of the river in a tumble, somehow still hanging onto my now saturated bag.

The bank on my right flashed by, an impossibly thick tumble of woods and scrub, the left side all retaining wall and the backs of buildings. I saw car bumpers above it in one spot, evidence of the parking lot behind the Ford dealership. I tried to yell, gained a mouthful of dirty brown water for my efforts, sputtered and coughed madly. This is it: this is how it all ends. I hugged my bag to my chest, feeling faint from all the trauma, my vision cloudy. This is it.....

It took a moment to realize I was seeing tree branches in the water ahead of me, branches that were attached to a huge sycamore tree that had collapsed into the river. Its roots had been undercut by the river until it finally slumped into the water, leaving a tremendous root ball clinging to the shore. I barely had time to register its presence before I was swept hard into the middle of the crown, little green leaves sprouting out all over it still. I finally reacted, grabbing at anything I could. I slammed to a halt against the trunk, my legs swept underneath, my upper body folded over the top, bobbing in the current, my bag wedged between me and the tree. I sobbed and held on, letting my face fall into the speckled white and gray bark.

Time passed. I floated and gasped, hanging on for dear life, too tired to move, frozen to the point of numbness from the water, my brain sludge from the overload of adrenaline. I felt the entire tree quiver. Oh no, God no, don't get swept away!

I felt more motion, heard a voice, opened my eyes and saw a work boot patched with duct tape gingerly sliding out the tree towards me. The crown dipped lower into the water at the weight. I sobbed and held on tighter. "I got 'er." Hands closed on my arm, hauling me up, I flailed and struggled, he hauled harder, slipping on the narrow surface he was perched on. "Cut it out!" He cuffed me on the side of my head, hard. Shocked back into awareness, I stopped struggling as a second pair of hands closed onto my other arm, grunting. "Mmmph! This is a heavy one!" I smelled something, something like rotting fish and mold.

They hauled me unceremoniously towards the shore, inching along the tree, then thigh deep in the water. I flopped and dragged over branches, my bag gone, having been taken by a set of hands. My brain was saturated, barely working. Numbly, I let them manhandle me to shore.

Ground, solid ground under my feet. I sagged towards it. My right arm jerked hard in the socket, pain spearing through the haze. "'Ay! Use yer own feet! I ain't carryin' ya!" Pushing, shoving, my rescuers hauled me rudely up the embankment. I smelled wood smoke.

I couldn't get my brain to fire on all cylinders again. My neck felt too weak for my head, my chin sagging onto my chest as I stumbled walked along a narrow path, leaf litter swirling around my dragging feet. Two pairs of feet bracketed mine; one in duct tape repaired work boots, the other in torn, dirty sneakers. I heard another voice, a woman's. The smoke smell grew stronger.

You're in Brownville, VT. You are in the center of Brownville VT. You are alive. You are in the center of town. So why the hell did this smell and feel like I was somewhere deep in a jungle?

My rescuers dropped me unceremoniously onto the ground. I sagged down, my face resting on the dirt. Oh sweet Lord, I was alive! My throat tightened and rebelled as water tried to come back up. I started coughing and retching.

"Dammit Willie! Don' let her yack all over our camp! What the hell were you thinkin'?" A woman's voice again.

Someone swore, male, heartfelt, and hands clasped under my arms again. The world swirled as I was hauled upright and deposited into a rickety lawn chair. I took several deep breaths, raising my head slowly to try to take stock of my surroundings. My right eye was swollen shut, depth perception gone. The figures around me were indistinct at first, then slowly they swam into focus.

Two men. One woman. A collection of blue tarps and pallets shoved between the trees, the ground beaten bare between them. A fire pit, remains of a fire still smoldering. Random bits of furniture, a tattered bicycle leaning on a tree, empty bottles stacked in pseudo sculptures, sunlight glinting through the green, amber and clear glass. Around the encampment, deep woods, impossibly green, the undergrowth thick and impenetrable, the canopy arching overhead.

The woman had taken my bag and was pawing through it eagerly. My head cleared fractionally.

"Hey! Get your freaking paws out of my bag!" I didn't want to think of what condition the contents were in. Thank God I hadn't put my laptop in there today.

The man with the duct-taped boots turned and cuffed me savagely on the side of my head, causing a loud ringing in my ears and black spots to dance across my vision. What the hell?

"Shut up! It's 'er bag now!"

Anger blossomed in my belly, adrenaline cutting through the fog. "Like hell it is, you walking shitstain! You give that back to me right now!" I tried to rise up from the chair.

He scowled at me, his heavy beard bristling out in all directions. "You don' tell ME what to do!" He shoved me back down in the chair, hard. "Ozzie! Gimme some tape!"

Tape? What the… I struggled against him, causing him to grunt and elbow me in my battered head. The smell of rotten fish was overwhelming, coming off him in waves.

My poor stomach had enough: I projectile vomited onto his duct taped boots. He swore viciously, dancing backwards from the mostly water splatter as Ozzie came into my line of sight, a roll of tattered duct tape in his hand. Grabbing it, he pinned me down and wrapped strands around my wrists, tying me to the chair, immobilizing me.

Oh, hell. This was not going to end well.

Across from me, the woman had not even looked my way during all of this. She rocked back and forth on her haunches, crooning softly to herself as she removed the entire contents, one by one. My wallet was opened and the few pitiful bills tugged loose and stuck in her pocket. A stick of waterlogged gum found its way into her mouth surreptitiously, her jaws chomping ferociously, triple time. She removed my gun, frowned at it and dropped it onto the ground. Water leaked out of the barrel. A sodden notebook was next, dropped onto the gun, concealing it. Then chapstick, another pair of underwear, (why in the world did I carry so many pairs with me? Make a mental note to research that in the psychiatric library… if I got out of here intact) pens and pencils. The pile slowly grew.

Willie and Ozzie were agitated, pacing around as she crooned and dug.

"We can't keep 'er 'ere!"

"She was in the river, so she's ours!" Ozzie was adamant.

Willie swore, "You dumbass! We can keep anything we find in the river if it isn't ALIVE!"

Both stopped and turned to stare at me, one pair of batshit crazy brown eyes, one pair of batshit crazy blue ones.

Uh oh.

I struggled against the tape, fear beginning to flower in my brain.

"Guys…guys come on. That isn't something you want to do."

"Why not?" Willie's voice was flat. "I don't like you much. You called me a name, and you puked on me."

"I don't like you either, but I wouldn't… kill… you." Bile rose in my throat at the word. I looked at Ozzie. "Come on Ozzie, you look like a gentleman. You wouldn't kill a defenseless woman, now would you?"

"You ain't defenseless. You came down here with a gun." The woman spoke up, still not looking at me, her attention focused on my now ruined cellphone.

Shit. Shit. Shit. Shit.

Ozzie and Willie bristled more. "A gun? A gun? Why in the shit would you need a gun? You a cop? I bet you are a cop! Why are you down here, cop woman? Huh? Everyone knows we own the river! You a cop! You a dumb cop!" Spittle flew from Willie's lips. His crazy eyes grew crazier. Oh, brother. Case, you really did it this time.

I looked at Ozzie, who glared back at me suspiciously, then at the woman, who rocked and mumbled, digging in my bag further. I realized I had seen all of these people before, just hadn't ever really looked at them though. They were part of the small population of homeless people who populated Brownville, drifting like smoke down Main Street.

My brain cleared a fraction. I was in deep shit now and would only get deeper if I didn't derail this line of inquisition. I stammered, "I'm not a cop! I'm a reporter! I was over at the warehouse researching a story and I fell in the river. My co-worker did too! And he's looking for me right now!"

Jorge....oh crap! I hadn't given him a thought since washing up downstream. Where the hell was he? My last view of him was waist deep in water, trying to catch my hand as I flailed past.

Willie drew back a fraction. "The warehouse? You can't get in the warehouse! Everyone knows that! You lying!"

"I am not! Two dogs attacked us and we fell down the bank, then we were stuck so we tried to get out by going through that tunnel. I got swept away and almost drowned! I work for the Brownville Reporter!"

They shared a look. The woman on the ground upended my now empty bag, water dumped out of it on the ground. Shaking it, she peered inside, then placed it on her head like a big, leather hat.

I gestured with my chin towards my sodden pile of belongings." Look. Look inside my wallet. There's a press pass in there with my name on it."

"A wallet? Hey!" Ozzie growled and grabbed it, glaring at the woman. "You didn't say she had a wallet!"

She shrank back, lips pulled back in a feral snarl. "Mine! Mine!"

He muttered a curse, then an aside to Ozzie. "She fucking crazy, you know that, don't you?"

Oh, brother…

Tearing open my wallet, he rifled through the contents, disappointment evident on his face. "She ain't got no money! 'Ow the 'ell do you have a wallet with no money?"

On the ground behind him, the woman rocked and muttered harder.

He pulled my press pass out, eyeing it suspiciously, his lips moving slowly. "Sandra Case….Brownville Reporter."

"See? I told you I was a reporter."

"Shut up!"

Ozzie chimed in. "What are we gonna do? What are we gonna do?"

"Shut up!" directed at Ozzie.

The tape pinched and itched, blood from the earlier cut was oozing down my face into my eye, the other eye was swollen shut. My head rang and pounded from the trauma. What a mother of a day this had turned into.

I heard feet shuffling, twigs cracking, a weird clomp, clomp, clomp. Ozzie and Willie turned to look at the front of the camp; the woman peeked up from her prayer like position. A familiar beanpole clomped around the bend in the narrow path, ice skates clomping on the dirt, his coat flapping around his knees. He stopped short when he saw me duct taped to the chair.

"Tahw eht lleh?"

Willie spoke first, suddenly fawning, obsequious. "Afternoon Guvner. We found a trespasser in our camp. Me and Willie were just discussing what to do with her."

One Eyed Joe stared at me for a moment, then turned his eye on Willie.

"You stupid, brain dead, dumb son of a bitch!" Whoa! No reverse tape recorder needed for that one!

Willie and Ozzie shrank back. The woman on the ground covered her head.

Joe gestured at me. "Esaeler reh!"

They scrambled over to the chair, grasping at the tape feverishly. Willie tried to explain himself. "She was in the river! And she had a gun! She has to be a cop!"

Joe glared, his anger evident without words. Tape tore loose from my wrists roughly, taking skin and hair with it. I yelped. On the ground, the woman rocked and muttered, my bag now clenched to her chest, eyes tightly closed.

Joe glared at her, then stomped over towards her on his white women's ice skates, the pom-poms dancing merrily. "Evig ti kcab ot reh!"

She rocked harder, started humming tunelessly. Joe straightened up and turned his glacier blue eye on Ozzie. "You do it."

This back-and-forth stuff was making me woozy.

Head hanging, Ozzie shuffled over to the woman and pried the bag loose from her arms. He scooped up the pile of sodden contents, shoveling them back into the interior. The woman wailed and wrapped her arms around her knees. His entire upper body bent in a posture of submission, Ozzie scrambled over to me and dropped the bag at my feet. Willie was sullen, standing a few feet away, twisting the duct tape strands in his hands.

I raised my head and looked Joe in the eye. "Thank you."

He considered me in silence for a moment. From the river, faintly, I heard a panicked voice. "Sandy! Sandy!" Everyone lifted their head at the sound.

"That's Jorge!"

Joe raised an eyebrow at me. I filled him in. "Jorge was with me when we fell in the river. We were attacked by some dogs at the warehouse." At the mention of the warehouse,

Joe's expression darkened. He reached out and nudged the woman with his foot. "Og teg mih."

She scrambled up awkwardly, greasy blonde hair matted to her skull, and scuttled towards the water.

Willie muttered something, causing Joe's head to whip around. He stepped across the intervening distance and cracked Willie upside the head with a flattened palm. Willie howled and covered his ear. Ozzie shrank into himself.

"Silence! If you want to stay here in the community, you will follow the rules!"

They fell into an uneasy silence. From the river, I heard crunching as feet tromped up the narrow trail. Crazy woman came into sight, with an even crazier looking Jorge behind her. Long scratches marred his face, his shirt was shredded, one shoe was missing. Relief flooded his face when he saw me. "Oh, thank God! Jesus, Sandy! I thought you were dead!"

I felt tears suddenly prickling my eyes. I thought I was dead too.

Jorge looked at Joe, gratitude on his face. "Joe. Thank you." He stuck his hand out to him. Joe nodded and shook Jorge's hand solemnly. Jorge looked over at me, his unspoken meaning clear. Slowly, I hauled myself to my feet, swaying momentarily, sticking my hand out. "Joe. I thank you for saving my life." A bit melodramatic perhaps, but true. Joe's hand closed around mine in a brief clasp.

Jorge's took ahold of my upper arm. "Sandy, I think we need to get you some medical attention."

I shrugged, "Hey, it's no worse than what date night with Ben used to be." I was trying for flippant.

Instead, it fell flat. Both men stared at me, my addled brain accidentally giving away a glimpse into my past. Shit.

Jorge's hand tightened on my arm, his lips pressed into a thin line. "Let's go Case."

CHAPTER 25

*J*orge hung up the receiver and scribbled a note on the pad in front of him. He shook his head. "The plate on the Oldsmobile is a dead end. It's not listed as stolen; it's registered to a Eugene Whitmore, on an Oldsmobile, but a different model."

"Then we find Eugene and see what his connection to the two morons is. Do you have an address?"

"Yeah." He glanced down at his note. "He's in Center Cemetery in Winslow, plot B9."

"Oh..."

I sat half turned to look at him. My swollen eye had finally subsided enough that I had the use of both again, the black turning to shades of green and purple. Two days had passed since our impromptu float trip down the Mill River. My aching parts were actually feeling half decent today. Jorge seemed like he was back to being himself again. You would think after almost losing your coworker that you would have some appreciation of them. Not Jorge. After his initial elation that I was still alive and that there wouldn't be all the endless forms to fill out, he turned sullen, bitter that I had created the chaos (as he called it) in the first place. For almost thirty-six hours, he had given me a cold shoulder, even threatening to pull himself out of the case. Today, however, he was finally back to normal.

Around us, the newsroom was humming the Friday afternoon song. On weekends, an expanded edition was printed on Saturday, with two extra sections, one devoted to Health and Lifestyle, the other to Home and Garden. In the fall, it expanded to three, with a special Outdoor Edition that featured hunting stories added in. We had a features editor, John Rufkin, who handled his stringers for those two sections, giving us an extra four people who normally weren't in the newsroom at any other time. Their little area was cluttered with people working to layout the pages. Our ad manager, Gus Johnson, was buzzing back and forth from the front room where advertising lived, making sure that the ads he worked so hard to sell during the week made it into the sections. The newsroom actually felt closer to capacity, more like what it would have been in its heyday when there were twenty people working in this space on a regular basis.

We were closing in on one week since the murder, six days since the melee in front of the Town Hall, five days since John Peckham disappeared, and two days since we had discovered Hal Morgan on Victoria Street. We now had four days until the impromptu debate scheduled on the common.

The police were stonewalling us. I was persona non grata, and Jorge was finding that even channels he had used in the past were now closed to him. He was getting frustrated. As far as we could tell, they were no closer on solving the murder than they had been when it happened. And as everyone knew, thanks to the age of internet and CSI shows, the longer it went, the higher the chances that they might never figure it out. What little info we were getting showed a police force that was increasingly pressured and desperate, grasping at straws. We had hit our own stonewall, with nothing concrete to work with other than a warehouse that had some sort of sketchy association, Hal Morgan in a tenement building, and a suspect who was now officially missing some five days.

John Rufkin made his way over to where we sat, a yellow legal-size envelope in his hand. "Hey Jorge, Sandy. How goes the story?"

We didn't have to ask which one; there was only one right now as far as we were concerned.

Jorge shrugged, noncommittally. "It goes, just not well."

John turned to me. "Sandy, this was in with my shots from the Baker Garden shoot last week. It's got your name on it."

Puzzled, I took the envelope from him, wondering what Karl had taken for me. "Oh, thanks, John."

"No problem. See you kids later."

Jorge looked up as I broke the seal and lifted the flap, peering in at the contents. "Oh...!"

"What?"

"It's the photos I took from the scene! I forgot I asked him to blow them up and enhance them!"

Jorge's' eyes lit up, the first I had seen in two days. He was definitely on the mend. "Bring those over here!" He cleared his desk off. Rolling my chair, I crowded in on his workstation and we laid the two photographs out side by side on his desk.

They wouldn't win any photo contests. The grain was large and blurry, some details were indistinct. But they gave us something we hadn't had for a week; a perspective from inside the scene while it was going on.

Jorge pursed his lips as he studied the shots; broken glass and chairs scattered, Sebastian O'Nary dead in the case, a bullet hole dead center of his forehead. You could see that the shop's walls and ceiling were stippled with holes. I had the number '23' in my notes as to how many bullet holes they had found. We looked at each other, Jorge voicing what we were thinking.

"Doesn't seem very professional now, does it?"

"No, not hardly. Why so many shots? Were they chasing him around trying to gun him down?"

Jorge looked at the chairs upended, the cases on the floor, candy everywhere. "I would say so. But the only wound was dead center to the forehead and..." he leaned closer, peering at the blurry scene, "It looks like there may be contact burns around it."

"Someone shot him point blank? That's cold."

"And inefficient, doing it from the front like that. A temple shot angled back is much more effective. Or going for the mass, aiming for the heart. They ran the risk of him surviving what essentially would be a frontal lobotomy via a gunshot."

I shuddered. The whole thing had a decidedly creepy edge to it. In Chicago, crime was matter of fact. Dead drug dealers, domestic violence, the odd random killer who targeted strangers, alcohol fueled rages. Not many cold-blooded, point blank executions, despite the city's shadowy past.

Jorge leaned back in his chair, in professorial mode. "So Case, what do we learn from this?"

"Ice cream is bad for you?"

"No, come on, think. What does this scene tell you?"

I picked up the nearest photo, my mind going back to the moment I had taken it, before the tasering, before the pit bulls and the near drowning. I lowered it down slightly and stared at Jorge over the top of the print. "The scene was chaotic and unprofessional, both during the murder and when the police were there. I remember there being lots of people tromping all over the place, hearing glass crunching under their feet, and seeing people just touching anything any old way they felt like."

Jorge was frowning, staring intently at me. "That's a bit out of character for our PD. Hanniford usually runs a tight ship."

"Well, he wasn't this night. And the State Police were in attendance, too, so it wasn't like it was all Brownville."

"Hmm. Strange." Jorge leaned over to look at the photos again.

Movement in the doorway caught my eye. Lizzy was coming in, the mailbag slung over her shoulder. Today's getup was summer themed, summer in Dracula's castle that is. Black leather miniskirt over bright green stockings, a black vest over a bright red short-sleeved shirt. Her hair was done up in a twist, with yellow feathers fluttering as she walked. I shook my head, smiling a bit. Turning to Jorge, I said, "I would sure hate to have to be her father, having to watch her walk out the door every day dressed like that." The words had barely left my mouth when the implication hit me, just as it hit Jorge.

Her father. Head of the State Police.

"Oh Case... we shouldn't."

"But Jorge... where else can we go?"

"Come on, what's she going to be able to find out?"

"I'm not talking about finding anything out, I'm talking what has been said, oh, I don't know, around the dinner table maybe?"

We both turned to look across the room at Lizzy. Feeling our eyes on her, she looked our way, a 'What?" expression on her face. I muttered to Jorge, "Let me handle this one."

Kicking my chair back, I rose and made my way across the newsroom to her. "Morning Lizzy."

"Good morning to you, Sandy." She pulled out a chair at the station she was using for her work. "What's happening with the story?"

I pulled the adjoining chair out and dropped into it. "Not as much as we would like. Still no breaks in the case that we know about. Captain Hanniford is being less than cooperative."

She was firing up her laptop as I spoke. I hesitated, wondering how to broach the subject.

She looked over at me, eyes guileless. "What about asking the State Police then?"

"Uh… I tried that too. They weren't all that interested in speaking with us."

"I see." Her screen flared to life, long fingers tapped her password in rapidly. She turned her eyes back on me. "So you are here to ask me to ask my dad, yes?"

"I… uh… well….." Shit. Was I that obvious? "Well, if you happened to hear anything that maybe you could tell me….but I'm not asking you to do anything you wouldn't be comfortable doing now. I mean, this is your family here."

Amusement crinkled her eyes. She sighed, "Well, being as you happened to ask, I might just have overheard some things at home that might shed some light on what's happening. I was wondering when you were going to get around to asking me."

Chastened, I edged my chair closer to her. "Well… I didn't want to put you in a spot. But now we are getting in a jam. No one will talk to us, not the locals, not the staties. The clock is running out."

Lizzy turned to face me, leaning over so her elbows were on her knees. I leaned in so our heads were inches apart. "Dad said they're frantic trying to find Peckham. There's no sign of him, it's like he dropped off the face of the earth.

They think he set up Sebastian at the shop, that he told him to meet him there and then the hit men went after him."

"Hit men? More like Laurel and Hardy."

"I know. Anyway, they've been all over John's house. He's gone, but nothing of his is. His wallet, car, clothing, everything is still there. They think he was abducted."

Oh... holy crap.

"What about his family, Lizzy? Is he married?"

She shook her head no. "Divorced a few years ago. Not a pleasant one either."

I could sympathize with that. Changing gears, I asked her, "What about the scene at the shop? Why was that so chaotic? That looked like a war zone."

"I know. Dad said that they thought it was an ambush. That maybe John was involved. Apparently Sebastian took a phone call late that night at home. He told his wife he had to go out and meet someone, that he would be back in an hour. She doesn't know who called or where he was going. Next thing she knew, the police were waking her up to tell her he was dead."

Ouch.

"What about ballistics? Any idea what kind of gun or guns were used?"

"Haven't heard anything about that yet. Oh, dad also said that the Brownville PD is in 'disarray' right now." She hooked her fingers into quote marks for the word disarray. I cocked my head, curious at this. "Really? What's going on?"

She glanced around us at the almost empty newsroom, then whispered to me, "He said Hanniford was really pissed at some of his officers for how they handled the scene and the aftermath. He's suspended one of them for a week. I guess he tried to discipline him by putting him on bike patrol first, but then a video surfaced about something the cop did after, so he suspended him. If it wasn't for the union, he would have fired him. Everyone's all in a tizzy about it."

My heart was sinking towards my feet. "Do you know which officer, Lizzy?"

"Yeah. Jim Pim."

CHAPTER 26

*L*izzy drove an old Chevy S10 pickup truck, a hand-me-down in her family. I fumbled with the shift lever as I rolled it out of the Reporter's parking lot. I really needed to get a car for myself, but still was no closer to deciding how than I had been the day I lost Peggy. I sighed heavily as I aimed the car up Elm Street, bucking a bit at the lights with the unfamiliar clutch. I didn't stop to think about what I was doing or why: I simply aimed it towards the Meadows again, this time using the conventional route in, and drove.

My mind chewed on what Lizzy had told me, mulling over the implications of various events as the town streets gave way to wide lawns and old homes, then to farm fields. I followed the route carefully, mindful of the borrowed vehicle. When I reached the street John Peckham lived on, I glanced down the road towards his house, and kept going.

Towards the Pim's family farm.

According to Lizzy, Jim still lived there with his parents and two siblings. The farm covered some 300 acres in the Meadows, like many in the valley, eking out a living running a small dairy and beef operation, and selling firewood. Jim worked at the Brownville PD as his full-time job and at the farm any time he was home. Lizzy had told me he was the first one of the Pims' to get full-time work off the farm, a fact that had caused some strife among his family. As he settled in and became a seasoned officer, they adapted to his new career, eventually becoming very proud of him. His suspension was sure to be causing tension at home.

I wondered again what the video was that Lizzy had referred to. I had a memory of the kids on the sidewalk with a smartphone aimed at us as we lay on the ground, their laughter tinkling in the air. An uneasy feeling rippled down my spine. Suspended over that? It couldn't be.

The sky was a cerulean blue bowl over my head as I sped down the dirt road alongside a rolling field, the long grass and daisies at the edge of the road bobbing in the draft from the little pickup truck. The river glinted through the trees, turkey buzzards circled lazily. The windows were down; dust billowed in around me as I drove. It felt peaceful, like another world out here. I spied the cluster of farm buildings down a lane, backed by the river, dark blue silos above an old, low New England barn, a white house set some distance away from the barn, a large maple tree dwarfing the front. I slowed, unsure, then taking a deep breath, turned down the drive.

Jim's mother was a handsome woman, about late fifties, tall with gray-streaked hair and tan arms. She straightened up from the massive vegetable garden as I approached, her face inquisitive but open. It shuttered up as soon as she realized who I was.

"He isn't here." She fidgeted from the unaccustomed weight of trying to be rude. I'm used to being sworn at, thrown out, challenged or otherwise dismissed, so I had no problem staring her down.

"Well, where is he then? I need to see him."

"Why?" She stood straight up again, bright blue eyes pinning me. "Why do you need to see him? Haven't you caused enough trouble for him?"

I spread my hands in supplication. "What are you talking about? What trouble? We were both just doing our job at the crime scene. There's no reason he should be in trouble for that."

"Well he is, all right? He's heartbroken over it. Dad's livid. Said he never wanted Jim in the police anyway, not when we need him here. And I'm sick over it! My son, my firstborn, humiliated like this! I know what it meant to him, this job. And now you come along and screw it all up for him!"

"Me?" I was incredulous. "If you think I screwed up his job, then you're mistaken!"

She shouted at me. "It was you! You're the one in the video his boss was so angry about! So yes, it was you!"

I stood silent a moment, before quietly asking, "What video?"

"You can't tell me you don't know what video…." Her voice trailed off as she looked at me. I looked back, wordless. She heaved a huge sigh. "Dammit. You don't, do you?"

I shook my head no. "Look, I came out to apologize to him, that's all. I only heard this morning that this all went down. I have no idea why or how it happened, but I felt bad. When you see him, would you tell him that for me, please?"

It was her turn to stare silently at me. Finally, she sighed, pushing a strand of silver hair off her forehead, her gardening glove leaving a muddy streak. "He's down the road, the field on the left. He's mowing today. You can tell him yourself."

I nodded my thanks. She turned her back to me and went back to the rhubarb.

CHAPTER 27

I slowed as the field in question came into view, grass falling in waves behind the lone tractor trundling back and forth across it. Suddenly I was tongue tied, unsure. What, I asked myself, in God's name was I hoping to accomplish, coming down here like this? What possible good could my apology do Jim now? I shoved the thought away, discomfited by it, and parked the truck. Light glinted across the cab of the tractor as it made the turns at each end of the field, obscuring the view of the driver. I could see his head craning to make out who was in the truck as he drove parallel to me across the field. From his viewpoint, he would see Lizzy's truck with a lone woman wearing sunglasses in it. Sitting back, I mulled over the problem of the murder as I waited for curiosity to get the better of Jim.

It only took him two more passes before he raised the mower deck and swung the big green tractor around to head towards me. The field lay flattened, neat mounds of green waiting to be raked into rows and baled into hay. I inhaled the scent; that was one thing Chicago never had. Sometimes

I felt like a refugee from two worlds, missing the city and yet loving the country.

The tractor thumped across the edge of the field onto the road behind me; the driver craning through the glass of the cab. I got out as he pulled alongside Lizzy's truck and stopped. Now I never studied body language, or lip reading, but I'm getting a lot of on the job instruction in it: even from here I could tell he was swearing. I stepped in front of the tractor to stop his flight. It jerked in place, hiccuped, then silence as he cut the motor.

"Jim... I just want to talk to you for a second."

"About what? I got nothing to say to you! Every time you show up, I keep expecting to get hit with an asteroid. You're just bad luck, through and through!" His voice was muffled by the cab. Sighing, I walked around to the side of the tractor, clambered up on the step, yanking the door open.

He was wearing cut-off shorts and a Brownville PD tee shirt, face dappled with sweat and a fresh tan. He eyed me warily as I stood in the door of the cab, hanging onto the door handle for support.

"Look Jim, I only just heard about what happened to you an hour ago, and I'm here to apologize for whatever role your department gave me in it. I didn't do anything wrong. And I doubt you did either, but that's small comfort right now."

He muttered sullenly, "It's Officer Pim, not Jim. Only my friends call me Jim."

"Okay, okay, whatever, Officer Pim. Either way, I wanted to say I'm sorry, okay? Look, I think you're a nice guy, maybe too nice for this department. I... I... also wanted to say I'm sorry for how I've treated you too. All I can say is I have a lot on my plate right now with this whole case, a new town, hell, everything, so I'm sorry if I was rude at any time." Sweat trickled down my temples.

He heaved a sigh. "Here, climb in here and sit instead of hanging on my door like that." He indicated the side of the cab where the fender curved over the wheel. I climbed in out of the sun, settling on the inner fender.

The cab was small, a radio on the dash, ball cap hanging from a knob on it. It smelled of freshly cut grass. Sweat stung my swollen eye. Without thinking, I pulled the glasses off and rubbed at it gently. He stiffened in the seat next to me. "What happened to your eye?" he asked quietly.

I barked a laugh. "The question would be what didn't happen to it? Rabid dogs, near drowning, crazy people…" I replaced the glasses, "Just another day at the Brownville Reporter."

"What in tarnation are you talking about? Who did that to you?" I realized belatedly that there was an undertone of anger in his voice. Looking full at him, I cocked my head, "Why Officer Pim! I do believe you are upset that I have a shiner."

He shifted uncomfortably, fiddling with the tractor shift lever. He muttered, "I don't like to see a woman get hurt, even a pain in the ass like you."

I smiled sardonically, "Well, that's a refreshing attitude, considering the number of people wishing me harm lately."

He stared at me in silence. Then, "What's going on, Sandy?"

I shrugged, unsure how much to say. I changed the subject instead. "Ji… uh… Officer Pim, I just heard about some video this morning. What happened?"

He heaved a defeated sigh. "Remember those kids in front of John's place the other day? Well, one of the little darlings filmed me crashing into you, dubbed music and subtitles to it, and posted it on YouTube and on TikTok. It's going viral."

"What?" Oh good Lord!

He nodded glumly. "Over 500,000 hits as of this morning,

probably be closer to 800,000 by the time I get home tonight."

I mulled this over for a minute. "Is it funny?"

"Is it... wha?" He looked at me startled, then paused. "I guess... you know, if it wasn't you and me, then I'd say hell yes."

I felt a smile at the edge of my lips. "Looks like we are stars then, Officer. You can't unring the bell." I frowned at him. "Although I can't believe your union let them get away with suspending you. What was the reasoning behind it?"

"Conduct unbecoming of an officer. Coupled with widespread public humiliation. And a serious lack of humor right now due to the murder investigation."

"Damn. How long is the suspension for?"

"The rest of the week. They wanted to boot me for a month, but the union wouldn't let them."

He laughed softly. "Guess being short staffed helped too. They need someone who can work doubles, and a lot of those guys cain't."

I sighed. "Again, I'm sorry. I just wanted to talk to you that day. I had no intentions of getting you in trouble, much less dumping you on the ground." That damned smile again, I felt it itching at my mouth. He noticed it too. "What? What are you grinning about?"

That sent me over the edge. I clamped my hand over my mouth as laughter, somewhat hysterical laughter, made its way out. "I'm sorry... it's just, we must have looked funnier than hell!"

He shook his head, smiling now himself. "We did. I hate to admit it, but we did. God!" he slapped his belly, "I've got to lose a few pounds! Working graveyard screwed up my eating habits. I looked like a beached whale landing on you."

Oh, lord! That was a visual I didn't need. He turned to

face me, asking quietly, "Now tell me what happened to your eye."

I shifted uncomfortably, wondering how much I could tell him. He folded his arms and waited.

Finally, I gave in, figuring being suspended himself, that there wouldn't be much he could do to me for the trespassing part of it, and told him a condensed version of what happened.

His eyes were saucers when I was finished.

"Holy crap! How come I never heard about any of this?"

I shrugged. "We never called it in, for one thing. The Brownville PD isn't exactly real happy with me right now."

He scowled. "You and me both. But still, you were assaulted and held against your will. Sandy, just an FYI, you cain't go down into the Glen like that. You're damned lucky Joe showed up when he did. Those folks you were with, they ain't wrapped too tight."

I laughed, "You're telling me? What's the Glen?" I had not heard that phrase before.

He fiddled with the shift lever some more. "There's that strip down on the river where you ended up, folks call it the Glen. Runs along behind the Po'Bank section of town." The lower income side of town was commonly called 'Po'Bank,'. "Folks who don't live down there know to stay out of there. It's been a place for the homeless people to live for the last twenty-plus years. We all turn a blind eye to it. They gotta live someplace, and we know where they are, so it works. Most of the time, they're peaceful. Joe is kinda like their mayor, he keeps them in line and looks out for them. But once in a while, all hell breaks loose, and we have to go in and break up a fight or cart one of them off to rehab for a while."

I looked out the cab across the wide green fields,

drowsing under the midday sun. "How many people live down there?"

He shrugged. "The number's fluid. Anywheres from six to as many as fifteen folks, usually."

I frowned. "Why so many homeless here? I've seen a couple here and there, but I didn't realize there were this many. Brownville's, what, 15,000 maybe?"

Jim nodded. "Yeah, well, we prolly got more than your average town this size, on account of the hospital closing down in the '90s."

"What hospital?"

He gestured over towards the western side of town. "Culberth Sanctuary. It was a mental hospital, real big in the '40s, '50s, then it shrank. By the '90s, it was outdated and had a lot of accusations of mistreatment and abuse. They finally shut it down, which was good and bad, because a bunch of folks had no place left to go except out on the street. For a while, we musta had twenty or thirty folks from there, people with mental illness and abuse problems and no families or anyplace else to go. So they migrated down to the Glen and set up their own community." He fiddled with the lever some more. "Every once in a while, folks get up in arms, demand that we evict them and cut down all the trees there so they cain't camp. 'Cept, one thing, where they gonna go?" He raised blue eyes to me. "They'd be all over town, and people wouldn't like that either. Chief says let them stay, we know where they are and they know we know."

His story left me vaguely depressed. "Christ, in this day and age, I can't believe we have people needing care living like that."

Jim shrugged. "I know. It's sad. A lot of us farmers grow extra vegetables that we leave down for them. And people leave them stuff at the edge of the woods too, like pallets and tarps. They won't go to the shelter, except for a few when it's real cold. Joe looks out for them, though. He's probably the most together one down there."

He leaned back in his seat. "So why were you in the warehouse? You kinda skipped over that part. Not to mention, you just told me you performed a B&E and were trespassing."

"I, uh, well, you know... we needed to see where my friends were coming from."

Jim folded his arms, looking out through the windshield. "I was looking into your 'friends' when I got set down. They're running a plate from another car, one that ain't stolen, so I was going to go for misuse of plates."

I felt a flush of unexpected gratitude. I figured everyone in the police department would be interested in seeing me hung like a piñata, with a bunch of drunken people beating on me with sticks.

Jim sat staring at me, arms folded. "The warehouse." He prompted again.

"What's so weird about the warehouse, Ji... Officer Pim?"

He dropped his eyes and mumbled, "Aw hell... you can just call me Jim."

Well. That was progress of sorts. I guess when you share an intimate moment on film with 500,000 other people, it brings you closer together.

"The warehouse?" I asked again. Two can play at this game.

"I asked you first." He turned blue eyes on me again. I smiled at him. "Well, I asked you now. So what's with that place?"

"If you ain't the most contrary woman I've ever met...!" He shifted in the tractor seat again, resumed fussing with the lever. I folded my arms and smirked at him. "How'd you get in? And what did you find?"

"Sorry. I can't tell you. I'm working on a story and that's confidential."

He looked up at me, dead serious. "Well, your investigation's gonna get you killed if you aren't more careful about where you go. You don't go into that warehouse. Period."

"Why not?" My curiosity was aroused. "I get attacked by a dog there and practically killed, and you tell me it's my fault? What's the story on that place?"

He shook his head. "I really don't know the whole story. We've all been told to steer clear of it other than to make sure the perimeter isn't breached. Boss say's heads will roll of anyone gets inside that place. They take their security pretty serious."

"Why?"

He shrugged. "I tell you, none of us know. I'm not even sure the Chief knows. But the orders came down from on high."

I cocked my head, confused. "On high? From who? And when?"

"I dunno. From the mayor, I guess. Boss didn't really say. And as to when, maybe eighteen months ago?" He looked out through the cab window a frown evident. "Some company came in and cleaned the place up and put new sections of fence up, did all new locks, boarded everything up. They always kept the place locked tight, but now they really have it tighter than a nun's bunghole." He flushed red when he realized what he had just said. "Sorry," he muttered.

I smiled at that. "I usually say it's tighter than a frog's asshole."

He turned blue eyes on me at that; the corners crinkling. "I heard they're watertight."

I smiled back at him. "It doesn't get much tighter than that. You've never heard one fart, now have you?"

I was suddenly aware of how small the cab was; our legs so close I could feel the heat from his through my jeans. He stared at me, his expression changing minutely, a puzzled look in his eyes. I suddenly felt flustered, tongue tied. Where the hell did that come from? Stammering a bit, I changed the conversation again.

"So has anyone heard anything about John Peckham? It's like he fell off the face of the earth."

Jim shifted in his seat, his eyes tracking back to the freshly mown field. He shook his head. "Nothing. No one had heard from him, no activity on his credit cards, nothing." He looked back at me dubiously. "Look... don't take this the wrong way, but you sure are stretching your credibility around the station being the last person who he talked to and all. Chief is of the mind to haul you in and sweat you a bit. Only thing stopping him is the newspaper connection." He broke off for a moment. "Shit. I shouldn't be saying this to you."

"It's not anything I don't already know Jim." Now it was my turn to look away and shift in my seat. "I said it before and I'll say it again, I don't know where he is or what happened to him. If I hadn't been late leaving Main Street, I wouldn't have gone that way, nor would I have lost my car."

He looked me in the eye. "You might not be sitting here right now either."

"I... uh... yeah. Maybe not." I really didn't like to think about what could have happened if I had reached him earlier.

He looked over at the S10. "Whose truck is that?"

"Lizzy Burnitis."

"She the girl with the funny hair, the college kid?"

I nodded, a smile on my lips. "Yeah. She likes to express herself through her clothing."

"Her dad's a big boss over to the State Police barracks in Westminster. Been there a long time."

"Yeah. She's a good kid. Smart as a whip."

"You getting another car soon? You really did a number on your old one."

"You're telling me?" I laughed wryly. "You should have seen the adjuster's face. I have to figure that out yet. I want to get a used one, something cheap and sturdy, but I haven't had time to look around, plus I don't know where to start here." It was a definite handicap coming to a new town where you didn't know the characters yet, especially when walking in bleating like a sheep waiting to be shorn.

He gestured towards town with his head. "Go see Jason over to Park's Towing. He's always got a couple used cars for sale. They're always tight and clean, plus Jason won't take advantage of you." Again that look directed at me. "Tell him I sent you."

What the hell was going on here? I wanted him to look at me that way. But why? Pudgy farm boys turned cops were not my usual type, even if he did smell good. Get a grip, Case. Or go buy a battery-operated toy. But don't go down this road.

Instead, I looked directly back at him and said nothing. He flushed, his eyes darkening. The cab was suddenly tiny and hot. The pulse beat in my throat. We stared at each other a long minute; I felt myself starting to lean towards him...

A car whipped along the road towards us, dust billowing up under it, the back end slewing out as it passed. I caught a glimpse of two kids inside, ball caps turned backwards, radio thumping. Pebbles pinged off the tractor. Jim muttered a curse. "God damn Barkley kids. They're gonna kill themselves someday."

The moment was gone, disintegrated like the cloud of dust behind the car. Disappointed, I sat back, muttering, "Well thanks for the tip. I really should get back now."

He looked at me, his eyes wide. "Ah... yeah... um. I, um, I'm glad you stopped out today. Glad we cleared the air."

"Yeah. Me too." I needed to get out of the cab before I made an ass of myself. "Thanks, Jim. See you around."

Popping open the door, I swung out and onto the step, leaving him with his mouth hanging slightly open, a bewildered look on his face.

"Hey!" he yelled after me as I dropped to the ground.

I turned to look back up at him. "What?"

His mouth moved a minute, then he muttered, "Shoot. Just…. just be careful out there, okay?"

I nodded slowly. "Okay."

CHAPTER 28

I've always hated Mondays. No matter where I worked, or how great the job was, Monday mornings always gave me a case of the hemorrhoids.

I had a feeling this Monday morning would be even worse than the usual case of butt itch.

Dana and Diane's cackles were audible before I pushed the door to the newsroom open. My eyes scanned the cubicles as I marched in, coffee firmly clenched in my right hand, my water stiffened bag over my left shoulder. They were at Dana's computer, the familiar red and black screen of Benjamin Shithead Morven's blog visible. Diane raised watery green eyes to me as I strode past.

"Good morning, Sandy."

I muttered something more or less intelligible. Beside Diane, Dana turned calculating brown eyes at me. "Hey, Sandy....have you seen this blog?"

Striving for nonchalance, I tossed my bag under my desk and resisted telling her to fuck off. Instead, I responded, "Probably. I've seen almost everything on the web."

She narrowed her eyes. "Aren't you even going to ask which blog it is?" Beside her, Diane dissolved into a paroxysm of giggling.

"Nope. Got things to do, stories to write." Jorge's seat was empty. I sat down at mine, attempting to end this conversation.

Dana sniffed, looking back at the screen, then turned back to me as if the thought just occurred to her. "Hey! Don't YOU drive a Volvo?"

"Actually, no, I don't. I have a Toyota Rav4." I had taken Jim's advice and stopped at Park's that afternoon on the way back, where I purchased a ten-year-old Rav4. It was somewhat dinged up but mechanically sound, and best of all, I could afford it. He was supposed to have my tags on it that afternoon.

Dana looked disappointed. "Well, what were you driving when you got trashed by the train the other day?"

I had had enough. "Dana, the only other wheels I've had lately have been on my menstrual cycle. Now if you don't mind, I have stuff to do, ok?"

Jorge chose that moment to arrive, catching my last remark to the evil bitches. He was shaking his head, a smile playing around his mouth as he reached his desk.

"Good morning, Case."

I muttered something along the lines of piss off, or maybe good morning, one of those things. He cast a glance at me.

"Having a good morning, I see?" His lips were twitching in a vain attempt to hide his smile.

I muttered, "Bite me." and popped the lid of my laptop open. Jorge smiled broadly and dropped gracefully into his battered chair, wheels squeaking as he rolled across the aisle to me. Leaning over, he stage whispered in my ear, "I have some news that will cheer your Monday up."

I raised my eyes to him. "The two hags are being transferred to classifieds?"

He smiled, "Nope. Better than that."

I sighed. "Give it up, Maxim. I have no patience for bullshit this morning."

"Your two friends? Igor and Ivan? Try Pyotr Vasilevich and Nestor Ivanovich."

"Pyotr and Nestor? Which is which?"

"The little greaseball is Pyotr. Nestor is the ox." He sat back, a look of smug satisfaction on his face.

"Where did you manage to pry this info from, Jorge?"

"I still have sources who aren't afraid to talk to me." The chair creaked as he rolled over to his desk, hitting the keys on his computer. "And want to try for what their careers are?" He looked like the cat with the canary firmly planted in his jaws.

I stared at him a moment. "Dare I ask?"

"If you said, 'Known Russian Mafia Connections', you would be correct." He smirked.

"Russian Mafia? In Brownville, VT?"

Jorge nodded, glancing over at Diane and Dana as another round of cackling cut through the air. "It's got the PD in a tizzy. They are looking for these two gentlemen with everything they have. Except they've apparently disappeared."

I sat back, nonplussed. The mob? Throwing headless chickens at my house? For the love of Christ, why?

Jorge wasn't finished. "They also are of the mind that they had something to do with the shootout over at A Pint of Peck's. For one thing, the hash was distinctly Russian. And for another, ballistics on the rounds they picked up over there show them to be Russian made as well." He folded his hands over his chest, triumphant. "This could be far bigger than anything we thought, Case."

I was staring off across the newsroom, my mind whirling. Frowning, I turned to Jorge. "They were at the press conference that night. Why?"

Jorge shrugged. "Half the town was there, Case."

"But why would you off someone and then go out into a huge public gathering right after? Wouldn't you lie low for a while?"

"No one said they were bright."

"Jorge, they were there for a purpose. They both looked pissed when John appeared. Why would they care? Why would they murder someone in his shop? And why was Sebastian there in the first place? I heard his wife said he received a call and said he had to go out for an hour. He was home for the night when he got that call."

Jorge cocked his head. "Where'd you hear that?"

I muttered, "I have my own sources too, you know."

Jorge eyed me and let it drop. "Well then, if they were at the last event, then I say we pay close attention to the debate that's been rescheduled for tomorrow."

"The debate is back on?"

Jorge nodded. "There was far too much outcry for them to quash it. So instead they bumped it back a few days."

"What time does it start?"

"Six o'clock. At the Town Hall, same as last time."

"Who is going to participate?"

Jorge picked up a piece of paper and scanned it. "Hal Morgan. Molly Bruce. David Gilson. Evan Matthews. Nancy Calligan. Ann Mullivan.."

"Who's that?" I hadn't heard her name before.

Jorge laughed, "Ann is somewhat of a whack job. She's never held a job, never been in politics, hadn't even registered to vote until 4 years ago. Now she suddenly thinks she can be the mayor." He laid the sheet of paper down on his desk. "I asked her what her qualifications were. Her answer was, 'I wiped the shit off the butts of three kids. I can wipe the shit off the butt of this town.'"

"Jesus." Every time I thought I had heard it all, I heard something even more bizarre. "How in the world are they going to get through a debate with that many people involved?" I had never heard of a debate with more than two candidates.

"Good question, Case. I haven't either. It says here the questions will be 'round robin' style, pairing off two candidates per question." He looked across the aisle at me. "There's also some disgruntled candidates who aren't participating that will be in attendance. Expect some political fireworks tomorrow night."

I sighed, rubbing my eyes. The constellation was finally fading around the traumatized one, but it still itched like crazy. "I have never heard of such a screwed up, ass backwards political race like this."

Jorge grinned broadly. "Why do you think I've stayed here so long? You can't find this sort of entertainment, much less get paid for it."

"I guess. How did they elect Silva all those years ago? Was it like this?"

Jorge laughed. "That election made this one look tame by comparison. The ones while he was in office weren't all that exciting, maybe three people going up against him in any given year. But we still had our moments."

I rubbed my itching eye again. "So Pyotr and Nestor.... tell me Jorge, why in God's name would the Russian Mafia be throwing dead chickens at my house? And why would they care about a pissant election in a small Vermont town?"

"If I had to guess, I would say money."

"Money? From what?"

Jorge swiveled to face me, dropping his voice. "Think about it, Case. Sebastian O'Nary... what was he promising the town?"

"He was going to bring the Lucky Plucker in..." my voice trailed off. Dead chickens. Sebastian O'Nary, also dead. The Lucky Plucker Chicken Plant... what the hell?

Jorge was staring at me, expectantly. "And who, I might ask, was so dead set against the plant?"

"The Liberals." He was shaking his head negatively before the words were fully out of my mouth.

"They really didn't care all that much, Case. Think harder."

"Hal Morgan." Champion of the plan to add green space and parks everywhere, all funded by mysterious 'donors'.

"Bingo." Jorge had a satisfied look on his face. "The same Mr. Morgan we happened to see in the area of the two bozos, I might add. And he happens to be the one person in the race who directly benefits from the untimely demise of Mr. O'Nary. Who is going to challenge him in the election? Molly Bruce? Peckham would have been a contender, except he happens to be MIA now."

My brain was buzzing along at warp speed finally. "The police..?"

He shook his head. "Haven't made the association yet. Or won't. They are leaning towards Peckham still being responsible. The drug angle has them off and running, the political one isn't being explored."

Holy shit. I sat back in my chair, staring off across the newsroom. "I'd really like to talk to John Peckham, Jorge."

"You and about half the police force." He drummed his fingers on the desk. "I suppose he could be dead too, but I just don't think so."

"Well, what about our two friends then?" I spun the chair

around again towards Jorge, dropping my voice. "Think we could find them ourselves?"

Jorge eyed me warily. "And how do you propose we do that?"

"We ask the Governor to help us."

CHAPTER 29

*B*ranches crackled underfoot as we made our way down the narrow path off of Springfield Street, over in the Po' Bank side of town. Jorge was muttering every stride, I was aware of my gun tucked firmly in the waistband of my jeans. I wasn't going through what I did last time if I could help it. I also knew I might be tempted to bust a cap in Willie's foot given the chance, so I made sure the safety was on.

"Case, I really don't think we should be coming in here like this. Can't you wait until tomorrow to find him on the street?"

I shook my head no. "Tomorrow's too late, Maxim. And besides, I think he acts crazier on the street than he is here. Come on, we've been all over town and he isn't in sight."

Jorge muttered something as he slid on the muddy bank, crashing into a low hanging maple branch. I ignored him, my nostrils picking up the scent of wood smoke.

"Someone's down there, Jorge."

Below us, I could see glimpses of blue tarp through the

leaves, could hear the rumble of the water. I shuddered thinking of the last time I was in this spot. I shifted my bag on my shoulder, emptied out except for some choice items I had placed in it. I could hear voices. Sharing a look with Jorge, we descended the last few feet, emerging out into the shabby clearing. I could see three figures around a small fire, one standing and gesticulating wildly, the other two seated in the rickety lawn chairs.

Joe, Ozzie and the woman.

Ozzie was up and prancing around, pantomiming something, Joe seated watching him impassively, wearing a battered fedora and his long trench coat. The woman rocked slowly in the chair, her arms folded over her belly, lank hair falling over her face. I felt a pang of pity looking at her.

Joe saw us first, raising his eyebrow in surprise, his one eye bulging and huge. Ozzie stopped mid twirl, the silence returning as he abruptly stopped his monotone monologue. The woman rocked in silence, not looking up or giving any sign that she saw us.

Aware of the tension suddenly around us all, I stepped forward. "Good afternoon. How are you today?"

Joe regarded me in silence, then nodded slowly. Ozzie's jaw moved, he cast a look at Joe and wisely held his tongue. Beside me, Jorge stepped forward. "Hi Joe. Hope you don't mind us barging in on you like this. We wanted to talk to you for a couple of minutes if we could."

He regarded Jorge for a moment. "Ok." He gestured towards a log set on two stumps. "Sit."

I was a bit surprised at how lucid he seemed, Jorge too raised an eyebrow. Sharing another glance with each other, we lowered ourselves on to the homemade log bench.

Joe slung one arm across the back of the chair, turning sideways in it, one long, skinny leg propped on his bony kneecap. The woman muttered and rocked. Ozzie shifted uncomfortably.

Taking a breath, I opened up the conversation.

"Joe, I wanted to take a minute to stop back down to thank you again for your assistance the other day. I was in big trouble when you guys found me. I think…" I glanced over at Jorge, "I think I was probably as close to dying in that river as I ever have been in my life. Ozzie and Willie saved me." Saying Willie's name as a savior stuck in my throat a bit. Ozzie stared at me, incredulous. His lips fluttered, but no sound came out.

I glanced at him, then back at Joe, who hadn't moved or changed expression. "Joe, I brought some things down for you folks, for the guys and for her," nodding towards the woman, "as a token of my appreciation for what you did."

Joe stared at me, expressionless. I met his gaze squarely. He sighed finally, "Siht sdnuos ekil tihsllub, tub ko. Tahw si ti?"

Unsure, I glanced at Jorge. He nodded at me, speaking softly, "Go ahead, Sandy."

I opened my bag and drew out the items I had brought with me. Four tee shirts from the newspaper. Two ball caps. A hairbrush for the woman. A dozen candy bars. And a bag of fresh blueberry muffins. I laid it all down on the ground between us and sat back in silence. The woman had raised her head, eyeing the bag of muffins hungrily. I looked at Joe. "What's her name?"

Ozzie answered instead, his gaze also riveted on the items on the ground. "April."

I leaned forward and picked up the hairbrush. "April. April… this is for you." I held it out to her. She sat still, her eyes roaming over the brush, lips moving slowly. She didn't unfold her arms from around her belly.

"Go ahead, it's ok. It's yours."

Slowly she reached a hand out, taking the brush gingerly. She turned it over and over, looking intently at the surfaces of it. Finally, she raised it up to her head and began to draw it over the matted snarls on her head. Joe watched her impassively, but I thought I saw something glimmering in his eye.

Ozzie looked at me, a puzzled expression on his face. "Why are you doing this, cop lady?"

Joe interjected, "She's ton a poc." He squeezed his eyes shut in frustration, repeating himself slowly, "She's.... not.... a...... cop."

Jorge spoke up. "No, she's not. Look, we are here for a couple of reasons. First, was that Sandy and I were very grateful for the help the other day. I know it was tough to haul her out of the water like that, especially given her size." I whipped around and glared at Jorge through narrowed eyes. What the hell was THAT supposed to mean?

Ignoring me, Jorge continued, "Joe, you and I have known each other a long time, and I have great respect for what you have done here. The fact is, I need help, and I think you may be the only one who can help me."

Joe stared at Jorge a long moment, the only sound the rushing growl of the water. April rocked slowly, pulling the brush through her hair over and over.

Finally, he nodded at Jorge to continue.

Glancing at me, Jorge continued, "You remember the other day when I asked you about seeing anyone new in town?" Joe nodded.

"Well, I... we... need to find them, and pronto. There's some seriously bad juju going on thanks to those two, and they seem to have disappeared. We've searched from one end of the town to the other, and they are no place to be found. I wondered if you and your citizens would be willing to keep an eye out for them and contact us if you see them?"

Joe frowned. Slowly he asked, "Why... do.... you... need... them?"

"They may have been involved in a murder and a kidnapping." A glance at me, "And they threatened Sandy. Threw a bunch of headless chickens at her house and wrote a threat on the wall in blood. "

Again the long stare with that enlarged eye. "Beware... the.... Right.. Wing."

I felt frustration welling up in me. "Joe, you say that but I don't get it. I'm sorry....I guess I'm dense. Look, these guys are probably Russian Mafia, bad dudes. All we need are some eyes and ears to find them. Don't go near them, please... I don't want to see anyone hurt." I looked at April again, who was exploring a knot in her hair with the bristles.

Joe kneaded his eye, tension around his jaw. Ozzie glanced at him, then hesitantly spoke up. "The Guv'ner's been tryin' to tell ya something here."

"What?" I spread my hands. "I understand his words, but I don't know what it means."

Ozzie looked at Joe, waiting. Joe finally nodded. Ozzie continued. "The Right Wing, them's the people at the old warehouse. They're no good. Them's the ones the people you be looking for are working with."

What? Jorge and I shared a look. Jorge spoke up. "What's the 'Right Wing'?"

Joe answered him, clenching his fist as he carefully enunciated his words with a metronome like precision.

"They are a chicken plant too. They been planning on opening up in Brownville. They are bad people. I tried to tell you that."

CHAPTER 30

*W*hen Brownville was chartered, the geographic boundaries of the town were set in a ragged triangle that stretched along the Connecticut river to the east, across the top of the valley to the north, and at a diagonal along the foothills to the west. The whole thing kind of resembled the shape of the state itself, but turned upside down.

The political process that had evolved over the years mirrored the shape of the town: turned upside down.

The common was teeming with people by 4:45, the atmosphere distinctly carnival like. I saw families toting coolers and chairs, kids raced after Frisbees, dogs barked and added to the general mayhem. Sprinkled across the common were the candidates who were not invited to debate, each one set up with their own campaign area, working the crowd, shaking hands and kissing babies.

Jorge and I shouldered our way through the thickening crowd, our plan to arrive early and stake out an ideal vantage spot ahead of time derailed by the throngs of partying townspeople. I ducked, narrowly avoiding being struck by a

Hackensack ball as we threaded our way through a gaggle of tween-agers. Looking around, I turned to him. "Well, Maxim? Now what?"

He didn't answer right away, his jaw tight with tension. "I don't know now. I wasn't expecting this many people here this early. Come on." He headed towards Elm Street, away from the town hall. I trailed along behind him.

Snippets of conversation hit me as I followed Jorge. Several times, I heard, "Hey… look. That's the woman from the video!" Cheeks flaming, I held my head up and followed Jorge resolutely.

He had heard the same remarks. Halting under an aging elm tree at the edge of the common, he looked back across the gathering and shook his head slowly.

"Not going to work, Sandy. You're going to have to stay up front and cover the debate."

Our plan, such as it was, was that we were going to take up positions along the edges of the crowd to watch for Pyotr and Nestor. Armed with cell phones, we would text each other if our quarry was spotted. My new found fame was putting a serious dent in that logic. I swore softly. I had watched the video; it was damn funny, but the amusement was lost on me now. Dejected, I looked around the common. "Do you think Joe will come through?"

Joe had reluctantly agreed to help provide surveillance with his crew. The more eyes, the better.

Jorge shrugged. "Hard to say. Look, I can still text you if I spot them and you can slip back here during the debate. People won't be paying as much attention to you then, anyway."

I shrugged. It wasn't much of a plan, but it was all we had.

The candidates involved in the debate began arriving at 5:30. Molly Bruce was the first, waving gaily at the crowd, blowing kisses and pumping her fists. I heard scattered cheers and laughter as she made her way across the stage. Don Silva with his entourage appeared, with Don being led carefully to his front-row seat. I noticed he appeared weak and unsteady on his feet. A woman I could only surmise as being Ann Mullivan appeared next, looking hassled and rushed, her hair windblown in all directions. She gave a curt nod to Molly Bruce as she passed her on the stage. I noticed she then began to count the chairs lined up, back and forth, then she began touching each one, her lips moving. Frowning, I texted Jorge.

WHATS UP W THS ROUTINE?

A moment later and my phone buzzed in my hand.

SHE HAS OCD.

Oh great. Another fine political candidate. Having reached some complex algorithm in her head, she had carefully seated herself on the edge of the next-to-last chair.

My bladder began to wake up, the last coffee I had consumed clamoring softly to be released. I swore in my head, and shifted in my seat, determined to ignore it, watching as the remaining candidates arrived for the show.

The noise from the crowd swelled as more people arrived for the fun. I twisted around, searching for Pyotr and Nestor. Instead, I found myself staring right into Jim Pim's eyes, two rows back from me, dressed in civilian clothing. Startled, I flashed him a big smile and a wave. He flushed, waved back shyly. I saw his mother and a man I could only assume to be his father, being as he was a mirror image of Jim, only twenty-five years older, seated to his right. Slightly rattled, I turned back around as my phone buzzed again.

MORGAN IS HERE

Craning over the crowd, I saw him stalking up the stairs, adjusting the sleeves on his sport coat. Quickly I texted back, ANY SIGN OF OUR FRIENDS?

The answer was almost immediate. NEGATIVE.

Shit. Was Joe going to go back on his promise? I chewed my thumbnail as the rest of the candidates made their way up onto the stage. I spotted Captain Hanniford, clad in his dress uniform, standing down at the base of the steps talking to two men. I frowned, wondering why he was so gussied up.

The answer quickly became apparent as he followed them up onto the stage and to the podium. I texted Jorge; WHAT IS THIS ABOUT?

IDK

U R THE POLITC GUY!

SHUT UP CASE

I cracked a smile at that. Glancing around, I switched my phone to camera mode and snapped a shot of my hand flipping the bird. I hit SEND.

A moment later: VERY FUNNY. NOW SHUT UP.

Captain Hanniford was still turned, speaking to the two men at the podium. He turned towards the crowd, his eyes scanning us all. I saw him flash across me, then flicker back, annoyance briefly visible. The noise that had swelled to a roar fell off as he cleared his throat and spoke into the mic.

"Ladies and Gentlemen; If I may have your attention, please.."

Relative quiet descended on the common. Satisfied he had our attention, he opened the program up.

"I have been asked by Mayor Silva if I could start tonight's proceedings with a brief update on the situation here in Brownville. As you all know, we wouldn't be gathered here this evening if it weren't for the tragic circumstances we encountered over the past two weeks. As of right now, I can assure you that we are actively pursuing leads in this case. This was not a random crime, so be alert, but not afraid. We will find and prosecute the perpetrators to the fullest extent.

And we are asking for your help in locating Mr. John Peckham, who is still missing. We ask if anyone has anything to offer that you call the special tip line at the police station to report it. That number is published online and in the newspaper, or you can call our regular dispatch line if need be."

He paused, scanning the crowd again. The mumbling from my bladder was turning into a louder, more insistent chant. I shifted in my seat, mentally cursing myself for that late day coffee. I scanned the crowd around me. Everyone was seated now, with people standing cheek and jowl behind the seated attendants. Maybe I could sneak up to the Town Hall and relieve myself and be back before the debate got underway. I dug the latest copy of The Brownville Reporter out of my bag and draped it across my seat back, to designate it as taken. Carefully, I got up and edged down the row, bumping knees and mumbling apologies. On the stage, Captain Hanniford was wrapping it up, turning proceedings over to Connor Murphy, Don Silva's press liaison. I hurried down the side of the Town Hall and into the side door, then up the short flight of stairs to the main floor.

It smelled of furniture polish and old wood inside, the air cool on my face. I pushed my way into the ladies room, listening to the rumble of voices outside. My bladder groaned in relief as I paid rent on the coffee. I sighed as I pulled my pants up, buttoning the top button, and stepped out of the stall door... right into the waiting arms of Pyotr and Nestor.

CHAPTER 31

*I*n novels, when the heroine is accosted it's while she is some place exotic, like at the crime scene, or at Nordstrom or something. They don't get attacked in a God damned public bathroom. Pyotr was grinning, a mean weasel grin, Nestor stared blankly at me, lips shiny with a brown substance I hoped to God was chocolate. I stared at them like a total dope for an instant, and an instant was all Pyotr needed. "получить ее!" Which sounded like "Nie-oth eor!" or something guttural like that. Nestor lurched at me, ham sized hands outstretched. I snapped out of my reverie and leapt sideways... unfortunately further into the ladies' room. The two goons were between me and the door.

His grasping hand missed me, banging on the stall with a thud, leaving a dent on the door. He recovered quickly, spinning and leaping at me again. I feinted left this time, my bag swinging and banging off my hip. I frantically spun as he crashed into the feminine hygiene dispenser, popping the door open with the impact. Tampons and maxipads cascaded down onto the tile floor. He drew back, his lips curling in disgust. Taking advantage of his momentary distraction, I pivoted and leapt back across the room, my eye on Pyotr and the door. Pyotr had lost his smile; now his lips were drawn back, revealing blackened teeth. He made a grab at me, just as I swung my bag at him, low and hard. I clobbered him across the kneecaps, sending him crashing backwards into the door with a rattling boom. I prayed the noise would attract attention.

Nestor had spun, surprisingly fast, and was coming at me from my left now, herding me back towards the rear wall. My foot slipped on a cylindrical object on the floor; a Tampon. Without taking my eyes from him, I reached down and scooped handfuls of Tampons and pads off the floor, flinging them at him while roaring, "Hee-YAAAA!"

Startled, the big ox staggered backwards, away from the onslaught of fresh and light all day protection, grimacing in disgust. He stepped squarely on Pyotr's leg, eliciting a yowl of pain as Pyotr tried to regain his feet. The two men went down in a crash.

Unfortunately, they fell against the door. Which opened into the room, not out.

I whirled around again, eyes racking the space. I could hear the PA system as someone spoke outside, the voice tinny and far away. There was a lone window set at about my head level, textured glass, two large panes. My gun was hidden under the seat of my new-to-me Rav4, leaving me with exactly nothing except my wits for protection.

Which meant I was in deep shit now.

Nestor was scrambling upright, managing to squarely stomp Pyotr with every move. Pyotr howled in pain, slapping Nestor on the back. I took advantage of the moment and swung my bag at the window as hard as I could. It bounced harmlessly off. Swearing, I swung it again as Nestor regained his feet. This time the pane cracked, a jagged line that glinted in the light. Stooping, I grabbed more Tampons as he lurched towards me again, flinging them in a cascade of white tubes. He squinted and grimaced, but kept coming. One more swing with the bag, the glass popped outwards with a crash. I was right behind it, leaping for the sink and then the sill, my bag tumbling over the edge.

My elbows hooked the outside ledge, my face hung over the edge for a brief moment. The ground swayed some ten feet below me, glass sparkling in the ragged bushes along the edge of the building. A face below mine looked back up in astonishment, mouth in a silent 'O' of surprise, a shard of glass glittering in her recently brushed hair, hair that now hung smoothly down her shoulder blades.

April.

We made eye contact as Nestor's hands closed around my ankle, hauling me effortlessly back into the destroyed bathroom. I felt a hundred places on my arms sprouting blood as I was dragged across the sill. Frantically, I kicked and twisted, clamping my teeth down on the hand that grabbed my mouth. I heard a grunt of surprise and pain, then I was violently swung around towards the sink. I caught a glimpse of my own face in the mirror, a face that was haggard and angry, lips drawn back in a snarl, then the two faces collided in a shower of glass as the mirror exploded under my cheek and everything went black.

CHAPTER 32

When I was a child, I used to play with anything that crossed my path. Sticks, stones, leaves, nothing fazed me. Until the day I spotted that cool looking, top shaped gray object on the back porch ceiling.

I had to be all of 5 or 6 I think, old enough to drag the old white side table that had been relegated to duty as my father's smoking table, underneath this new and strange object that had grabbed my attention. It was a chilly morning, probably the only reason I survived to remember this now. Tottering precariously, I reached up trying to knock the top down so I could play with it. My little arm came up about a foot short. Undeterred, I had clambered down, casting around until I found my brother's old wiffle ball bat. Armed with my tool, I climbed back up and balanced on chubby legs, then took a mighty swing. This time I connected squarely. Unfortunately for me.

The hundreds of white-faced hornets that called the paper top their home were not amused at being rudely awakened on a cool morning like that. While many tumbled out and crawled harmlessly around the floor, enough came out fired up that they launched a full scale assault on my upper arms.

I shrieked and wailed madly as the stinging turned into a merciless burning that spread up my arms and into my body. Flailing, I tried to escape the pain, searching desperately for my mother, who then, like now, was never around.

"Shut dat beech up!"

Acrid chemical fumes burned my lungs as I slipped back into oblivion again.

The ground jounced and swayed under my back. I moaned softly, pain lancing through the fog again. Hands closed on my arms, more pain spearing me somewhat awake. Hanging limply, I was hauled along, flashes of yellowed grass under my feet, soda cans, dirt. Darkness as a door thumped shut behind me, then stairs, endless stairs. Pain roared through my head. I tasted blood as I started to come out of the fog a bit more. I tasted a weird chemical taste in my mouth; wanted to be oblivious again.

Wooden floor thumped under my cheek as I was dropped on the ground, hard. Another door slamming, then silence. I groaned again, hot tears sliding down my swollen face to the floor. I heard a rustling noise.

"Oh, shit…" A hand touched my arm. I gasped, yelping in pain and surprise.

"Stop! Stop! Shhhh! It's okay… stop now!"

I stilled, opening my eyes, er eye, only one working, the other a sticky mess. Far overhead a ceiling rotated slowly in my whirling vision. I closed my eye again.

"Sandy? Is that… you?"

Struggling to keep my equilibrium, I carefully opened my eye. The silhouette of a man was over me, his face hidden in the glare that was coming from the barred window behind him.

"Who are you?" I asked. Except it sounded like "Igo ere foo?"

He moved slightly, allowing the glare to fall on his face instead of backlighting him. His eyes were sunken, cheeks hollowed and unshaven. Even in my state I could smell stale body funk.

"Shh. Don't try to talk. You're pretty banged up."

It was John Peckham. Holy shit!

I struggled to move, to sit up. He pressed me down. "Don't move, please! You're bleeding like crazy! Let me try to stop it."

The underside of my upper arms was coated in sticky blood, the hundreds of tiny cuts souvenirs of the trip through the window sill. I looked at the blood and fainted dead away.

My second reawakening wasn't much better, except this time, my arms were swathed in dirty sheet that had been ripped into strips. My upper body resembled a partial Egyptian mummy. Slowly I sat up, ignoring the twirling floor. I was getting to be pretty good at this beaten up thing.

John Peckham watched me anxiously, seated on the dirty mattress that was thrown on the floor. He offered me a bottle of water. "Here. Just sip a little bit."

I took it, swirling loose sticky gobs in my cheeks that I spat onto the floor. I watched the red globs puddle out.

"Where am I?" or, "'Er em ee?" My tongue was three sizes too big for my mouth. John frowned. "I'm sorry, what?"

"Er Em Ee!" I figured if I tried to speak louder he could hear better. I looked around the little room in bewilderment. There was the dirty mattress, the window, a cardboard box with bottles of water and packages of food. On the other side of the space, I spied a 5-gallon pail and a roll of toilet paper, a pail that smelled foul.

Oh Lord.

Taking a deep breath, I tried once more. "Ere am eI?"

"Oh." John nodded as he realized what I was trying to say. "We are at the old mental hospital."

"Uh?" The Culberth Sanctuary. I remembered Jim Pim telling me about it.

Shit! The events came flooding back to me. I cast around the room. No bag, nothing on me except what I had in my pockets. I fished in them. Empty. The goons had frisked me before dumping me here. My phone was gone. Shit! Shit! Shit!

John Peckham was watching me warily. "What's going on?"

Frustrated, I gestured at my swollen mouth. He frowned, then rose from the mattress. Digging through the box, he came up with a paper bag, then from under the cot a gnawed up pencil. He handed both to me.

I quickly scribbled out what had happened, and that we had been searching frantically for him. He closed his eyes briefly when he read that.

"I thought you set me up."

I shook my head no and was rewarded with a spinning room. I waited until it stopped, then wrote how I had been hit by the train on the way over. His eyes widened. "Holy crap! I heard that! I wondered what that noise was, and I went out onto my back patio, only to find those two goons there. Next thing I knew, I was here."

If I hadn't been late, I would have been there too. I wondered how the two of us would have done against them.

I hoped I had a shot at them again myself. I was seriously pissed off now.

I looked at Peckham and explored the back of my teeth with my tongue. One felt loose in the socket. I gestured for the paper again.

"What is going on here?" I scrawled. John read it, then looked up at me. "Well, as near as I can figure, this is what is happening..."

CHAPTER 33

*I*t took him the better part of an hour to spill out his theory, in part because he had spent so much time thinking about it, and in part because he had been alone more or less for the past eight days, and was starved for human contact. Some parts he repeated several times, but when he finally wound down, what I got was this.

Sebastian O'Nary had received a call telling him to meet with John Peckham at A Pint of Peck's on Main Street that night. Purportedly, John was going to concede his place in the mayoral race to O'Nary, but that he wanted to fill him in on some inside information too, perhaps cut a deal of some sort.

Intrigued, O'Nary went. When he arrived, he saw what he thought was Peckham through the window, so he entered the store, via the same back door I would later enter by. Instead of Peckham, he found the cardboard cutout of him (free ice cream and lower taxes for all) propped behind the counter. O'Nary was then confronted by the Russian version of the Keystone Kops. A fierce firefight erupted, one that ultimately ended Sebastian's life, the two goons fleeing as Peckham slept peacefully at home in the Meadows, unaware of the carnage that was about to turn his life upside down.

He learned about it, and about some of the theories of the setup, when the police arrived at his door.

Rudely pulled from a deep sleep, he was carted down to the scene and grilled, then to the station where he was held until his lawyer finally tracked him down. "They wouldn't even let me call him!" he griped as he sat on the filthy mattress.

William 'Bilkem' Chem had instead heard about the attack on his scanner, one that was set up in permanent residence in his house. Rolling out of bed, he had tracked his client down at the police department on his own and had finagled his release. Upon storming back into town, he had found us all at the press conference. Against 'Bilkem's' advice, he had confronted everyone, inadvertently putting himself squarely in the goon's sights.

Once he learned about the drugs and agreed to speak to me, he had been prepared to tell me everything he had heard and surmised, when he instead opened his back door to find Pyotr and Nestor on his bluestone patio. Knocked out, most likely with chloroform, he had been abducted and deposited here, where he now cooled his heels.

But there was one important fact about Mr. John Peckham that Pyotr and Nestor didn't realize: John could speak and understand Russian. Very well, in fact.

I gave him a questioning look at that. "Why?" was what I wrote.

In the late 1980s, John had worked as an importer, and specialized in Russian and Asian imports. As part of his career, he learned Chinese and Russian. "I knew the Chinese gave me an edge whenever we went out to a Chinese restaurant, Lord you wouldn't believe what I've heard them say about the ingredients in the dishes, like 'Here Kitty Kitty with Beansprouts'! But I never thought the Russian would come in handy again!"

The goons had been set up here ever since they grabbed John, usually in the next room. With nothing to do, and all day to do it, he had strained to listen to conversations through the wall, both by phone and in person. Slowly, he began to fill in the blanks about what was happening.

Sebastian O'Nary was the biggest threat in the mayoral race to the employers of the two goons, a threat that had to be eliminated. John himself was the second biggest threat. They thought they had neatly tied up both threats, only to be nonplussed when 'Bilkem' sprang him from the police so easily. They thought the killing coupled with the drugs would put him away for a long time.

I scribbled on the piece of paper, paper that was rapidly filling up. "Who is supposed to win and why?"

I wasn't entirely surprised when he told me that Hal Morgan was the handpicked choice. What did surprise me was why. It turned out that all the green spaces, the parks, dog parks, shuffleboard courts, and more importantly, the mortgage on Hal's new acquisition, his 4,000 square foot home tucked off the edge of the golf course was all paid for by the Russian mob. For their payment, Hal would kill the plans of the Lucky Plucker Poultry Producers plant in favor of their own; The Right Wing Chicken Federation.

I tried to move my tongue. Frustrated, I grabbed the bag, clumsily erasing prior sentences to scrawl: "But why?"

John shifted uncomfortably on the thin mattress, grimacing at some unseen pain. He told me, "It's just a front for a drug running operation. Every chicken that leaves that plant will be packed full with their own special giblets." He laughed sourly, "Who's going to inspect a load of dead chickens at any checkpoint?"

Continuing, he told me how they had already made a

significant real estate investment in town, an investment that I had already wondered about myself: the old Miller's warehouse.

I scribbled the question that had plagued me from the beginning; "Why me?"

John laughed, a short bark that ended in a cough at that one. "You are a threat to them, Sandy. First you wouldn't stop hounding everyone about the killing. Then later, they thought I had told you everything I know. The skinny one, Pyotr?" He looked questioningly at me. I nodded. "Pyotr said, and I quote, 'That crazy bitch has got to be neutralized. She's throwing a penis into the entire works.'".

Oh, brother. Even in their own language these were a couple of buffoons. I looked at John for a long moment, then scribbled in the remaining border on the bag.

"Really. Well, they haven't seen a penis in their works yet."

CHAPTER 34

This time of year, so close to the solstice, the daylight lasted until almost 9:00. I watched the far wall as the last of the light finally extinguished itself and faded to total blackness. I was seated on the mattress next to John, neither of us speaking, just sitting.

I was also brooding. I imagined the scene back at the newspaper, Jorge's reaction to my disappearance. I wondered if Jim Pim was aware that I never came back. I thought of One Eyed Joe, and April, who was the last person to see me.

I thought of what I would do when Pyotr and Nestor returned.

The night crawled. Unseen creatures scratched and squeaked in the walls, scrabbled across the floor. My bladder came back to life, I tried to ignore it. Finally, cheeks burning with shame, I used the 5 gallon pail that was a malodorous presence in the corner, John turning his face away even in the darkness.

By dawn, I was in a murderous mood.

I poked my tongue gingerly. It seemed to be working

better now, the swelling lessened. I made an attempt at speech.

"John." That was clearer. He looked up from where he had curled in a ball on the mattress, bleary and out of it. "Unh?"

"How offen do the ass hoos come to check on you?" I still sounded like I had a mouth full of marbles, but at least I could speak now.

He rolled over and slowly sat upright, running a hand over his bristly face. His eyes were spent, far away. I wondered how much longer he would last in here.

His voice crackled, dry lips hindering him. "Sometimes they came daily, sometimes not for a couple days."

I was feeling my face, for lack of a mirror. Strips of red-stained sheeting hung off my upper arms from John's makeshift bandaging attempt. My cheek was puffy, my formerly good eye now swollen shut. Son of a bitch. Another shiner. John rummaged through the box, coming up with a bottle of water. He swigged off of it and handed it to me. I choked down a blood flavored mouthful, then another, cleaner one. Giving the bottle back, I pushed myself to my feet and made a circuit of the cell which was an old ward-room from the mental hospital. The early morning light showed metal sprinkler heads in the ceiling, cast iron rings in the floor, marks where furniture had once been bolted down. The door was a solid, puke green painted thing, with a slot at the bottom for sliding trays through. I tested it without hope. Locked tight, of course. I crossed over to the window.

Years of grime had blurred the glass, the frame was warped and splintered in places. John shrugged when he saw me examining it. "I tried to open it." I wiped a clean spot in the glass and examined the countryside.

You know how creepy old mental hospitals look from the outside? They look worse from the inside looking out.

Everywhere was blight and decay. Windows along the wing that I could see from my perch had shattered gaps like lost teeth. Vines climbed the side of the building, an old smoke-stack tilted to one side, the upper bricks having loosened enough that the top looked jagged. Wires to the building hung almost to the ground, the driveway from the hospital stretched down through an avenue of overgrown trees and undergrowth, limbs and an entire tree clogging the entrance.

I caught a glint of metal in the heavy trees to the right of the driveway as the sun rose higher. Frowning, I rubbed a wider circle in the glass. Behind me, John spoke, "We're doomed. I can feel it in my bones. We aren't getting out."

I saw motion near the glint, tree branches rustling and moving. John droned on. Exasperated, I snapped, "Shut the hell up!" which came out more like, "Ut the 'ell up!"

I strained to see what the glint was as the branch moved, pushed to one side by an unseen force.

"Holy shit!"

"What? What?" Peckham had bounded up to his feet. I clapped a hand over my mouth, aware that the goons might be close, held a finger to my lips for silence. He crept to my side at the window, whispering, "What is it?"

I pointed….at my Rav4 parked deep in the underbrush.

John looked bewildered. "Whose car is that?"

I pointed at my chest. He looked at the car, then back at me. "But… how did it get there?"

I wasn't sure, but I hoped that the cavalry had arrived. I pointed at the underbrush, looking for Jorge, for Jim Pim, for anyone searching for me. I found them then, my would be rescuers, and my heart dropped into my shoes.

One Eyed Joe, Willie, Ozzie and April.

Oh shit. I had a memory of my bag tumbling out of the bathroom window as Nestor hauled me back inside, April standing below gaping up at me. I had hoped that she might run to the police, alerting them and by default, alerting Jorge to my predicament. What I could see had instead happened, was that she likely grabbed my bag and scampered back to her crew. The same bag that contained my car keys. Which meant that they were now in possession of my car. The question remained; why were they here? Coincidence? Or by design? I sure hoped it was to find me, not to strip my car and sell it for scrap. I prayed that one of them, any of them, had some sort of sanity and good will towards me. I pushed on the window, with no result.

John had spied the four who were creeping along the edge of the tree line at that time. "Hey!" he yelled. I clapped a hand over his mouth, shaking my head. Belatedly, he realized that we weren't alone on the floor. We both heard a chair scrape in the other room, a mumbling in Russian. I wheeled away from the window and dropped face down on the mattress, John stumbling behind me. I heard a key in the lock.

"What's de racket?"

John was quick on his feet. "I had a bad dream. Listen, she needs medical care, she's going to get an infection."

Pyotr laughed. I tensed on the mattress, wishing I could see him, wondering if I could lure him close enough to grab him around the throat and give him a great, big giant penis in his works. Perhaps feeling my tension, John laid a hand on my forearm and squeezed gently, a subtle warning. Pyotr sniffed. "I care not. Dat your problem. Not mine. Shut up in here." The door slammed shut behind him. I heard the lock rasp into place. John exhaled. "Jesus."

I lifted my head. "What?" I whispered.

"He had a gun this time. I haven't seen him with one before now." John sounded rattled. I was too; a gun was a game changer. In the room beside us, we heard the rumble of the two men, conversing in low voices.

Quietly, I rolled off the mattress and crept back to the window.

The edge of the woods was empty and still in the morning light, my car no longer visible. I swore softly under my breath.

I cast around the room for something, anything that could be used to catch attention. We had no mirrors, no lights, nothing brightly colored….. I stopped, considering. John looked at me, a silent question.

Leaning over to him, I hissed in his ear, "'Urn aroun for a minut."

He looked at me, puzzled. Irritably, I gestured at him to turn his back to me. With a grimace, he finally did. I kicked off my shoes, unbuttoned my jeans and wiggled them over my hips. John chose that moment to glance over at me.

"Jesus, Sandy! I know it's been a while, but I'm seriously not in the mood for that!"

"Ut up! An urn aroun!"

Muttering, he complied.

I scooted my bright red thong underwear off, and hauled my jeans back in place, scrounged for my shoes and popped them back on. From the mattress a muffled, "Can I turn around now?"

I ignored him, choosing instead to peer out the window in search of my rag tag team.

The minutes ticked past. Just when I thought they were long gone, I spotted motion in the overgrown ditch running along the edge of the ragged lawn. I spied a fedora and long hair; Joe and April. Afraid to knock and draw attention from next door, I raised the red thong to the window and waved it frantically.

April saw it first. Looking up, her mouth opened in a

silent 'O', and she stopped moving. Joe noticed me when he stopped to see why April had halted. Following her gaze, he craned up the building to the second-story window where I stood waving my shorts like a fool. We made eye contact, us one eyed warriors. Grimly, he nodded once. I held my finger to my lips, and pointed with exaggeration at the room next door, praying he had enough sense to get it.

He did. He cast a long look at the window next to mine and nodded again, then he melted back into the brush, pulling April along with him.

CHAPTER 35

I hate waiting. I have the patience of a gnat. But waiting was all I could do right now. The sun slowly rose higher. The voices came and went in the room next door. Once I heard yelling, great guttural whoops in Russian. I looked a question at John, who sat with his back to the wall, knees drawn up to his chest. He cocked his head.

"They have dissension between them."

"Well, no shit Sherlock, I 'ot 'hat, but why?" In a completely foul mood now, I made an irritated sound. John shifted, drawing his legs closer to him, refusing to comment. I pointed at the ruckus, he stared resolutely ahead, letting me know he was miffed. It hadn't taken long for our patience with each other to wear thin.

I closed my eyes, well, one eye anyway, in frustration, took a deep breath, asked him as nicely as I could, "Will you please 'ell me 'hat they are figh-ing about before I squeeze your nuts off?"

I told you I was in a rotten mood.

He drew his legs closer, but answered me petulantly,

"Pyotr is telling Nestor he's stupid. Nestor wants to go to town. Pyotr says they can't. They are waiting for word from their bosses.." he listened a moment longer. "Now Nestor is threatening to snap Pyotr's dick off..ooo!" he grimaced as we heard a slapping noise through the wall, "That sounded like it hurt!"

I grunted. "'Ood." I hoped Pyotr incapacitated Nestor. One on one odds were more to my liking anyway.

The noise stopped. Silence filled the old hospital. Then, I heard a door slam, feet stomping down the hallway. John and I shared a look. One set of feet, heavy, probably Nestor. John whispered, "They go down to the old solarium on the back to smoke. They also can watch the back of the building from there."

In the room beside us, we heard a mumbling male voice again. John strained to listen, shook his head in frustration. "I can't hear what he's saying. I think he's on the phone."

I scrambled to my feet and went to the window again. Peering through the glass, I scanned the empty front entrance area, searching for anything.

Nothing moved in the late morning sunlight, except for foraging birds. I braced my hands on the window and pushed with all my might. Nothing. Even if it opened, there were still the bars on the outside to contend with. Agitated, I started pacing the room. John watched me from the mattress.

"John, why 'aven't they 'illed you too?" I stopped and stared at him. He looked miserable, even worse than he had last night when I arrived. He shook his head. "I heard them say they had to wait until the primary election was over, and then they would arrange an 'accident' for me."

I narrowed my eyes at him. "Really. Well, I 'ink 'ey might 'ave one first."

He looked up at me, a spark of hope in his eyes.

I heard a new voice, female, high pitched, far away. It sounded like she was singing. I whirled away from the window at the sound. John scrambled to his feet, confusion evident on his face. "What the hell is that?"

I cocked my head, listening. The voice rose and fell, the cadence like a nursery rhyme. I looked up at John, met his eyes and smiled a grim smile. "I think the cavalry is here." My tongue, finally back to a more normal size, allowed freer speech now. John's eyes lit up, and he opened his mouth to yell. "Shhhh!" I lunged at him, grabbing his arm.

He closed his mouth.

I heard muttering in Russian next door, then the creak of the door as Pyotr went out to investigate.

As far as we knew, Nestor was still sulking down in the solarium.

The voice grew louder, echoing through the hallway. I pressed my ear to the door, realizing that the singer was inside the building.

I could make out, faintly, the rhyme that the singer was chanting over and over; "Jack and Jill went up the hill, so Jack could taste her candy, Jack got a shock and a mouthful of cock 'cuz Jill's real name was Randy." The last part of the chant rose until it was a shriek, then trailed off to start over again.

I wondered if it was April.

I met John's eyes, round and astonished, and surprised him by grinning widely at him. "It's showtime!"

"What the hell?"

From out in the hallway, we heard Pyotr call down to Nestor. John translated. "He says; What's this crazy bitch doing here? Nestor answered, 'She just walked in and started singing." He paused, listening. "Pyotr says, 'Well grab her and get her ass out of here!'" We heard footsteps thumping down the staircase, the voice fading away. Out in the hallway, Pyotr

WRITE ON MAIN STREET

swore, a heartfelt sentiment that even I could translate. Then he started down the stairs after Nestor. Voices echoed through the building, too faint to make out what they were saying.

I heard a new noise in the hallway, furtive, shuffling. It stopped outside the doorway. The knob rattled. John and I drew together in front of the window, watching it. I grabbed the odiferous metal pail, the only weapon I had, and held it ready to fling. Scratching sounds, the tumblers finally clicking over and the knob twisted down. I tensed, ready to act..... and the door cracked open, revealing Willie's face.

My breath exploded out of me in an exhale; I hadn't realized I was holding it. I dropped the pail to the floor with a wet splat. Willie eyed me with distaste. "Ah still don' like you."

I stepped forward. "Yeah? Well right now, I LOVE you!" and planted a kiss square on his lips. Flustered, he staggered back, wiping his mouth. Behind me, John was scrambling towards the open door. Willie pushed it wide, waving us out. "Guv'ner says get out, get out now." He handed me my car keys, pointing towards the front. "Yer car's out there. Under the trees. Get out. These bastards are crazy!"

Voices echoed through the building, the hallway a creepy mess of dark shadows and scabrous peels of paint hanging like ribbons from the ceiling, souvenirs of past water damage.

I looked towards the noise, then back at Willie. "What about you guys? I can't leave you here."

He grew agitated. "Go! Guv'ner says go! He takes care of us!"

Footsteps echoed in the staircase again, heavy tread; Nestor. Willie froze. "Shit!"

"Exactly!" I darted back in the room, grabbing the handle

of the pail. Willie drew back, lips crinkled in disgust. "Eww! Whose ass did that come out of?"

I ignored him, running to the head of the staircase where I could look down over the half wall at the staircase as it wound around through the floors. Feet echoed a flight below me. I caught a glimpse of a beefy arm as Nestor turned to make the last flight up. I looked up at Willie, whispered, "How do we get out of here?"

He pointed down the hallway, "Another stair case in the next wing." I nodded. John danced behind Willie, frantic, "Come on!" he hissed. I held a finger to my mouth. "Wait." I mouthed.

Nestor's head appeared, facing up the stair towards the last landing, away from where I crouched behind the half wall waiting. I let him get centered right under me, then rose. In one smooth motion, I tipped the pail, dumping half the contents squarely onto his head. He let out a bellow, flailing his arms, looking straight up at me, his mouth gaping wide open...

Which was when I dumped the remainder of the contents directly onto his face, right into his opened mouth, followed with an overhead fling of the metal bucket as hard as I could.

Anger gives me good aim. I hit him squarely in his now shit filled mouth, sending him tumbling ass over teakettle down the slick stairs, the noise booming through the stair-case. Willie jumped straight up in excitement. "Ooo-RAH! Good shot!"

I was already running down the hallway, pushing John ahead of me. "Go! Go!"

Our footsteps thudded and echoed off the walls, debris littered the way, walls half collapsed, doors sagging in the frames, spider webs tore across my face. Behind us, I could hear gagging, shouting and running footsteps as Pyotr and

Nestor took up the chase. There was a loud crash, followed by swearing in Russian, then Willie's high pitched cackling.

John and I skidded around a corner into a labyrinth of halls and doorways. We slammed into each other as we stopped. "Which way?" John's voice was high pitched, verging on hysterical.

"Shit! I don't know!" Black hallways stretched off both sides, another one dead ahead. No sunlight came directly into the large room we were in, maybe a lunchroom at one point? I saw what looked like it had been a kitchen, appliances long gone, the roof semi caved in. Graffiti covered the walls, black, red and white streaks covering the institutional green, splintered tables lay on their sides, legs broken and hanging. I spun, trying to orient myself to where we were. Behind us, we heard a gunshot, then another. John's face paled; mine probably did too. "Come on!" Blindly choosing, I plunged down the hallway straight ahead, feet thundering in the enclosed space. I heard John panting behind me, almost hyperventilating. We plunged on through several zig zags of corridor then… a locked door barred our way.

"Shit!" I tugged frantically on the knob. The noise of our pursuers grew louder. John grabbed my arm. "We have to go back to the last hallway!"

Dammit, he was right. Back… towards the two goons. I grabbed a piece of broken door jamb that was lying on the floor and tore back down the hall the way we had come, back to the old lunchroom.

From the other hallway, the thunder of their steps grew louder. I sprang to the side of the doorway, my back flat to the wall, John dropping into a crouch behind an old table that lay on its side and waited.

Pyotr was first through the door, followed by Nestor the shit-covered goon. I was ready for him. I swung hard and from the shoulder, swinging my body on my hips the way I used to in baseball so many years ago. My chunk of door-jamb connected solidly with Pyotr's nose, exploding it under the impact. He crashed backwards into Nestor, taking him down with him. The thought flickered across my mind about taking his gun, but in the end, discretion won out.

I whirled and sprinted down the other hallway, John hard on my heels.

CHAPTER 36

*T*his time we had the right hallway. Sunlight began to flicker across the walls, light streaming in from the broken windows we could see from our prison cell. I spied another half wall, signaling the staircase. We sprinted hard around the edge and started thundering downstairs. Behind us, I heard shouting and running feet, the two goons back in the hunt. I smiled grimly. Bring it on, boys.

Down we raced, leaping over chunks of concrete, and some sort of dead, gray furry creature on one of the landings. The door slammed outward into the hallway under my flying body, my feet and arms flailing; the ground floor, sunlight streaming through the door that was open to the outside, being held open by Joe.

He waved frantically, "Og! Og! Og!"

I tried to slow, to speak to him, but he shoved me through the doorway, pointing towards the woods where Ozzie gestured from the trees. We ran full bore at him.

I heard yelling behind us, then a gunshot. A zing like an angry hornet buzzed past my ear. I risked a glance back. Pyotr, his face a bloody mess, was leaning out of one of the windows in the staircase, aiming at us again. I pushed John, and we hit the deck as more shots zinged past.

"Damn!" John yelped.

Understatement of the day. Ozzie had taken cover at the shots, now he whistled from the woods. "Here! To the left! Hurry up!!!"

We scrambled through the tall grass, adrenaline fueling our flight. No more shots rang out, but I heard yelling as the goons burst out into the daylight. I spied my Rav4, probably the most welcome sight I had ever seen. We sprinted the last forty feet to it; I shoved John rudely towards the passenger side.

I plunged into the driver's side and began rummaging under the seat. John was fully hyperventilating now, gasping, "Get out of here! What are you doing?!"

My hand closed around my gun, and I drew it out. I turned to face him with a nasty smile. "I'm leveling the playing field. Wanna play some Russian Roulette?"

His jaw dropped. "Holy shit... you're nuts!"

"No. Actually, I'm not. And I'm not leaving those assholes here to hurt my friends." I fired up the motor and stomped on the gas. Dirt flew as we slewed around under the trees.... heading towards the old hospital instead of away.

I burst through the woods on the edge of the old lawn in a shower of leaves and branches, catching a glimpse of Ozzie's astonished face as he dove for cover in the old drainage ditch. I let out a whoop.

In front of the building, Pyotr and Nestor froze, halfway across the lawn as I roared towards them. I fired off a shot from the window, not caring if it was wild.

It worked. They turned and ran for the back of the building, surprisingly fast. I whooped again and laid on more throttle; the car slewing sideways as we made the turn. As I had hoped, they were tumbling into the gray Oldsmobile as we rounded the corner. I stomped on it and burned a donut in the grass, heading the nose back the way we had just come. We tore out from behind the building with the gray Olds in pursuit and headed for the driveway. I thought I could hear Willie's voice over the din, shouting, "OOO-rah!"

John was hanging onto the door, his head bouncing off the roof as we slammed through holes in the pavement, his mouth working, a high-pitched keening noise coming from his lips. I ignored him, my attention on the Oldsmobile in the mirror. I really didn't have a plan, other than to not leave them there to hurt any of Joe's crew. Ducking and dodging, I yanked savagely on the wheel to avoid all the downed trees as we roared back towards the road. I heard another shot coming from the car behind us.

"Assholes." They were starting to make me mad.

We hit the roadway in a shower of dirt, the roads in this area of town being mostly undeveloped. I slewed the car east in a storm of gravel and hit the gas.

The Oldsmobile followed suit. I heard another shot, and the rear window of my new-to-me Rav4 exploded in a shower of glass.

"God damn son-of-a-bitch!" I hadn't purchased glass insurance on this one.

Beside me, John shrieked and covered his head. I thrust the gun at him. "Here! Shoot back!"

He shook his head. 'I can't!"

"Why the hell not?" I was screaming over the roar of the wind in the car, the speedometer pushing 60 mph.

"I think I just shit myself!"

"Oh, for Christ sakes!" I pointed the gun over my left shoulder with my right hand and fired, wincing at the boom in my ear. The Olds swerved, but stayed hot on our tail. I had to get more room. I poured the gas on harder.

The network of roads was unfamiliar to me, so I chose

turns at random, always trying for ones that looked better traveled. We flashed over a low rolling hill, hayfields on both sides, a tractor trundling across one of them. I thought it looked familiar, then I saw the white house with the big maple tree.

Pim's family farm.

Behind us, another shot rang out from the Oldsmobile. I heard a solid thud as it hit metal. But I had a plan now.

I skidded through the center of the Meadows, praying there wouldn't be anyone out walking on this lovely June afternoon, then whipped the wheel hard to the left, off the pavement and onto another dirt road, one that showed few signs of recent travel. I banged off another shot at the two Russians, aware that I had two left. Hopefully, I wouldn't need them. Fields gave way to trees, then I caught a flicker of gray metal and a spark of light through the forest to the right.

No way….

I slowed a hair and let Pyotr and Nestor climb right up on my tail. I could see Nestor trying to steady himself to take another shot at me.

I prayed Lizzy was right.

The road doglegged back in a hairpin, a short steep slope dead ahead of us. John yelled something unintelligible, I nailed the throttle, the little Rav4 leapt forward, motor whining.

I hit the short steep slope to the train tracks at 40 mph, yelling at John, "Hang on!!!" Out of the corner of my eye, I saw the flare of light from the train's headlights, much closer now than it had been the first time I tried this crazy assed stunt.

The battered Toyota crested the hill and went airborne like a rotund Gazelle. I let out a whoop, John let out a scream, Nestor let out a shot that passed by harmlessly, then we were slamming down on the other side of the tracks, the soft suspension wallowing, threatening to send me sideways. I fought the wheel, struggling to keep the car under control as I watched my rearview mirror for the Oldsmobile.

The gray nose shot into sight, pointing straight up, then the car slammed down hard, all forward motion checked abruptly, two spiderwebs of cracks blooming on the windshield where our Russian mafia friends slammed their skulls against the windshield. The car stopped dead in a shower of sparks. Right on the tracks, high centered like my Volvo had been. I hit the brakes and skidded to a dusty halt, watching in fascination as the train loomed into the crossing, sparks flying from the wheels, the poor engineer yelling, "Shit! Shit! Shit!" again.

The Olds exploded in a shower of metal and glass, Pyotr and Nestor still in the car. I heard a new screeching of metal as the train shoved them across the road and out of sight into the woods. Beside me, John breathed one word.

"Damn..."

CHAPTER 37

$\mathcal{I}$t took a surprisingly long time for the relatively short train to slide through the crossing, the screaming from the locked up steel wheels overwhelming. John and I had gotten out of the Rav4 and stood still, watching in silence. I surely didn't like Pyotr and Nestor, maybe even hated them, but watching someone die was still kind of a bummer.

I figured I would get over it with the help of a hot fudge sundae.

The last car on the train skidded through, a flatbed with a truck trailer strapped on it, and I found myself staring across the tracks at a parked pickup truck, the driver out of the truck, his mouth hanging open, a gun clenched in his right hand.

It was Jim Pim. He saw me standing on the other side with John and let out a yell.

"Holy Shit! Sandy!"

To my astonishment, he sprinted across the rails and down the other side, grabbing me in a huge bear hug, pulling me off the ground and spinning me around, his pistol still clenched in his hand, thumping me in the back. He smelled like laundry soap and freshly cut hay. I hugged back, hard, tears prickling my eyes.

"Oh my God, oh my God, oh my God." He stammered over and over into my hair.

Finally, John cleared his throat. Jim finally realizing who he was. "Holy shit! John!"

John held both hands up, warding him off. "I've been shot at, shit at and held captive, but I am not hugging you!"

Jim laughed, still with me firmly in his grip. "I ain't hugging you… just her." He pulled me against him again, his face buried in my hair.

Geez. A girl could get used to this.

CHAPTER 38

The parking lot of the Brownville Valley High School was filled to overflowing. Cars circulated, searching for backup lights signaling an exit from a coveted slot. More were parked haphazardly on the grassy fringes, the dust churned up from the wheels, a fine coating on everything. Jorge and I made our way across the packed lot until we could see the entrance to the high school itself.

The candidates were not allowed within 100' of the entrance where the voters were filing in for this, the primary election. They had all set up camp on a strip of sidewalk that everyone had to walk through, a veritable political gauntlet. I spied Molly Bruce, her hair shining in the sun, darting about on the walkway hugging people. Ann Mullivan glowered from the sidelines, firmly ensconced in her lawn chair, her son holding a cardboard sign endorsing her. John Peckham was also fully in evidence, standing facing the lot where no one could fail to see him, shaking hands and greeting people face to face. His dramatic reappearance had been covered by every newspaper on the east coast, although he still faced a lot of overt suspicion over his role in the death of Sebastian O'Nary.

Standing twenty feet behind him, studiously ignoring him, was Hal Morgan. I felt the vein in my forehead begin to pound as I watched his smug expression. He pressed palms and kissed babies, laughing heartily. His entourage milled around with placards on their chests, endorsing him.

I had taken to calling him the Teflon Candidate. Nothing we had learned about him was sticking. For one, our two sources had been shoveled up and dumped into two boxes over at the morgue. That left John Peckham as our only source. And he was hardly an unbiased one.

Jorge read my expression correctly. "Case... don't."

"Dammit Maxim! Look at him!"

"I know. Be patient."

Patient. Yeah... right. The girl who microwaves PopTarts because the toaster took too long, patient? Good one.

I heaved a sigh, leaning back against a scraggly maple tree perched haphazardly in the median of the parking lot. Jorge, looking like a male model even though he wore jeans and a tee shirt, put his hands in his pockets, his eyes scanning the crowd. Finally, he decided it was time.

"Come on Case. It's showtime!"

We threaded our way back through the jammed lot, reaching the nondescript Ford Taurus Jorge had borrowed for the day. I was dressed in torn jeans, a black tank top, my hair pulled back and under a paint-splattered ball cap. A pair of glasses with plain glass lenses perched on my nose, a pair of brown contact lenses covered my normally hazel eyes. Even I had to do a double take to realize it was me. I felt naked without my bag though. A small backpack waited for me in the back of the car.

Jorge mashed the car into gear, wallowing over the curbing to get out of the lot. We knew that Hal would be here for the duration... a fact we were counting on. I felt a fission of energy tingle up my spine. This could make... or break us. Beside me, a bead of sweat popped out on Jorge's forehead.

"This is suicide, you know that Case?"

Oddly enough, his words calmed me. "No, it is not. Come on, Jorge. You told me yourself that this is the time for bold moves. Now let's roll!"

Pavement hummed under the Taurus's worn tires as we sped across town. Blocks of homes gave way to rolling lawns and large fronted homes. The undulating greens of the golf course appeared on the left. Jorge took the freshly paved roadway marked 'Birdy Lane' and followed it to the cul-de-sac at the end. A large, gray shuttered mansion loomed over the road, wisteria trees draping scented flowers over the flagstone pathway that marched up to the massive front porch. A pea stone driveway sat empty, the occupants busy at the high school. Late morning sun glinted off the windows. Jorge swung the car around and slotted it along one side of the cul-de-sac, behind an aging Porsche 944. Our doors thumped in the quiet morning.

Nerves jangled in my spine. I shot a look at Jorge. "Okay Maxim. Like we belong."

Popping the trunk, I pulled out buckets, mops, and cleaning supplies, distributing them between us, my little backpack slung over my shoulder. Laden with these objects, we marched up the drive, through an ornamental garden gate that opened onto the bluestone walk, flanked by over-flowing gardens, heavy flowers nodding on their stems. A tidy glass-paned door peeked under an arch of clematis vines, the side entrance into the kitchen.

I produced the key I had made from the spare I had, um, accidentally found under a fake stone some three nights earlier, while Morgan and his family were busy at a last-minute press conference. Slotting it into the knob, I paused, rapping three times sharply on the mullion paned windows. "Acme Cleaning! Hello?"

Silence greeted us. With a glance back at Jorge's sweating face, I opened the kitchen door… and we were in.

I let out a low whistle when I saw the expanse of stainless steel and granite that stretched around a room larger than my entire apartment. "Holy shit.."

Jorge was taking it all in, the copper pots hanging from a huge central rack, the island with the range in it. "Damn…. there's good money in politics, huh?"

"I don't know about politics, but there certainly is in drugs."

He swiveled around, looking for the entrances. "Okay Case. You take the left side of the house, I'll take the right. No more than two minutes per room, then we meet back here before we go upstairs."

I swallowed, my throat suddenly dry. Damn! This was B&E, the real thing. Excitement coursed through me. Jorge held up his cellphone silently, the meaning clear. I patted my pocket and nodded.

With one last look at each other, we split up.

CHAPTER 39

*L*arge rooms, lushly carpeted, looked out over tall arched windows to the rear. Beyond the labyrinth of gardens and a row of evergreens, the golf course was visible, emerald green waves disappearing towards the club-house. I spied a golf cart parked under a portico in the back, a small bricked pathway leading to direct access to the course. The dirty bastard could have his coffee and lumber out into his private cart for a short round every morning. Anger bubbled up in me.

Focus, Case... focus.

Pivoting, I looked across the enormous drawing room I stood in, noting the bookshelves that stretched to the ceiling, leather-bound books filling them. A gigantic stone fireplace filled one wall, an elaborate family crest in mosaic tile above the mantle. Not this room; this was for public show. I headed towards the dark wooden door that led off the left side.

Hinges creaked as I cautiously pushed it open, peeking into the mahogany-paneled room. Silence greeted me. This room was not a public one; in fact, it looked like Morgan's man cave. One large, arched window sent sparkles of sunlight across the roll-topped desk that stood in front of it, daisies and roses leaned against the bottom of the glass; he would have a clear view down the golf course from where he sat. I wondered what the price of this place had been.

Moving quickly, I started with the right side drawers. Bills, receipts, folders of household expenses neatly organized. Nothing.

The left side was locked. I tugged in frustration, then glanced at my watch. Two minutes up. A quick scan around the room, I headed back out the little door.

This time, I took the large arched entryway to the rear of it, a short hallway spilling out into a formal dining room on the right, and a front sitting room on the left. I ignored both.

The front foyer opened into the area just past the sitting room. I couldn't help myself: I stopped dead, staring at the three-story atrium, gracefully spiraling staircase and marble flooring. Holy crap! Was I in the wrong business or what?

Pushing it aside, aware that time was sliding past, I hurried on to the next set of rooms. These were more intimate, not for the public. One was a television room, with a large flat screen dominating one wall, soft sofas and cushy chairs spread around. A small bar took one wall. The other was a small downstairs bedroom, the bed showing evidence of use. Women's items were visible; makeup and perfume on the dresser, in the small bath connected to it, hair products and a brush. A white linen robe hung from the back of the door. I frowned. As far as I knew, Hal and his wife lived here alone.

Quickly, I rifled through the drawers in both bedroom and bathroom. Other than an assortment of women's clothing and toiletries, there was nothing. I cringed when a scan of the bedside table drawer revealed a worn looking dildo. I had seen Hal's wife; I really didn't need to have this visual. My cell phone vibrated with an incoming text. Jorge.

'DONE. ARE YOU?'

'COMING' I wrote back. With one last puzzled look at the bedroom, I hustled back through the house to rejoin Jorge.

He was in the kitchen when I arrived. "Anything?"

"Maybe. He has an office back there. One side of his desk is locked up tighter than a nun's bunghole."

A smile cracked Jorge's serious demeanor. "Little redneck creeping in here, Case."

I flushed. "Shut up, Maxim."

He gestured towards the other door out of the kitchen. "We'll go back to it. I found nothing downstairs. Time to go up."

A dark paneled back staircase ascended from the utility hallway we stood in. "Time?" I asked him. He checked his watch. "10:38."

I checked mine, nodded. "Rock-and-roll."

Our sneaker-clad feet whispered on the smooth wooden steps. Light spilled across the top of the staircase from the open door to the bedroom at the top. A quick glance revealed tightly drawn covers, unadorned dresser top, empty closet. Guest room.

Jorge gestured to my left. "Two minutes per. Meet you back here."

I nodded and took off on crepe-soled feet.

The house was a warren of rooms upstairs, most of them unused. Bedrooms, sitting rooms, a game room. The front stairs wound through, heading up to the top story. I craned over the railing at the top floor, wondering what we would find up there.

Twelve minutes later, I was waiting as Jorge reappeared. "Anything?"

He shook his head.

"Was the master bedroom on that side?"

"No. Just a bunch of guest rooms, a small kitchen area, and a kind of living room."

We both looked towards the sunlight that streamed down from the atrium.

"Come on." I headed out.

"Case... wait."

Stopping, I glanced over at him. "What?"

He was frowning. "Not the front. We'll be visible from the course. The back stairs go up over here."

I followed him down the darkened hallway.

CHAPTER 40

J felt short of breath as we ascended the last flight, my heart thudding in my chest. I could smell sweat on Jorge, saw the dark circles under his armpits, felt them on mine.

We had been in Morgan's house for 22 minutes now. We both had hoped to find a smoking gun long before this.

The door creaked open into a short hallway. To the right was a huge walk in storage area, cabinets and cupboards lining the walls. I noticed a laundry area complete with a laundry chute tucked inside a large louvered door closet. I peeked into the chute: a basket mounded with linen located on the next floor down, a holding area for the laundress to collect from.

To the left was the bedroom.

Leaving the storage area, we both headed left, into Morgan's most private space. Jorge shoved the mahogany door open cautiously.

Holy shit!!

The room was enormous, a huge glass walled sanctuary. A king-sized bed dominated the back wall, floor to ceiling

242

windows framing it. I noticed a telescope perched in one window, aimed down at the course. The other side of the room had a railing that overlooked the foyer three stories below. More glass fronted the outside wall, windows that created an illusion of being outside. A glance up revealed a small cupola, a spiral staircase joining it to the main room. Off to the opposite side, a huge bathroom stretched, raised Jacuzzi tub surrounded by more glass, walk in his and hers closets. I scanned the bathroom, noticing only male accessories visible in it. I frowned.

Jorge caught my expression. "What is it?"

I gestured at the bathroom. "I don't think he's sleeping with his wife. I found a room on the first floor with women's stuff in it. There's none here."

"Case, we don't have time to worry about his marital problems. Start searching."

"But Jorge... his wife was his alibi the night Sebastian was killed. Said they went to bed around 10:30, remember?"

Jorge stopped, his eyes narrowing. "File that. We'll come back to it." He nodded at the row of dressers along one wall. "Hit it."

I quickly pawed through an assortment of male undergarments, wincing as I realized he was a tighty whitey kind of guy. Drawers of polo shirts, button-down shirts, holy Christ, suspenders?

Across the room, Jorge was quickly rifling through the other dresser, distaste in his expression.

My fingers found a small wooden box, third drawer down on the right. Pulling it out, I opened it to find a small key chain.

"Jorge!" I hissed.

His head popped up from where he had been peering under the mammoth bed. "What?"

I held up the ring. "Bet you a buck one of these goes to that desk downstairs."

He rose to his feet, coming around to me and taking them from my hand. I saw a small smile. "Let's go!"

We tore down the stairs, feeling like the time we had left was slim to none. I couldn't have told you why; it was a gut feeling that was growing with each revolution of the second hand. Jorge felt it too.

I grabbed his sleeve as we hit the downstairs, tugging him along with me to the small den off the dining room. Jorge noticed the golf cart under the portico. He shook his head.

With trembling hands, I tried one key after another. A small bronze one finally slid in, turning with a snick. I slid the top drawer open.

"Hell yeah!"

A gun lay on top, cradled in a soft cloth. Bundles of papers below it. Grabbing one, I scanned it quickly as Jorge grabbed the next one.

"Case..."

I looked at him. He held up the blue topped stationary in victory. "The smoking gun. Bank statements from a Bermuda Bank."

I snatched it out of his hands, scanning the deposit amounts, same sum, regular payments, all of them large.

"I take it these didn't make it when he released his financials earlier this year?"

Jorge shook his head. "Hell no. The IRS doesn't even know about these."

I was frustrated. "But they still don't tie him to the mob."

Jorge was shooting cellphone photos of each statement as he pulled them out.

"Keep looking."

Papers flew under our hands. Bank statements, a deed for

the house (2.7-million, paid in full) deeds to other holdings. Jorge paused, frowning at one piece. "Look."

It was another deed, for the building we had seen Morgan in, the one we crawled through to reach the warehouse. The deed was made out to Sunline Industries, LLC.

I looked at Jorge. "Did Sunline Industries ever make it to any of the financial reports Morgan filed?"

Jorge shook his head no. "No association before now." He quickly snapped a photo of the document.

I heard the crackle of gravel under the wheels of a car outside. We froze. "Shit!" Jorge hissed. A car door thumped. We scrambled, sliding paperwork back in, locking the drawer, aware that our mops and pails sat in the kitchen entrance.

Crunching footsteps in the gravel as we skidded back to the kitchen at high speed. Our supplies sat in the entryway in a jumble. We heard a scrape as the garden gate was slid open.

"Leave it!" Jorge spat as I fumbled for my backpack. I ignored him.

He grabbed my shirtsleeve, pulling me into the hallway at a dead run. We sprinted into the darkness, then I was jerked sideways as he sprinted into the back staircase. We ascended in three leaps, tumbling around the corner into the hallway, my heart pounding so hard I could barely hear.

Downstairs, the kitchen door hissed as it opened.

Silence.

My heart thudded in my ears. Jorge crouched beside me, breathing through his open mouth shallowly.

A footstep, light, stealthy. A clink of the pail. Then, "Consuela?"

Jorge and I made eye contact, both of us with eyes widened in shock.

The voice was Chief Hanniford's.

CHAPTER 41

$\mathcal{H}$e moved through the kitchen into the drawing room. We heard another car motor outside, the door thumping shut. With a look at each other, we carefully rose to our feet and crept down the hall towards the front staircase foyer.

The acres of carpeting were our friend. Sneakered feet sank into the plush pile, our movements soundless. Downstairs, we heard a shoe squeak on the marble flooring as the back door was opened. A man's voice, muffled. Hanniford's responding. Then: "Damn woman, leaving her stuff like that. I have half a mind to fire her ass. Why is it so hard to get good help?" Hal Morgan's voice.

We looked at each other in shock. "What is he doing here?" I mouthed at Jorge.

"Never mind him, what the hell is Hanniford doing here?" Jorge mouthed back.

Holy shit. We were stuck upstairs, red-handed in Morgan's home, with Morgan and Hanniford between us and the outside.

"This is not good!" Jorge mouthed.

"No shit Sherlock! Tell me something I don't know!" I hissed back.

More footsteps below us. Voices floated up the atrium, the acoustics clear as a bell.

"Come in, Bill." Hal's voice. Footsteps clattered across marble tiles.

"Would you like anything to drink?"

"Cut the shit, Hal. This isn't a social call."

"Well... you..." Hal blustered.

"You know why I am here. You owe me and I want my payment."

"The primary isn't over! The deal was when the primary is done you get another third, then the last one third after the election."

"You know as well as I that you are a lock. I want my money and I want it now."

"Jesus, Bill! We can do this tomorrow when it's done."

A rustle of leather. "Now."

"Christ! Calm down! Okay, okay, I get your point. Now it is. Put your God damned gun away!"

Jorge and I shared round eyed looks.

"Let me go get it then. It's in my safe."

Footsteps. The squeak of the door leading to his den, muffled voices... then silence.

I strained to listen, heard a voice. Hal Morgan's. "Bill... someone has been in here."

We heard the rustle of metal sliding out of leather again. "You better not be bullshitting me."

Hal's voice, louder, "That stuff in the kitchen? Consuela isn't due until tomorrow. I just assumed she was a day early."

"Fuck!" Hanniford spoke from the heart.

I heard a drawer slide shut. "Come on, let's go look."

His gun. Top drawer. I knew it was in his palm now.

Frantic, we looked back and forth down the hallway. Where the hell could we go?

Hal, whispering now, "I'll take the back stairs, you take the front."

I was fishing in my backpack as Jorge rose to the balls of his feet, panic evident in his eyes. I found what I was looking for, my cellphone. I quickly thumbed a number into it. Downstairs, a loud musical chime started. Both men started and swore.

Tugging Jorge by the sleeve, we sprinted up the staircase onto the top floor.

CHAPTER 42

"What the fuck?" from downstairs, impossible to tell who said it. Jorge looked over at me and mouthed the same thing. I had seen Hal Morgan with his cell phone before, had noticed his clumsiness with it. I was banking on him taking a moment to find it, then silence it, the noise a cover for us to get to the top floor.

Jorge tugged my sleeve again. "What the fuck are you doing?" in a hiss. I shook my head, pushing him to go faster. Our feet sank into plush carpet just as the phone went silent.

Acres of bedroom. Huge bathroom. I ignored both, pushing Jorge towards the storage area instead.

Below us I heard a hissing sound, a shushing noise, then footsteps, stealthy, quick, coming up the stairs.

Shit! They heard us!

Breathing through my mouth, sweat trickling into my eyes, Jorge's face drawn and scared. We sprinted into the laundry area, halting at the louver door closet that held the chute. "Now what?" Jorge asked.

I was pulling my gun out of my backpack. "Oh shit, oh no! No Case! That's the Chief of Police out there!"

"And he's a dirty son of a bitch!" I racked a round into the chamber.

"Get in!" I pointed at the chute. Jorge looked at it. "What?"

"I said, get in! Now! Hold on and wait until I tell you it's OK."

"Are you crazy?" he hissed.

I swung the gun towards him. "YES!"

"Holy shit!"

"Just shut the hell up and get in the chute until I tell you!"

Footsteps were scuffing off the top of the stairs into the bedroom.

"Jesus!" Jorge swung his legs in, sliding partway into the chute, hanging onto the edge with pale knuckles.

I took up a stance behind the partially opened door, peering through the louvers at the entrance to the hallway. I saw a shadow move. Judging from the height and build, it was Hanniford. He moved carefully, his gun held in front of him, sliding down the wall. I didn't see Morgan. I held my breath.

I heard Jorge's breathing behind me, amplified in the chute.

Hanniford reached the room where the light hit him when Morgan loomed behind him. In a normal voice, Morgan said, "There's nobody up here."

"Jesus Christ!" Startled, Hanniford swung towards Morgan, his gun coming to bear on him.

Several things happened simultaneously. I hissed, "Go!" at Jorge, heard him slide free, Hanniford and Morgan heard it too, then I was swinging my gun up and around the doors, aiming straight for them.

The gunshot was an explosion in the small space.

Hal Morgan crumpled in a heap, then Hanniford was swinging around turning his still smoking gun towards me.

In desperation, I let loose a shot. Sparks flew as the bullet pinged off the muzzle of his gun, his yell ringing in my ears. He staggered backwards, off balance, and I took advantage of the moment's grace and dove into the laundry chute.

Dark metal walls banged on my face and body, the scent of dirty underwear strong in my nostrils. I hit the basket like a pile of dead weight, praying Jorge was clear of it.

He was. He was lying on the floor, holding his ankle.

"I fucked my ankle up!"

Shit! "No time for namby pants, go, go, go!" I hauled him upright. Above us, we heard feet sprinting for the back stairs. I shoved Jorge into the staircase and down to the first floor, taking the steps three at a time. We skidded out into the marble-topped kitchen... and right into Jim Pim's outstretched gun.

Holy shit! No!

His eyes widened as he saw us, then we all heard thundering feet in the hall. He made eye contact with me. "Under cover! Now!"

I pushed Jorge over behind the kitchen island where we fell in a heap. I heard Hanniford's feet thunder into the kitchen and slid to a halt.

"What the hell...?"

"You stop right there, sir!" Jim's voice trembled.

"Pim! What the hell are you doing here?"

"The question is, What the hell are YOU doing here?"

Hanniford drew himself up. "Officer Pim. Lower your gun right NOW!"

"No sir. I cain't do that. You are under arrest, sir."

Jorge and I looked at each other. Oh no...

I heard a barking laugh from Hanniford. "Oh really? On what charges?"

"Conspiracy to commit murder, sir. In the death of Mr. Sebastian O'Nary. You have the right to remain silent..."

I was scrambling out from behind the island as Hanniford pulled his damaged gun up to bear on Jim Pim. I saw Jim flinch, and steel himself even as he pulled the trigger. The explosion echoed off the copper pans with a ringing sound as Hanniford collapsed to the gray-tiled floor, his blood pooling out beneath him.

We froze, a moment in time suspended. Wide, scared blue eyes on Jim Pim. Wide temporarily brown ones on me. He swallowed noisily. "Oh, shit…. I'm gonna be sick!"

"Holy crap! Jim… you just saved our lives!"

He turned white as a sheet, his hand trembling. His lips moved. "I killed him…"

I stepped over to Hanniford, felt his neck. I could feel a pulse beating under my fingers. "No, you didn't. Jim, he shot Hal Morgan upstairs!"

Beads of sweat ran down Jim's face. "We need backup and an ambulance now!"

Jorge rolled out from behind the island. "Already calling it in." his cellphone clenched in sweaty hands.

I looked at Jim. "Why are you here?"

He stared at me a moment. "I followed you here."

"What? Why?" I felt a flash of annoyance. We hadn't noticed the tail.

"I was worrying about what you were gonna do, so I decided to kinda keep an eye out, case you needed backup. I saw you guys come in here, and I didn't know what to do, so I just decided to wait and watch." He looked at Hanniford, who was starting to moan softly. "Then I saw them come in behind you and I knew the shit was going to hit the fan. I knew Morgan was dirty.." he gazed at Hanniford, disappointment visible on his face. "I just didn't realize he was too."

"None of us knew, Jim."

Jorge had pulled himself to his feet, well foot, and was

hanging onto the kitchen island. We heard sirens climbing in the breeze.

Jim looked at me. "Sandy. Give me your gun."

"What? No!"

"Sandy, just do it." Jorge interjected.

I sighed and handed it over to him. He checked the chamber and wiped it down. "Go."

What? We looked at him, bewildered.

He gestured to the door. "Git out of here. It'll be easier for everyone this way."

With a long last look at him, we got out of there. He called after me. "I'll see you later."

A promise.

I nodded and left.

CHAPTER 43

*N*o one was more surprised than Molly Bruce when John Peckham conceded the election to her before the results were fully tallied. Standing in the November chill outside the high school, he called an impromptu press conference among the newspaper and television crews that waited in the cold leaf scented air. The local political pundits had already released predictions of the early tallies giving him a slim lead over Molly in a race that was surprisingly tight right down to the wire.

I watched from the edge of the crowd of reporters, convinced that he was going to give, in my opinion, a premature victory speech. Instead, his opening statement shocked us all into silence.

"I would like to congratulate my opponent, Molly Bruce, on her clean, well-run campaign and to hereby formally cede any claim to office I might have had in this race. Furthermore, I am announcing my retirement from politics, effective immediately."

Beside me, Jorge said, "Whoa! Even for Brownville, that's a new one!"

I heard mumbling from the crowd that started to rise in volume. John held his hands up, silencing them. "Please direct all questions to my lawyer and political consultant, William Chem. Thank you."

"Well, no shit." I turned to Jorge. "Hello Mayor Bruce."

Jorge looked over to where Molly Bruce stood, her face a mask of shocked delight. He smiled. "We could have done worse."

Could we ever! Hal Morgan, currently cooling his heels in an upstate jail on racketeering charges, could have plopped a drug running facility smack in the middle of town. Sebastian O'Nary, for all that he meant well, was trying to put a large processing plant in town as well. The jobs it would have created would have been limited and the headaches huge.

To everyone's surprise, in an eleventh-hour move Molly Bruce had brought to the table a huge player for the town, one that was currently in the process of negotiating to buy the old Culberth Sanctuary on the outside of town. Diamond Resources was a nationwide clinical program that specialized in outpatient and therapeutic programs for a wide range of conditions. Part of their regimen called for a jobs center where people could receive specialized training in technical skills, as well as support for people with mental illnesses and addiction problems. I hoped fervently that Joe and his crew would take advantage of the services it had to offer.

Their business plan also called for an IT based office park in the center of town, utilizing the many empty storefronts and upstairs spaces for offices already pre-wired for international access. Rumor had it over 50% of the available space was already spoken for.

It was a major coup for Brownville.

The old Miller warehouse had been suddenly and myste-riously abandoned. Only scant days after Pyotr and Nestor had met their end under the wheels of the locomotive, state police had snapped the padlocks on the gate and cautiously fanned out around the grounds. All they found were piles of dog shit and responses from the drug-sniffing dogs that drugs of some sort had been stashed inside the warehouse. The only sign left behind were the marks where hundreds of crates had sat on the floor. Attempts to trace ownership of the building had come to a dead end in the Cayman Islands.

Chief William Hanniford was in federal custody, awaiting a trial on conspiracy to commit murder, attempted murder, and the attempted murder of a police officer. Jim Pim was being hailed as a local hero for taking down the corrupt police captain, a case that made national news. Already a minor star on YouTube, he was having to adapt to his new national celebrity status. He and I both hoped it would blow over quickly.

The video had gained steam again, garnering another million hits, after the news had broken of Chief Hanniford and Hal Morgan's involvement in the mob. Morgan had sung first, giving up Hanniford in a heartbeat, tying him in so tightly to the mob there would never be any going back.

The Lucky Plucker Poultry Producers were rumored to be looking to the north, at another little town along the river. I hoped that maybe they could bring jobs and hope to that area.

Our own newspaper had received a stimulus package of its own in the aftermath of that wild June adventure. Russ White had his first orgasm of the decade when he realized the full extent of involvement that Morgan and Hanniford had. The Brownville Reporter was front and center on one of the largest news stories on the national scene. Even Jan Petersen was smiling these days.

Our sales had doubled, then tripled. Offers to speak on news programs and shows like Larry King had poured in. I

WRITE ON MAIN STREET

had declined, sending Jorge out to face the bright lights on his own.

After all, he was the one who had received a nomination for a Pulitzer for this story.

I was too close to it. You can't be part of the story and write about it too. I basked in his reflected glory, both of us knowing the award was something we shared.

I caught up to John as he was trying to sneak away from the gathering, a dark shadow in the high school's parking lot. On the other side of the lot, the football field blazed under klieg lights, brightly shirted players running in herky jerky motion.

"I told you, I have no..... oh! It's you!" He gave me a brief hug. Spending time locked in a cell brings you closer together.

Holding him by the upper arms, I cocked my head at him. "What gives?"

He shrugged. "I lost my taste for it all, Sandy. I kept watching Molly, who is so innocent and wants to do a good job, and I realized that I just don't want it. She's going to be a good mayor, much better than I would have been."

"Well, I don't know about that, I think you would have been great at it too, but I respect your decision."

"Do you?" He stared at me in the light from the ball field, searching my face. I nodded. "I do. It takes guts to do what you did."

He looked down, discomfited. I knew why. "John." I shook his upper arm. Slowly, he raised his eyes to mine. "John, you did an amazing job back in June. Don't ever tell yourself otherwise."

He was already shaking his head negatively. "Sandy, I was a pantywaist. You can't tell me different."

I sighed. I knew better than that, but he didn't. "Look. All I am going to say is that you handled it a lot better than most men would have. You didn't lose your head; you listened and gathered information that helped keep us alive." I shrugged. "Who knows if I would have made it out if you hadn't been there?"

He stared out at the players a moment, biting his lower lip. Slowly he nodded his head. "Thanks."

I patted him on the arm and watched him walk away between the rows of cars, knowing he wasn't convinced.

CHAPTER 44

*T*he newsroom was illuminated by only a few lights at this hour. I glanced down the rows of empty cubicles, relishing these few moments alone, the day shift done and the night shift consisting of one person, who was out right now. Dropping my bag on the floor, I booted up my laptop and stared intently at the screen, feeling my inner self go calm and Zen like.

Which is why, when the lights blazed on and people popped up around me shouting, 'Surprise!' that I almost spit my lungs out.

"Jesus!" I clutched my chest, convinced that this was the big one, the one that would stop my heart forever. I stared, befuddled, at Lizzy, Jorge, Jim and Russ, all of them grinning like idiots. Lizzy held a small, lopsided cake, a candle sputtering to life as Jorge lit it.

"What the hell is this?" My voice squeaked. Jim stepped forward, kissing me squarely on the lips. Our first intimate moment had been played out in front of over 4.5-million viewers now; the rest of them took place with a far more intimate audience.

STEVIE LYNNE

I leaned into his chest as Lizzy set the cake down on my desk. She was wearing gold eye shadow, red feathers in her hair, a long leather skirt and a sparkly black sweater, her Indian Gypsy Circus combination. I looked at the cake, then the little group, utterly bewildered. Lizzy smiled wider. "It's your birthday!"

"What? No, it's not!" My birthday was in May. "Well, it is now!" Russ said, and plopped the paper on my desk. I looked at it, then back up at the little group. "What's this?"

"Read it, Case!" Jorge shoved it over to me.

I shook my head. These people were losing it. Leaning forward, I picked up the paper, noting that it was The Chicago Tribune. I frowned, looking at the date. Today's. Where the heck did they get this?

There was a front-page article circled in red pen; 'Transvestite Prostitution Ring Sting Nets Numerous Celebrities.'

'Police today confirmed that they had taken down one of the widest reaching prostitution rings known to Chicago after they conducted a pre-dawn raid on a three story brownstone. Authorities arrested Olga and Bolga Korkavech, two men posing as blonde sisters. The Korkavech's had an extensive collection of documents and videotapes chronicling their sexual adventures with many of Chicago's leading luminaries, a list that included political figures and A-list celebrities. Arrested at the scene was Pulitzer winning journalist, Benjamin Morven, a well-known figure on the national scene...'

"Holy shit!" my yell echoed through the newsroom. "Transvestites? Ben? Oh my God!" My hand rose to cover my mouth. Lizzy smiled, a megawatt smile, folding her arms across her chest. I eyed her body language a moment, my eyes narrowing.

"Lizzy? Is there anything you want to tell me about this story?"

"Huh? Moi?" She batted her eyes at me. Beside her, Jorge smirked. I eyed him too. Something stank here.

I resumed reading, skimming the article to the end, noticing where it mentioned vaguely how a tip received last summer set the sting in motion. Finishing up, I sat back and eyed my group again. They all wore smug grins.

"A tip, eh?" Again, the innocent looks. "I don't suppose this tip originated in New England?"

"Feh." Russ couldn't hide his grin. "Here, blow your candle out before it lights the cake on fire."

He pushed the cake over to me, hot wax dripping on the frosting. I looked at the group once more before pursing my lips and blowing the candle out.

Behind us, the police scanner crackled to life. Heads cocked, we listened as static voices speaking in code reported a naked man leading a goat on a leash down Main Street. Jim smiled. "The Brownville Rams musta won the game. Gotta go, babe." He leaned over, kissing me again, a kiss full of promise. "Wait up for me. I shouldn't be too late." He spent more time at my home than he did at his parents now.

Home. My home. Right here in Brownville, VT. I grinned and cut into the cake.

THE END

ABOUT THE AUTHOR

Stevie Lynne is the alter ego of S. L. Funk, a rather twisted individual. With the Brownville Series, Stevie allows herself to explore the sometimes hilarious antics and personalities found within small towns all over the country. Stevie celebrates life in these small towns in a tongue-in-cheek manner while saluting those who make life there worthwhile.

Stevie (aka S.L. Funk) holds a creative writing degree and has a background in journalism at a small town newspaper. She lives in a small New England town with her husband and several four legged family members.